ECHOES OF AWAKENING

THREE STORIES

Hector M. Rodriguez

Library of Congress Cataloging-in-Publication Data
Rodriguez, Hector M
Echoes of Awakening/ Hector M. Rodriguez
p. cm.
ISBN: 978-1-7355584-6-2 (Paperback)
ISBN: 978-1-7355584-7-9 (eBook)
1. Young Adult 2. Action Adventure – Thriller 3. Social Fabric

Printed in United States of America
First Printing: January 2025
For permissions requests, email the author/publisher at:
hcsm@comcast.net

DISCLAIMER
This is a work of fiction. Names, characters, businesses, places, events, locales, and incidents are either the products of the author's imagination or used in a fictitious manner. Any resemblance to actual persons, living or dead, or actual events is purely coincidental. The information in this book is provided for educational and entertainment purposes only. The author and publisher assume no responsibility for errors or omissions. Neither is any liability assumed for damages resulting from the use of information contained herein.

10 9 8 7 6 5 4 3 2 1

TABLE OF CONTENTS

ADDITIONAL WORKS
BY THE AUTHOR

What Happened to Joe French?

The Path Taken:
A Father and Son Journey on the Camino de Santiago

24 Stories- A Collection of Short Stories

A Story
(The Gift of The Tiger)

The Awkward Optimist's Guide to Human Connection
(A Field Manual for the Socially Ambitious)

INTRODUCTION

Thanks for stopping by. I want to tell you a little bit about what you are about to read and enjoy, I hope. There are several common elements you will encounter across all three stories. First, all draw upon ancient knowledge and secrets. All three stories involve the discovery or protection of profound secrets from humanity's past. Each contains hidden wisdom that could change our understanding of human history. You will see archaeological and historical discoveries drive key plot points in each of the tales.

There is a consistent evolution of consciousness. What I mean by this is each story deals with moments when human consciousness takes a leap forward. The characters, mostly human, experience heightened awareness or special abilities. They explore what they have not understood. They are curious creatures. There is transformation of understanding about what humans are capable of. The protagonists don't always win but they do seek something.

I will also introduce you to the concept of a spirit or Jakkar (the tiger in one story). This spirit appears symbolically in each account as a significant concept. There is a representation of both primal power, and spiritual or mystical elements embedded in each of the novellas. In some respects, the symbol acts as a guardian of ancient wisdom. Some may see this a Godlike figure.

There is a strong connection to our genetic legacy, past, present and future. DNA and bloodlines play crucial roles as each character has deeper connections than what is originally reveled. There is a consistent connection to the earth. We, as humans, are the culmination of special sometime random genetic traits or in other words, genetic mutations. Those mutations affect the characters in the novelettes. It is common theme that is slowly revealed. I also look into the future. The stories look at the concepts of heritage and inheritance as pivotal themes.

I hope you will see that I take outsider protagonists to a new level. The main characters are often overlooked or underestimated by their respective society. They are all children in a sense. All are outcasts, or those who don't quite fit in. The forgotten or lost ones. I developed characters who see what others miss and capitalize on opportunity.

There is also a profound protection of sacred knowledge. The characters become guardians of important secrets or abilities. I try to always build tension between revealing truth and protecting dangerous knowledge. I impose responsibility of safeguarding ancient wisdom to those who would not be expected to.

I also play with time. I work with dual timelines. Time, being a construct of homo-sapiens should not limit our imagination. I often move, almost secretively, between past and present. I explain how ancient or past events may have affected modern circumstances. A resemblance would be the domino effect. Or why something happened the way it did and where historical actions have present-day consequences.

Given these common elements, a title that captures the themes of ancient wisdom, transformation, and genetic legacy would be most appropriate. That is why I call this collection *"Echoes of Awakening"*. I hope you enjoy my stories.

Hector M. Rodriguez
Writer

These stories are dedicated to my family and friends,
and their friends, and their friends....

THE GIRL IN THE PAINTING

For My Mom
She taught me to appreciate art.

"*M'Liss*"

CHAPTER 1

THE PAINTING

SOME STORIES FIND YOU WHEN YOU LEAST EXPECT THEM. Mine found me on a bitter autumn morning in 1994, tucked between cast-off memories at a yard sale in Kamloops, British Columbia. I almost missed her—a girl's face emerging from layers of aged varnish, her eyes so alive they seemed to follow me between tables of tarnished silver and moth-eaten quilts.

The painting wasn't beautiful in any conventional sense. The canvas was torn along one edge, paint flaking from its corners like autumn leaves. But there was something in those eyes that stopped me cold—a fierce intelligence, an old soul's wisdom trapped in a child's face. She couldn't have been more than eleven, this girl from another century, her untamed black hair framing features that managed to be both wild and aristocratic.

She sat before what appeared to be a cave mouth, though something about the darkness behind her suggested a mine entrance. Her clothing told its own story: a frayed red wool shawl that might once have graced a fine lady's parlor draped over a forest green dress with a turned-up hem. No shoes. Golden maple leaves swirled at her feet, each one rendered with obsessive detail, as if the artist had been trying to capture something more than just falling leaves.

"Five loonies," said a quiet voice. I turned to find a young woman watching me, her expression oddly like the girl in the painting. "She's been in my family since my great-grandmother's time." Her fingers traced patterns on her sleeve—a nervous habit, or something more? "Mom used to say there was blood in that painting's history. Said it brought both fortune and misery to those who owned it."

I handed her the five loonies, trying not to notice how her hand trembled apprehensively as she took the coins. As I lifted the canvas, something fluttered from behind the frame—a scrap of paper that danced on the morning breeze before I could catch it.

"Might want to be careful with that one," the woman called after me as I carried the purchase to my car. "Some stories are better left buried in the California hills."

Later, under the harsh light of my study, the painting began to yield its secrets. Hidden in the shadows of the cave entrance, almost lost in the artist's heavy brushstrokes, were what appeared to be numbers—coordinates perhaps, or a date. And there, in the bottom corner beneath flaking paint, a signature emerged: Edwin Long, 1872. But it was what I discovered in the original frame that changed everything. Tucked into a careful hollow in the wood was a fragment of paper, its ink faded to near-invisibility. Only two words remained legible: "Remember Melissa."

I didn't know it then, but I had just purchased my way into one of the gold country's darkest stories—a tale of murder, greed, and revenge that had waited over a century to be told. The girl in the painting was

Melissa Smith, and she had been both witness and avenger to events that would shake the California gold fields to their foundation. That night, I dreamed of her eyes watching me through layers of old varnish, waiting for someone to finally uncover the truth she had buried beneath Red Mountain's blood-stained soil.

The next morning, an envelope arrived with no return address. Inside was a single gold flake and a yellowed map fragment. Scrawled across it in faded ink were words that would launch me into months of research: "Smith's Pocket lies deeper than any mine." The mystery of Melissa Smith was just beginning.

SHADOWS OF RED MOUNTAIN

HISTORY LEAVES CLUES, IF YOU KNOW WHERE TO LOOK. Red Mountain itself still exists, though you won't find it on modern maps—just another ghost town lost in the folds of the Sierra Nevada, two hundred miles east of Sacramento. But in 1872, when Edwin Long first set eyes on it, the town pulsed with gold fever and darker hungers.

My research led me first to the California State Archives in Sacramento, where yellowed newspapers and mining records painted a portrait of a place where fortunes rose and fell between sunrise and sunset. But it was in a dusty courthouse basement that I found the documents that would change everything—the personal papers of Dr. James Clapp, Red Mountain's doctor and coroner.

Clapp's cramped handwriting revealed a town built on fault lines deeper than geology: two saloons facing each other like gunfighters across the main street, the "respectable" National Hotel and the notorious Empire Hotel, a Presbyterian church whose white-washed walls stood in stark contrast to the rusty iron-rich soil that gave the mountain its name. But it was his notes about the cemetery, perched on the northern edge of town, that first mentioned Melissa Smith—specifically, the mysterious circumstances surrounding her father's grave.

The town's population fluctuated with each new strike and disappointment: 268 souls at its peak, a babel of languages and hopes. Chilean miners worked claims alongside freed slaves from the South. Chinese laborers-built railroads and worked spent-out claims. Mexican miners, who remembered when this was still their territory, kept to themselves, guarding old secrets about the mountain's true wealth.

But it was the story of one child that seemed to echo through every account. Melissa Smith moved through Red Mountain like a ghost in reverse—not haunting the town but witnessing its hauntings. She appeared in mining records, church documents, even criminal complaints, though never as the accused. Always as the witness. The town's children feared her. The adults spoke of her in whispers. Some called her "M'Liss"—a name that would later appear in Bret Harte's famous stories of the gold country.

As I studied the painting under different lights, I began to understand Long's obsession with the shadows behind her. The cave entrance—which I now knew to be the opening to Smith's Pocket, her father's infamous claim—seemed to shift and deepen the longer one looked at it. Using specialized photography, I discovered layers of earlier brushstrokes beneath the final image—different positions of the hands, subtle changes in the angle of the cave mouth. It was as if Long had been trying to capture something that kept slipping away.

The painting's provenance raised more questions than it answered. It appeared in a Hearst Castle inventory in 1887, then vanished during a suspicious fire that many whispered was set deliberately. Rumors placed it in a San Francisco gambling house in 1906, just before the great earthquake. Each time it surfaced in historical records, death or disaster followed.

Why had Long, at the height of his London career, traveled to a remote California mining town to paint one portrait? Why did Brett Harte, who made his fortune writing about the gold fields, become so obsessed with this one child that he commissioned the painting in the first place? And why did Washoe Smith, on the very day he supposedly discovered a new motherlode, end up dead with his gun in the wrong hand?

The answers, I suspected, lay in the very pigments of the painting itself. Under ultraviolet light, the shadows in the cave mouth revealed more than just artistic technique. Hidden in those layers of paint was a map—one that someone had gone to great lengths to conceal.

Two weeks after purchasing the painting, I received another anonymous letter, this one containing a newspaper clipping from 1873. It detailed the mysterious collapse of Red Mountain's Presbyterian church and the disappearance of several prominent citizens. In the margin, written in a shaky hand that matched the writing from the painting's frame, were the words: "Some truths stay buried. Others rise like poison from the ground."

The mystery of Melissa Smith was becoming something darker than I'd imagined—a story not just of gold and greed, but of secrets that had claimed lives across centuries.

The next morning, I booked a flight to California. I had to see Red Mountain for myself, to walk the ground where Melissa Smith had orchestrated her revenge. I didn't know then that I was following a trail she had laid out over a century ago, leading to a truth that some would still kill to keep buried.

CHAPTER 3

THE PRICE OF GOLD

WINTER CAME EARLY TO THE SIERRA NEVADA IN 1872, as if nature herself conspired to keep the mountain's secrets. Through Washoe Smith's mining journals, which I discovered in the University of California's special collections, I learned how the first snow fell in September, dusting Red Mountain's peaks with white while the valleys still clung to autumn's gold. By October, the miners knew this would be one of those winters the old-timers feared—the kind that could entomb a man in his claim until spring, if he survived at all.

But Melissa Smith wasn't afraid of winter. Born to the rhythm of pickaxe against stone, she read the mountain's moods as easily as other children read rote bible verses. While they huddled by their mothers' hearths, she prowled the maze of tunnels that honeycombed the mountainside, learning their secrets by candlelight.

Smith's Pocket was unique among the claims surrounding Red Mountain. Washoe Smith had discovered what the Mexican miners called a bolsada—a natural pocket where ancient rivers had concentrated gold over millennia. The nuggets pulled from Smith's Pocket were distinctive, wrapped in milky quartz that seemed to glow in the lamplight. But there was something else about the claim, something that made experienced miners uneasy. More than one swore they could hear strange sounds in the deeper tunnels, like music played on glass strings.

The town's archives told stories of claim jumpers found frozen solid in their tracks, of partners turning on each other over a single flake of color in their pan. The winter of '69 had been particularly brutal—twenty-seven crosses added to the cemetery, though old-timers whispered that not all the bodies had been found.

Dr. Clapp's diary, dated just weeks before Washoe's death, revealed the first hints of what was to come:

"Young M'Liss came by again today, fever-bright and full of questions about her father's claim. She speaks of the mine as if it were a living thing, with moods and secrets of its own. The girl has her father's gift for reading the mountain's signs, but there's something else in her—a wildness that makes even hardened miners uncomfortable. She told me she's been dreaming of gold deeper than any mine, though what she means by this, I cannot say. W.S. was in earlier, paid his bill with two sizeable nuggets. Mentioned something about a new strike but seemed nervous. Said things would be better for M'Liss soon. I fear what this winter may bring."

Among Washoe's recovered possessions was a crumpled map covered in cryptic notations. Most were indecipherable, but one phrase stood out: "The deeper the gold, the darker the price." The paper itself was unusual—Chinese-made, available only in San Francisco at the time. How it came to be in Washoe's possession became clear only when I found Wing Lee's ledger, recording a specific purchase just three days before Washoe's death.

The painting captured Melissa at this precise moment—poised between childhood and something darker. Long's obsessive attention to the shadows behind her wasn't artistic flourish; he was documenting something he'd seen in those tunnels; something that made him write to Brett Harte: "There's something in her eyes that I cannot quite capture—a knowledge of things no child should comprehend. Sometimes, when I work late into the night, I swear the painting changes. The shadows in the cave mouth seem to deepen, and her eyes... God help me, but her eyes follow me across the room."

As winter tightened its grip on Red Mountain, hydraulic mining was transforming the landscape. Massive water cannons tore entire hillsides apart, their operation echoing through the canyons like artillery fire. But Smith's Pocket remained untouched by these modern methods. Washoe worked his claim the old way—with pick, shovel, and an intuition that seemed almost supernatural.

What he found in those depths would soon transform Red Mountain forever. By spring, when the snow finally released its grip on the Sierra Nevada, the town would be changed beyond recognition. And at the center of it all was Melissa Smith, a child of the gold fields who would become something far more dangerous—an avenger with nothing left to lose.

The brutal winter of 1872 marked more than just another season in the gold country. It marked the beginning of a story that would be whispered around mining campfires for generations—a tale of murder, betrayal, and a revenge served as cold as Sierra snow.

CHAPTER 4

A FATHER'S BLOOD

WHEN MELISSA FOUND HER FATHER'S BODY IN THE frost-rimmed gully, her world didn't shatter—it crystallized. Three details told her this was no suicide, despite what the town would soon whisper: the missing leather pouch of fresh gold, the gun clutched in the wrong hand, and most tellingly, the torn page from his mining journal with coordinates to what would become known as "The Last Pocket."

Through Dr. Clapp's detailed coroner's report, I pieced together that bitter morning. He'd arrived within the hour, his breath clouding in the mountain air as he examined Washoe Smith's body. Melissa had watched his face with an intensity that unnerved him—she'd learned to read men's expressions as easily as she read the mountain's moods. Something in the doctor's eyes confirmed what she already knew: this was murder, carefully disguised.

"The pistol," she'd said quietly, her voice steady. "Pa always wore it on his left side. Said it was quicker to draw cross-body with his right hand." Clapp's personal diary recorded his response: "Clever girl. Like your father that way." But in the margins, he'd written something more revealing: "God help those who think her just a child. There's something in her eyes today that reminds me of the mountain itself—patient, watchful, and utterly merciless."

The torn journal page burned in her mind like a hot coal. She'd recognized it instantly—not just her father's hurried scrawl, but the distinctive Chinese watermark in the paper's corner. Only Wing Lee's shop in Red Mountain carried such paper, and her father had purchased a full journal just three days before. The coordinates weren't meant for claim registration; they were a message meant for her alone.

As winter tightened its grip on Red Mountain, Melissa began her own investigation. She moved through the town like a shadow, collecting whispers and secrets. The miners who'd worked her father's claim spoke freely around her, seeing only a grieving child. They didn't notice how she cataloged their words, their gestures, their inconsistencies in a journal of her own—one I found decades later, hidden in the walls of the collapsed church. Three names emerged repeatedly in her careful notations: Chaco, the Mexican miner who claimed Washoe owed him forty dollars; James McKenzie, owner of the Empire Hotel who'd been buying up failed claims at suspicious prices; and most surprisingly, Reverend Cole, whose church fund had mysteriously grown wealthy enough to commission a new bell tower just days after Washoe's death.

But it was Brett Harte's arrival that changed everything. The writer brought with him not just his notorious curiosity but also the English painter Edwin Long. Their interest in her story might have seemed innocent—just another tale of the gold fields for Harte's magazine—but Melissa recognized opportunity when it appeared.

"Tell me about your father," Harte would say, notebook ready. And

Melissa would tell him carefully curated pieces of the truth, watching how her words rippled through the town like pebbles in a mining sluice, shifting what lay hidden beneath.

The painting sessions with Long provided perfect cover for her true work. While the artist captured her likeness, Melissa studied the comings and goings at the Empire Hotel across the street. She noticed how McKenzie met with Reverend Cole late at night, their discussions hidden behind drawn curtains. She watched Chaco disappear into the mine registry office with documents that shouldn't have existed. But most importantly, she began to understand the deeper mystery of Smith's Pocket. The coordinates on that torn page didn't lead to a new gold strike—they led to something far more valuable. Something that had transformed Red Mountain from a simple mining camp into a den of conspiring thieves. The truth lay in the geology itself. The ancient riverbed that had created Smith's Pocket hadn't stopped at her father's claim. It continued beneath the town itself, directly under the foundation of the Presbyterian church. The new bell tower wasn't just a symbol of the town's prosperity—it was a clever way to hide the sound of late-night mining.

As Long worked to capture her likeness, Melissa made sure he captured something else as well—in the shadows of the cave mouth behind her, she positioned herself so that the angle would reveal just enough of the rock face to show the true strike line of the gold vein. To most eyes, it would appear as simple background detail. But to anyone who knew mining, who understood how gold moved through rock, it was a map. The same evening Long finished the painting, Reverend Cole's church caught fire. In the chaos that followed, no one noticed a small figure slipping into the mine registry office. By morning, when the town discovered that all claim records for Red Mountain had vanished, Melissa Smith had already begun the next phase of her plan. She would use Harte's growing obsession with her story and Long's painting to set her snare. The men who killed her father would soon learn that the daughter of Washoe Smith had inherited more than just his claim—she'd inherited his cunning, and a patience as deep as the mines themselves.

CHAPTER 5

THE SPIDER'S WEB

Red Mountain harbored two kinds of poison that winter—the obvious kind that men whispered about in saloons, and a subtler variety that only Melissa understood. Through her journal entries, which I found hidden in a rusted tin beneath her father's cabin ruins, I learned how she wove her web of vengeance with the patience of a widow spider. "Pa taught me that finding gold isn't about luck," she wrote. "It's about reading signs. A bent twig, a displaced stone, the way water moves differently when it hits certain rocks." She applied these same lessons to hunting killers, tracking her prey through the hidden passages of Red Mountain with a hunter's precision.

They thought she was just another mining camp calamity—a half-wild orphan girl who'd soon be shipped off to some distant relative or church home. Nobody noticed how she kept her father's old mining journal, not for the coordinates or claim notes, but for the names. Washoe Smith had recorded everything: who borrowed tools, who worked shifts, who paid their debts and who didn't. More importantly, he wrote down who started asking questions about the new strike just days before he died.

The mystery deepened when I discovered Dr. Clapp's correspondence with the California Geological Survey. His letters, written in a cipher that took me months to crack, revealed something disturbing. The groundwater near the church had begun to show traces of what he called "La Muerte Plateada"—the silver death. The Spanish had found it first, centuries ago, and had sealed their tunnels rather than face its effects.

Melissa began marking her own codes in the margins of her father's journal. A dot next to names of men who visited the church at night. A small cross beside those who suddenly had money for new equipment. A wave pattern when she spotted someone carrying mining tools in or out of the bell tower construction site.

But it was her observations of the Empire Hotel that proved most revealing. Through a crack in the dining room wall, she overheard McKenzie and Wade planning something bigger than mere claim jumping. They spoke of a man named Hearst, of government contracts, and of something beneath the church that would "change the face of mining forever." The church itself became the center of her investigation. Every Sunday, she sat in the back pew, watching Reverend Cole preach about greed and redemption while his eyes kept drifting to the new floorboards near the altar. The same floorboards that had been replaced just days after her father's death.

Through Wing Lee, Red Mountain's Chinese merchant, she learned that Spanish missionaries had built the original church not to save souls, but to seal something away. The native people had warned them about "the water that burns"—springs that could dissolve gold and poison the land for generations. Then came the night that changed everything. While pretending to sweep the church steps, Melissa overheard a conversation between Wade and an elegantly dressed stranger whose voice carried the weight of money and power:

"The mercury is the key," the stranger said. "Control that, and we control every mining operation from here to the Comstock. No one can process gold without it." Mercury. The vital ingredient in gold processing, worth its weight in the precious metal it helped extract. And beneath Red Mountain lay the largest deposit ever discovered—one that could make a man master of the entire gold industry.

The sporadic painting sessions with Long became her cover. While he worked to capture her likeness, she made sure he also captured the geological truth in the cave entrance behind her. Each shadow, each rock formation, when properly understood, revealed the location of the mercury deposits. It was a map hidden in plain sight, one that would only make sense to someone who knew what they were looking for. But someone else was watching too. Through her hidden passages, Melissa caught glimpses of men she didn't recognize—professionals with expensive boots and careful eyes, measuring the town's buildings and testing its water. The government survey team her father had mentioned in his final notes had arrived early.

The stakes were suddenly higher than mere revenge. What had started as a daughter's quest for justice had become something far more dangerous. Because beneath Red Mountain's streets, in tunnels older than memory, lay a secret that could destroy not just a town, but an entire industry. And in her small cabin room, Melissa added one final notation to her father's journal: "The deeper the gold, the darker the price." She was beginning to understand what those words truly meant.

DEVILS IN THE DEEP

THE FIRST BODY WAS FOUND ON A BITTER December morning, half-buried in fresh snow behind the Empire Hotel. Thomas Chen, Red Mountain's youngest assayer, lay frozen with his throat cut. Most dismissed it as another mining camp murder, but Melissa knew better. Two days earlier, she'd watched Chen talking to Dr. Clapp, passing him papers bound with red silk—papers that had vanished by the time Wade's men "investigated" the scene.

In the California State Archives, I found Chen's last letter to his father in San Francisco. Written the night before his death, it contained a cryptic warning: "Something worse than gold lies beneath this mountain. The Spanish knew. That's why they sealed the lower tunnels. If these men succeed in their plan, they will poison half the Sierra."

The murder changed everything in Red Mountain. Fear crept through the town like winter frost, and with it came a man who would alter the game entirely: Augustus Wade, claiming to be a U.S. Marshal investigating mining fraud. Tall and razor-thin, with eyes like chips of Sierra quartz, Wade carried authority the way other men carried guns— naturally and with lethal intent. Through her network of hiding places in the walls, Melissa watched his first meeting with McKenzie in the Empire Hotel's private dining room:

"Quite the operation you've got here," Wade said, studying the hotel's gilt-framed mirror. "Interesting how many claims seem to change hands just before they strike color." McKenzie's smile never wavered, but his fingers tightened on his whiskey glass.

"Mining's a risky business, Marshal. Men get desperate, sell too soon. Can't blame a businessman for having good intuition."

But Wade wasn't really a Marshal. Melissa had seen his type before—a Pinkerton detective, hired by someone with deep pockets and darker ambitions. The question was: whose side was he really on? The answer came three nights later when Dr. Clapp was found dead in his office, his medical records scattered and his safe cracked open. The official story was robbery, but Melissa had watched Wade slip into the doctor's office an hour before sunset. More importantly, she'd seen what Wade carried out – the worn leather satchel with her father's original claim documents, which Clapp had been keeping safe.

"Such a tragedy," Reverend Cole announced from his pulpit that Sunday, his congregation gleaming with new wealth. "First poor Thomas Chen, now our beloved doctor. These are dark times, my friends. Dark times indeed."

That same week, Edwin Long began acting strangely. He'd taken to working on the portrait at night, claiming the lamplight captured Melissa's essence better. But she saw how he studied the cave entrance behind her, how his hands shook slightly as he added layers to the shadows. He knew something—or had figured something out from the rock formations she'd carefully positioned him to paint. Then Long disappeared. The official story was that he'd returned to San Francisco, but his art supplies remained in his hotel room, including a sealed letter addressed to Brett Harte. Before anyone could read it, Wade appeared and claimed it as "evidence."

Through a crack in the wall of Wade's office, Melissa watched him read the letter by lamplight. His face went pale. "Hearst needs to see this," he muttered, reaching for his coat. But as he stood, something fell from the letter—a small diagram showing the church's foundation and what lay beneath it.

The next morning, Harte's room at the Empire Hotel was ransacked, his notes stolen. A warning had been carved into his desk: "Writers should stick to fiction." That night, hidden in the church's bell tower, Melissa overheard another conversation that changed everything:

"The girl knows too much," McKenzie said.

"She's just a child," Cole protested weakly.

"Children grow up," Wade replied coldly. "And this one's too much like her father. We all know how that ended."

But the real shock came when they mentioned her mother: "Marion Smith is starting to remember," Wade said. "The laudanum's wearing off."

"She's in Sacramento?"

"For now."

"Make sure she stays there. Permanently if necessary."

Her mother was alive. All these years, they'd kept her drugged and hidden, another piece in their deadly game. But why? What did her mother know that was worth destroying her mind to keep secret? The answer, Melissa realized, lay in the Spanish tunnels beneath the church. Wade's men had been digging deeper, following old maps that predated the gold rush. They weren't just after mercury—they were looking for something else, something the Spanish had tried to seal away forever.

That night, Melissa made her decision. It wasn't just about revenge anymore. She had to stop them before they breached those ancient barriers, before they released something that could poison every mine from Red Mountain to the Comstock Lode.

The game was changing, and so were the stakes. Because somewhere in Sacramento, a woman was beginning to remember the truth about Red Mountain's darkest secret—and the real reason Washoe Smith had to die.

CHAPTER 7

DARKEST WINTER

J ANUARY OF 1873 BROUGHT THE KIND OF COLD THAT MADE MEN
question their sanity. Through three weeks of relentless blizzards,
Red Mountain lay buried in silence. But beneath that pristine
blanket, corruption festered like gangrene. In Wade's private correspon-
dence, which I discovered in the Hearst Mining Company archives, he
detailed his methodical takeover of the town. He'd created the posi-
tion of special mining commissioner—a title that didn't exist in any
California law book but carried the weight of Hearst's gold behind it.
What fascinated me most was finding Reverend Cole's journal, hidden
in the collapsed church's cornerstone. His entries revealed a man tor-
tured by guilt:

*"What manner of shepherd have I become? Each Sunday I
preach against greed while men die in tunnels beneath my*

feet. The bell tower was my sin—my pride made manifest in wood and stone. But what we've found below... Dear God, the Spanish were right to seal it away."

Wade moved quickly after Melissa's apparent departure. New "deputies" appeared daily—hard men with eyes like broken glass who wore no official badges. They started with the Chinese camp, burning shanties and driving residents into the storm. Next went the Chilean miners, then the Mexican families. Red Mountain was being cleansed of witnesses.

Brett Harte tried one last time to expose the truth. His final dispatch to the San Francisco Chronicle never arrived—the printer's office mysteriously burned down. The next day, Harte was found beaten nearly to death in an alley. Wade's personal physician declared him "unfit to travel" and confined him to a back room of the Empire Hotel. The painting had vanished from Long's room, but Melissa discovered its new location—hanging in Wade's office, though he'd had it reframed. The original frame, she learned, had been burned. Through her network of passages in the walls and under the building, she watched Wade study it late at night, measuring distances on maps, comparing angles. He knew there was something hidden in those shadows, but he couldn't quite grasp what Long had captured. Then came the night that changed everything. Following one of Wade's lieutenants through her secret alleyway passages, Melissa overheard a conversation that chilled her blood:

"Marion Smith's starting to ask questions in Sacramento," the man reported. "The laudanum's wearing off. She remembers having a daughter." Wade's response was ice: "Ensure she has an accident. Make it look natural."

But there was more. The lieutenant mentioned something that made Wade's mask slip: "The Chinese prisoners we put in the lower tunnels... they've found something. Something older than the Spanish works."

"Show me," Wade demanded.

Melissa followed them down into darkness she'd never known existed. The ancient tunnels beneath the church dropped deeper than any mining shaft, their walls smooth and unnaturally cold. In places, strange symbols had been carved into the rock—warnings in languages even the Spanish hadn't understood. What she saw in the lowest chamber defied explanation. A vast cavern, its walls gleaming with threads of mercury that moved like living silver. But it was what lay at its center that made her understand why her father had died trying to keep this place sealed. The mercury wasn't just seeping from the rocks—it was flowing upward, against gravity itself, forming patterns that seemed almost deliberate. The Spanish hadn't sealed these tunnels to protect their gold. They'd sealed them to protect the world above.

In her hidden nest high in the bell tower, Melissa added new notes to her father's journal. She'd thought Wade and his men were just greedy murderers. Now she understood they were something worse—they were fanatics who'd convinced themselves they could control forces the Spanish had fled from in terror.

But she had one advantage they didn't suspect. Her father hadn't just taught her how to read the mountain's moods—he'd taught her about its weaknesses. Where pressure could be applied and taken away. Where water could be redirected. Where ancient supports, carved by Spanish hands, could be removed to bring the whole system crashing down. The mountain itself would be her weapon. But first, she had to find a way to reach Sacramento. Because somewhere in that city, a who could be her mother was remembering things that scared these men. Melissa had to find out why some secrets were worth killing an entire town to keep buried.

CHAPTER 8

WHEN MOUNTAINS FALL

THE DISASTER BEGAN WITH A SINGLE CRACK—A SOUND LIKE breaking glass deep beneath the church. In studying the old Spanish mining records, preserved in Mexico City's archives, I discovered why they'd built their support beams in such a peculiar pattern. They weren't just holding up the mountain—they were containing something that lived within it. Through Wade's mining records, recovered from the wreckage years later, I pieced together that final morning. His men had pushed too far, too fast, their greed making them careless. Blackwood, the Cornish miner with thirty years' experience, had tried to warn them.

"The timbers are wrong," he'd said during the dawn shift change, his voice echoing off the damp tunnel walls. "Listen to the mountain—she's singing a death song. We're undermining the whole bloody town." They found his body two hours later, neck broken, at the bottom of the main shaft. "Mining accident," Wade declared. But Melissa, watching from her hidden perch in the bell tower, had seen Wade's men following Blackwood after he'd spoken up. She'd heard the struggle, the sharp crack of bone. From her vantage point, the town lay spread before her like a chess board. The morning sun painted Red Mountain's iron-rich soil in shades of rust and blood. Steam rose from the mine ventilation shafts, carrying the sharp mineral tang that locals had learned to associate with wealth. But today, there was something else in that mist—something that made the horses stamp nervously in their stables and set dogs to howling.

When they brought up Blackwood's body, something fell from his coat pocket—a folded paper that fluttered into a snowbank. Hours later, Melissa retrieved it. It was a letter to the U.S. Geological Survey, but not about the mercury seeping into Red Mountain's water supply. Blackwood had discovered something far worse in the depths: evidence that the liquid mercury deposits were moving and could easily enter groundwater flow patterns.

That's when the second body appeared. Brett Harte, still weak from his "accident," had finally managed to send a detailed story to San Francisco. They found him face-down in the snow behind the Empire Hotel, a half-written exposé clutched in his frozen hand.

"God's judgment falls on the wicked," Reverend Cole preached that Sunday, his voice quavering. But his eyes kept darting to the new cracks appearing in the church walls. The whole building had begun to settle ominously as the tunnels beneath it expanded. The church bell tolled unexpectedly at noon, though no one was in the tower. The sound had changed—deeper, with a resonance that made windows vibrate and children cover their ears. Some swore they could hear whispers in its echo, voices speaking in a language older than Spanish.

Wade's desperation showed in his actions. His men doubled their shifts, forcing the Chinese prisoners to work eighteen hours a day. The sound of picking never ceased now, and neither did the screams when someone collapsed from exhaustion.

But before Melissa could move, the timber beneath her cracked. Wade's reckless mining had undermined her secret passages. The collapse started slowly—a groan of tortured wood, the tinkle of falling debris. Then everything happened at once. The church bell began to toll on its own as the tower listed like a dying tree. Deep below, something ancient stirred in the Spanish tunnels, awakened by Wade's dynamite. The mercury wasn't just rising now—it was flowing upward through the rock like living silver, following patterns that matched the strange symbols carved on the tunnel walls. What followed would be whispered about in mining camps for generations. A girl running across snow-covered rooftops, pursued by killers. Shots fired in the darkness. Blood on the snow—some of it Melissa's from a bullet that grazed her arm. But she led them on a calculated chase, drawing them exactly where she needed them to be. Melissa Smith had learned more than just mining from her father. She'd learned that every mountain has its breaking point. And she had spent months finding Red Mountain's.

THE DEVIL'S BARGAIN

The final act of Red Mountain's tragedy began at dawn. Through Melissa's recovered journal, singed but intact in the ruins, I learned how she orchestrated every detail of that fateful morning. The timing had to be perfect—she needed Wade's men deep in the tunnels when the mountain's own weight became their executioner. Through the night, she had moved like a ghost through her memorized maze of passages, strategically weakening key support beams. Not enough to cause immediate collapse—just enough to make the mountain hold its breath. Each placement was calculated, using everything her father had taught her about how pressure moved through rock.

The morning crew descended at first light: McKenzie leading the way, followed by Reverend Cole and five of Wade's thugs. They carried new drilling equipment, determined to breach the final barrier before the government survey team arrived. Above ground, frost-covered timbers creaked under the weight of fresh snow as Wade paced the church steps, issuing orders like a general before battle.

"Something's wrong," McKenzie's voice echoed up the main shaft. "The water level's too high." Of course it was. During the night, Melissa had redirected the underground streams, using her father's detailed knowledge of the mountain's waterways. It was done by a simple re-routing of a stream by moving some rocks to make the water diversion. The poisoned groundwater was rising, driving the mercury's invisible threat upward with it.

"Keep going!" Wade shouted down the shaft. "Hearst wants that sample today!" That's when Melissa pulled the first lever—a simple wedge in a wooden beam triggered a cascade of falling timber. The crash echoed through the mountain like thunder. Screams erupted from below as the first tunnel collapsed. "It's coming down!" Someone shouted. "Dear God, it's all coming down!"

But this was just the beginning. The second phase of her plan was already in motion. The water she'd diverted wasn't just rising—it was following old Spanish paths, soaking and weakening crucial support points throughout their illegal mine. McKenzie emerged first, gasping and covered in mud. "She's flooded the Spanish works! Everything we dug... it's gone!" Wade drew his pistol, but Melissa was ready. A third wooden wedge type lever sent a carefully balanced load of mining equipment crashing down, narrowly missing him but cutting off his escape route. The look of realization on his face almost made up for everything she'd endured.

"You don't understand what you're doing," Wade shouted into the chaos. "This is bigger than you, bigger than revenge!"

"I understand perfectly," she called back, her voice echoing off the walls. "Pa didn't die for gold. He died trying to keep your poison buried." That's when she revealed her final hand. From her hiding place, she withdrew the journal—not her father's journal, but Dr. Clapp's record of their operation. Everything was documented: the mercury poisoning, the disappearances, Hearst's master plan to control California's gold industry by monopolizing the mercury supply.

"Looking for this?" She held it up where Wade could see it. "Dr. Clapp kept better records than you knew. Everything's in here—and copies Mr. Harte made are already on their way to every newspaper from here to San Francisco."

The ground trembled again, but this time it wasn't from collapsing tunnels. Something older was stirring below—something the Spanish had tried to warn them about. The mercury wasn't just seeping up through the rock anymore; it was flowing like quicksilver rivers through the ancient passages, following patterns that matched the mysterious symbols on the walls.

Wade's face went pale. Behind him, Reverend Cole stumbled from the mine shaft, coughing up black water stained with silvery threads. The others never emerged at all.

"Hearst will hunt you to the ends of the earth," Wade snarled, raising his gun.

But Melissa was already gone, disappearing into passages she knew better than her own heartbeat. Behind her, the mountain groaned one final time. The supports she'd weakened gave way with a sound like the world ending. What happened next would become mining camp legend. The entire church simply... descended, swallowed by the earth as though the mountain itself had opened its maw. Wade and his remaining men went with it, their screams cut off as abruptly as justice. The mercury remained sealed in its ancient tomb, just as the Spanish had intended. Just as her father had died trying to ensure.

WHAT LIES BELOW

THE AFTERMATH OF RED MOUNTAIN'S COLLAPSE RIPPLED through California like aftershocks. When the snow finally melted that spring, little remained of the town except the stories—and one painting that seemed to hold all their secrets. Through my research in the Hearst Foundation archives, I discovered letters revealing the true scope of what had been lost. Hearst's plan had been brilliant in its simplicity: control the mercury, control the gold. Without mercury for processing ore, every mining operation in California would have been at his mercy. But he hadn't counted on a girl who loved her father more than she feared his power. The official investigation found only what Melissa wanted them to find: evidence of illegal mining beneath the church, mercury contamination in the water supply, and enough proof of corruption to end several political careers. But the deeper mystery—what the Spanish had originally sealed away in those ancient tunnels—remained buried with Wade and his men.

Melissa's own account of the aftermath, which I found in a letter to Brett Harte's widow, revealed what happened next:

> "I reached Sacramento five days after the collapse. Found my mother in a laudanum haze at St. Mary's Hospital. Her mind cleared slowly once the drugs left her system. She remembered everything – including being kidnapped so long ago. But it took a long time. The mercury wasn't just valuable, it was alive in some way. Moved with purpose. The Spanish hadn't built their missions to save souls, but to guard places where the earth itself seemed to wake up. Pa discovered this truth too late. When he refused to help them access the lower tunnels, Wade gave him a choice—his life or mine. He chose. But he left me the tools to finish what he started."

The painting played its own role in the aftermath. When I had it professionally restored, we discovered something remarkable beneath the flaking paint. Long hadn't just hidden a map in those shadows—he'd documented the ancient Spanish warnings, recording them in the very pigments he used. Under ultraviolet light, symbols emerged that matched those found in the sealed tunnels of three other abandoned mercury mines across California.

Melissa and her mother disappeared from official records after 1873. But I found traces of them in unexpected places—property deeds in Virginia City, mining claims in Colorado, all held by a company called "Smith & Daughter." They'd used Hearst's own money—recovered from Wade's office—to build something legitimate from Red Mountain's ashes.

The last confirmed sighting of Melissa Smith was in 1922. A

geological survey team, investigating reports of strange lights near the old Spanish mission at Nueva Almadén, encountered an elderly woman walking the mercury mine's abandoned tunnels. She carried an old mining journal and seemed to know every passage by heart. When they asked her name, she smiled and said only, "Some secrets are best left buried."

As for the painting that started my investigation—I finally understood why the young woman at the yard sale had trembled when she sold it. It wasn't just a portrait; it was a warning. In those deep brown eyes, Long had captured not just a moment in time, but a truth about justice: sometimes it comes not from laws or guns, but from the earth itself.

The site where Red Mountain stood remains oddly empty. No trees grow there, and prospectors report their compasses spin wildly near the old church foundations. Sometimes, after winter storms, locals swear they hear a church bell tolling deep beneath the ground. But only I know what really lies below—because last month, I received an anonymous package. Inside was an ancient Spanish map and a modern geological survey, showing something extraordinary: the mercury under Red Mountain isn't dead. It's still moving, still following those strange patterns, still guarding whatever secrets made Melissa Smith choose the mountain over mercy.

Some say you can still see her there on cold autumn evenings, a small figure in a red shawl, watching from the shadows of the mine entrances. Watching, and waiting, in case anyone else decides to dig too deep into Red Mountain's heart. But as I learned from my long search through history's shadows, some stories don't end—they just go deeper, like veins of gold in living rock, waiting for the next seeker to discover their gleam in the darkness.

THE PAINTING'S LEGACY

2025—My Study, Vancouver, British Columbia

The painting hangs in my study now, restored but still bearing its battle scars. The tear near the red shawl, the flaking paint along the bottom edge—I've left these imperfections untouched. They're part of its story, just as much as the hidden symbols and mercury-laden pigments that Long used to record his warnings.

Last week, I received an anonymous envelope, postmarked from a small town in Nevada. Inside was a newspaper clipping about unusual geological readings about two hundred miles east of Sacramento, near Red Mountain. Seismologist have detected something moving deep beneath the collapsed town—something that follows patterns they can't explain. They're planning to drill exploratory wells this summer.

Along with the clipping was a single page torn from what appeared to be Melissa Smith's original journal, the paper aged but the ink still sharp:

"There are two kinds of secrets in this world. Those that die with the keeper, and those that must be kept alive. What lies beneath Red Mountain is the second kind. That's why Pa had Long paint the warning signs into my portrait—not just for his generation, but for all that would follow. Some treasures are worth more buried than found."

The letter was signed only with an elegant 'M', written in a hand that seemed impossibly familiar. Enclosed was a small key that matched the age and style of the painting's original frame. A while later, I took the painting to be analyzed using modern spectroscopic techniques at Cal-Tech. The results were astonishing. The pigments Long used contain traces of mercury in configurations that modern science can't explain—arrangements that echo the mysterious resonating density patterns now detected beneath Red Mountain.

But it's not these scientific mysteries that keep me awake at night. It's the way the girl's eyes seem to follow me in the darkness, carrying the same warning they did in 1872. The way the shadows in the cave mouth appear to shift when no one's watching. The way the painting seems to grow colder to the touch whenever news arrives of fresh drilling plans near the old mining site. The last thing in the envelope was a deed to a small parcel of land near Red Mountain and a single playing card—the Queen of Hearts, yellowed with age. On its back, in fresh ink, was written: "Your turn to keep watch."

I understand now why the young woman at the yard sale trembled when she handed over the painting. She wasn't just selling a family heirloom—she was passing on a responsibility. A duty to ensure that some secrets stay buried, that some treasures remain uncounted, that some stories continue their work across generations. Tonight, as I write these final words, I swear I can hear a bell tolling, faint and deep, as if carried on the wind from somewhere far below the earth.

And in the painting, Melissa Smith keeps her endless vigil, guarding mysteries that some say are better left in darkness. But that's the thing about darkness—it has a way of preserving what light might destroy. Just ask Red Mountain. Its secrets are still there, still waiting, still moving like quicksilver through ancient Spanish tunnels, watched over by a girl in the painting whose revenge became something far more important: a legacy.

And now, that legacy is yours to protect.

THEY WERE ONLY KIDS

Hector M. Rodriguez

Dedicated
To
The Children

PROLOGUE

THE FIRST PULSE OF THE ELECTROMAGNETIC DISRUPTOR killed the security cameras. The second took out the motion sensors. In the darkness of Portland's "Elegant Gems & Jewels," Oliver Drake watched the tiny red dots on the security panel fade to black, one by one. His mop of unruly black hair fell across the Google Glass display showing the store's security grid. At thirteen, he was already one of the best hackers on the West Coast—not that anyone would know it. That was the point.

"Emily, you're up," he whispered into his comm unit. Thirty-five pounds of concentrated grace and skill, eight-year-old Emily Chow slipped into the ventilation duct like a shadow. Oliver had measured it himself: 12 inches by 12 inches. Too small for an adult. Perfect for her.

They'd been planning this heist for weeks. Not for the money—though the diamonds and precious gems would certainly help fund their operation. No, this was about sending a message. The same message they'd been sending for months, from museum vaults to private collections: "Look closer. We're right here. We've always been here."

Michael, their eleven-year-old tech prodigy, kept his modified Xbox controller steady, maintaining the electromagnetic field that blinded the store's security systems. "Two minutes until automatic reboot sequence," he warned.

Through his earpiece, Oliver heard Emily's controlled breathing as she navigated the duct work. They'd rehearsed this a dozen times in the mock-up Mr. W had built in their hideout. Every turn, every junction memorized. A clang echoed through the store as the ventilation grate hit the floor.

"Hold!" Oliver commanded, his heart racing. One minute passed. No alarms. No response.

Emily dropped silently into the office, her Hello Kitty backpack incongruous against her black tactical gear. With practiced precision, she withdrew the bottle of concentrated sulfuric acid—their signature. The lock tumblers didn't stand a chance.

THE DETECTIVE'S BURDEN

Detective Leo Fibber studied the molten brass pooled beneath the display case, his leg throbbing with phantom pain from an injury that should have killed him. The lock's remains gleamed like liquid mercury under the jewelry store's harsh lights, its molecular structure altered in ways that defied conventional physics.

At fifty-two, Fibber wore his years like a threadbare coat—comfortable but showing signs of wear. His perpetually rumpled suit had seen better days, much like its owner. Peppered gray hair refused to stay combed, and his tie bore evidence of this morning's hurried coffee. But his eyes missed nothing, cataloging every detail with a precision that had made him legendary in military intelligence. Before joining Portland PD's Special Investigations Unit, Fibber had served as a Special Operations Intelligence Officer in Afghanistan. His photographic memory and intuitive grasp of patterns had made him invaluable in tracking insurgent networks. Until the night everything changed.

The memory surfaced unbidden: December 12, 2009. The moonless sky over Kandahar province. His team tracking an unusual energy signature that matched nothing in their databases. The explosion that defied every known law of physics, twisting reality itself around them. He unconsciously rubbed his left leg, remembering the White House ceremony where President Obama had presented his third Purple Heart. "Captain Fibber's actions saved his entire unit," the citation had read. But it hadn't mentioned the impossible lights, the way space itself had seemed to bend, or how his wounds refused to heal properly despite modern medicine's best efforts.

"Detective?" Officer Martinez's voice pulled him back to the present. "Forensics found something odd about the lock's molecular structure." Fibber knelt carefully, ignoring his leg's protest, to examine the melted brass more closely. Like the others, this lock hadn't been forced or picked—its tumblers had been strategically altered at the atomic level. Just like the locks at the OMSI heist last month, and the Egyptian artifact case before that.

The museum job had been particularly bold. During a charity gala benefiting youth programs, someone had accessed the secure wing through maintenance tunnels that should have been too small for an adult. The only clue: more pools of molecularly melted metal, and security footage that showed impossible things—shadows moving against light sources, spaces bending in ways that made his head hurt.

"Sir?" Martinez handed him a preliminary report. "Lab says the molecular changes would require temperatures over 1700 degrees Celsius. But nothing else was damaged. No scorch marks, or other evidence of tampering."

Fibber's perfect memory cataloged every detail of the crime scene: display cases opened with surgical precision, only certain items taken, and those impossibly small access points. A pattern was emerging, one that resonated with memories he'd tried to forget. His secure phone buzzed: a message from a blocked number.

"They're awakening, Leo. Just like you did in Kandahar. -D"

His leg throbbed harder as he accessed a hidden partition in his mind where he stored certain classified memories. The energy signature in Afghanistan had matched readings from a classified DARPA* project—research into enhanced human abilities and genetic modification. Research that had been suddenly terminated after producing unexpected results in children.

A security camera caught his attention. Like the others, it showed signs of sophisticated tampering. But something else nagged at his enhanced perception—a pattern in the digital noise that reminded him of codes he'd seen in classified files about genetic engineering and quantum computing.

"Detective?" Martinez pointed to a small vent near the ceiling. "We found blood traces. Minimal amount, but enough for DNA analysis." Fibber studied the vent opening. Barely twelve inches square. An adult would never fit, but a small child...

His phone buzzed again: "The lock is just the key, Leo. Look deeper. Remember what you saw that night. -D"

He did remember. The impossible lights, the way reality had bent around them, and most importantly, the children they'd found in the compound. Children with abilities that shouldn't have been possible. Children who had vanished without a trace after the explosion. Children who would be teenagers now.

The melted lock caught the light like a mirror reflecting possibilities. Whatever had happened in Afghanistan wasn't over. It was evolving, spreading, awakening in new generations. And somewhere in Portland, children with impossible abilities were pulling off heists that defied logic and left little traces.

The game wasn't just beginning. It had been in motion since that night in Kandahar when reality itself had shown its true nature.

*DARPA—Defense Advanced Research Project Agency

THE NEST

DETECTIVE LEO FIBBER SAT IN HIS DIMLY LIT OFFICE, SUR-rounded by holographic displays he'd "borrowed" from the FBI's VIVO* computing lab. His leg ached—not from his old war wound, but from something else. Something the doctors couldn't explain. The same something that made his military medical records classify as top secret.

The displays showed genetic sequences he shouldn't have access to. Data that pointed to a truth he wasn't sure he could understand. Each sequence contained markers that emulated conventional genetics—patterns that appeared in DNA samples from archaeological sites around the world, and now, impossibly, in a group of street kids in Portland.

Across town, Winston Blackwell III ascended to the Nest, his Cobalt-encrypted tablet analyzing those same genetic patterns. The elevator's hidden scanner read not just his biometrics but his cellular structure—patterns that matched those of the children he protected. Patterns the Consortium had been tracking for centuries.

The Nest's security systems made military installations look primitive. Quantum entanglement sensors could detect intruders before they entered the building by reading probability states in local spacetime. The technology had been reverse-engineered from artifacts found in sealed chambers beneath ancient sites—places that shouldn't exist according to conventional history.

Oliver's workstation housed processing cores that made government supercomputers look like pocket calculators. The system didn't just process data—it manipulated energy states across multiple probability timelines, allowing him to predict security responses before they happened. His augmented reality glasses, recovered from a dark web black site, could perceive fluctuations in electronic systems and exploit them.

"The Consortium's network is active," Oliver reported, his fingers dancing across neural-linked keyboards. "They're using entangled particles for instantaneous communication. But there's something else..." His screens showed energy patterns pulsing through hidden networks beneath major cities—networks that predated modern civilization. Pre-Neanderthals.

Winston pulled up the Consortium's history on a holodisplay. The organization's roots traced back to ancient secret societies, but their true origin was even stranger. They appeared simultaneously in multiple cultures, always watching, always searching for children with specific genetic markers. Always collecting artifacts that defied scientific explanation.

In 1876, they established the first genetic research laboratory hidden beneath London's Natural History Museum. By 1923, they had facilities on every continent, all searching for what they called "the convergence pattern" in human DNA. A major breakthrough came in

1954, when they discovered latticed crystalline structures in certain human genetic sequences—structures that resembled engineering more than evolution.

"New data from the Vatican site," Michael called out. His game controller-shaped device was actually a magnetic energy field manipulator, using principles that wouldn't be discovered by public science for decades. "The energy signatures are similar to what we found in the Shanghai tomb. Some kind of quantum-level information storage in piezo-electric crystalline structures."

Back in his office, Fibber's displays showed similar readings from sites around Portland. Energy patterns that shouldn't exist. Magnetic fluctuations that seemed to center around specific children. His leg throbbed as he pulled up footage from the jewelry store heist. The security cameras had been looped, but his borrowed screen sensors showed something else: probability distortions around the ventilation ducts, as if someone had been manipulating Bluetooth frequencies to avoid detection. The same holographic energy aura patterns appeared at every crime scene.

In the Nest, Emily and Lucy studied their target through the holo-table's imaging system. The Vatican's security wasn't just physical—it included encryption patterns that could detect any technological intrusion. But they had something the Consortium didn't expect: the natural ability to manipulate energy frequencies and resulting states, and the ability to code into their DNA.

"The Consortium's getting desperate," Winston noted, showing them centuries of data. "The convergence pattern they've been tracking for millennia is accelerating. More children are being born with active markers. The quantum processors in their genetic code are waking up." He brought up images from their previous heists: the Egyptian necklace that contained etched and encrypted data, the DaVinci Cipher that could manipulate probability fields, the crystalline keys that responded to specific genetic sequences. Each piece part of a larger puzzle the Consortium had been trying to complete—or prevent.

"Incoming microwave burst transmission," Oliver announced. The message appeared in multiple probability states simultaneously:

"GENETIC AWAKENING ACCELERATING.
CONSORTIUM DEPLOYING DROID SUPPRESSORS.
PROTECT THE CHILDREN. -T"

Winston's security systems flashed warnings. Detective Fibber had accessed restricted databases. He was getting closer to understanding what made his leg ache, why it had never healed properly. Why the military had classified his medical records. He was beginning to remember what he'd seen in Afghanistan before the explosion. The strange lights. The impossible readings. The children with abilities that defied explanation. The same abilities he was tracking now in Portland.

"Sir," Gibson called urgently. "Sensors detect Consortium agents converging on the city. They're using probability tracking to find us." Winston studied the faces of his young charges. Each carried processors in their DNA that humanity wasn't supposed to develop for thousands of years. Each held keys to unlocking technologies that could reshape civilization—or destroy it.

"Prep for Operation Blackbird," he commanded. Around the room, systems spun up, probability fields shifted, and artificial intelligent technology hummed to life. "We move tonight. Before they realize what these children really are."

Outside, Portland's rain fell hard through entangled air, each droplet carrying information in probability states between past and future. Between what humanity thought it was and what it was about to become.

And in his office, Detective Fibber's leg throbbed with recognition as he finally understood what connected him to these impossible children. He had been one of them once. Before the Consortium tried to burn the imbedded processors from his DNA.

*VIVO—Visionally Integrated Value Observer

HIDDEN CONNECTIONS— THE ART OF DECEPTION

Giovanna Torielle's fingers traced the ancient Egyptian necklace beneath her blouse as she navigated Lisbon's crowded airport terminal. Each gemstone pulsed with faint warmth—impossible technology disguised as archaeological treasure. Just like the processors hidden in certain children's DNA. Her phone vibrated: an unlisted number. Her heart stopped when she saw the message: "The boy in Portland. He has David's eyes. -N"

David Romanov. She hadn't allowed herself to think that name in fifteen years. Brilliant physicist, passionate lover, and according to official records, killed in a lab accident at CERN. But she knew better. She'd seen the strange lights in his lab that night. Heard his frantic message about crystalline patterns in human DNA. About children with impossible abilities. When the Consortium had tried to eliminate him,

Romanov had uploaded his consciousness into quantum states using technology recovered from ancient ruins. Now he existed as pure information, able to communicate through digital networks but unable to take physical form. This partial existence was both his prison and his protection, allowing him to guide events while remaining beyond the Consortium's reach.

She'd been pregnant when he disappeared. The child given up for adoption through an agency that, she now realized, had connections to the Consortium.

The necklace grew warmer against her skin as she approached customs. Its translucent structure responded to her elevated heart rate, to patterns in her own DNA she hadn't known existed. Patterns David had been studying before they took him.

"Package received," she texted her new employer. "Proceeding to Naples. -G"

Tobias's response was immediate: "The boy is safe. For now. But they're getting closer. -T".

In Portland, Detective Fibber's sensors recorded an invisible energy spike from the jewelry store. Similar to the signature he'd detected in Afghanistan, before the explosion that shattered his leg. Before he'd seen children doing impossible things and then vanishing without a trace. His secure terminal chimed with an encrypted message from a ghost he thought long dead:

"The processors are awakening, Leo. In all of them. Even you. -D"

David Romanov had been his handler on that classified mission. Before the Consortium tried to burn the tech from their DNA.

In the Nest, Oliver's head snapped up from his screens. For a moment, he'd felt something—a resonance with someone else's neural patterns. Someone with the same genetic markers. Someone close.

"Energy spike in terminal 4," Michael reported. "Signature matches the artifacts." Winston studied the pattern analysis. The necklace was active, responding to proximity with compatible sequences. He hadn't told Ginny the truth about why he'd chosen her for this mission. About what connected her to these children. About whom her son had become.

"Incoming high frequency ultra-violet burst transmission," Oliver announced. The message fragmented across multiple screens:

"ROMANOV PROTOCOL ACTIVATING. GENETIC CONVERGENCE ACCELERATING. PROTECT THE BLOODLINES. -T"

Winston's secure phone buzzed with a message from his old friend: "She's ready to know, Winston. Tell her about David. About the boy. Before the Consortium realizes what they've awakened. -T"

The rain fell harder outside the Nest, each droplet carrying information between past and future, between what humanity was and what certain children were about to become.

And in a hidden lab beneath CERN, David Romanov's consciousness, preserved in thin sectioned states, reached out across neurological energy fields to touch the minds of those who carried his enhanced DNA. The game wasn't just beginning. It had been in motion for generations.

Giovanna Torielle's fingers traced the ancient Egyptian necklace hidden beneath her silk blouse as she cleared customs at Lisbon International. The gold encrusted almost translucent lapis lazuli felt cool against her skin—priceless, stolen, and completely invisible to the security scanners. Just like the kids who had taken it. Three days earlier, she'd found the jewelry store ransacked, Kingston mentor and manager dead, and her career in shambles. Now she was on a plane with a stolen artifact, working for a mysterious employer who seemed to know far too much about her past. About her father. Her phone buzzed: a message from her new boss.

"Package received. Proceed to Naples. Details to follow. -T" She recognized Tobias's preferred signature—always just the single letter, a habit he'd maintained across centuries of secret communications. She didn't know it yet, but she was being drawn into a web that had been decades in the making.

CHAPTER 4

DIGITAL BREADCRUMBS

ETECTIVE FIBBER'S OFFICE HUMMED WITH HIGH-SPEED liquid processors as rain streaked down the windows of Portland's Central Precinct. His modified SQUID magnetometer—salvaged from CERN's abandoned Lab 23—detected distortions in local spacetime. Each pulse matched patterns he'd seen in Afghanistan, before everything went wrong.

"You look like hell, Leo," Martinez said from the doorway. "When's the last time you slept?"

"Sleep's overrated." Fibber manipulated a holographic display of DNA sequences. "Look at this. Quantum-level structures in human genetic code. Not random mutations—engineered changes."

Martinez crossed to the desk, careful to avoid the web of red string connecting photos on the evidence wall. "Like what they found in the Basel incident?"

"Exactly." Fibber pulled up classified files on the Basel containment breach. "2007. CERN detects some type of ethereal processors in human DNA. Natural ability to manipulate probability fields. Then their top scientist vanishes."

"David Romanov," Martinez said quietly. "My sister worked with him. Said he was on the verge of something revolutionary. Something about enhanced genetic sequences."

Fibber's three-dimensional display pulsed with new data. The jewelry store security footage showed impossible probability signatures around the ventilation shafts.

"Watch this," he said, overlaying sensor data. Reality itself warped around the entry points, as if someone was manipulating local spacetime.

"Jesus," Martinez whispered. "Just like Basel."

"That's not all." Fibber pulled up Dr. Ringo Tut's personnel file. "Former NSA quantum cryptographer. Worked with Romanov on Project ORACLE—classified research into human genetic enhancement." His secure encrypted line activated:

"The children are awakening, Leo. The processors we designed are becoming active. -D"

"Romanov's alive?" Martinez stared at the message.

"Not exactly," Fibber explained. "Before the Consortium could eliminate him, he used recovered ancient tech to upload his consciousness into quantum states. He can communicate through our systems, appear in digital spaces, but can't take physical form. It's a half-existence— enough to help guide us, but not enough to directly intervene.

"In a manner of speaking." Fibber brought up more classified files. "After Basel, CERN discovered a way to preserve human consciousness in LED frequency states. Romanov uploaded himself before the Consortium could eliminate him."

"The Consortium?"

"Shadow organization. Been suppressing all kinds of technology for centuries. Trying to prevent what they call 'episodic convergence.'" Fibber's leg throbbed—burned tissue that had never healed properly. "Some of us survived their purge. Had children carrying the enhanced patterns. I was able to recognize this early on. And there is more." His sensors detected massive energy spikes downtown. Probability fields warping around ancient networks buried beneath the city.

"There's more," Martinez said. "Before she disappeared, my sister sent me data about something called the 'Romanov Protocol.' Genetic markers activating in specific bloodlines. Children with abilities that could reshape reality itself."

Fibber's screens flickered with interference. A new message appeared, fragmenting across multiple pixel states:

"Remember Lab 23, Leo. What you saw before the explosion. The children need protection—especially Oliver. He carries upgraded sequences. My sequences. And Giovanna's. -D"

"Giovanna Torielle," Martinez breathed. "The jewelry store manager."

"Now in Lisbon with artifacts that resonate on piezo-electric frequencies." Fibber unconsciously reached for his sidearm. "It's all connected. The heists, the children, the ancient tech." His display showed new pulses beneath the city. Patterns matching technology that shouldn't exist for centuries.

"Sir," Martinez pointed to a data stream. "These readings... they're identical to the Basel containment breach. But stronger."

"Because it's not just one child now." Fibber studied probability projections spreading across his screens. "They're all awakening. Every enhanced bloodline Romanov created. Every processor encoded in their DNA."

The secure line crackled with David Romanov's voice, preserved in isoelastic states: "The Consortium fears what these children represent, Leo. The next step in human evolution. What we designed them to be."

"Why now?" Fibber demanded.

"Because the stars are aligning. Literally. Resonance patterns in their DNA respond to specific astronomical configurations. Configurations that repeat every thousand years."

Martinez checked readings from the frequency sensors. "Energy levels are off the charts. Whatever's happening, it's accelerating."

"Find them, Leo," Romanov's voice urged. "Before the Consortium realizes what they've become. What they'll allow humanity to become."

In the Nest, Oliver's enhanced consciousness detected the exchange. For a moment, he touched his father's preserved mind across neurological energy fields.

And beneath CERN's Lab 23, in a hidden containment chamber, David Romanov's consciousness reached out to all his children—genetic inheritors of humanity's next evolutionary leap.

The game wasn't just beginning. It had been in motion a long time.

"What do we do?" Martinez asked.

Fibber checked his gun for ammunition. "We protect the kids. Find out what the Consortium is really afraid of."

"And Romanov?"

"He engineered these children for a purpose." Fibber's sensors detected more probability distortions spreading through the city. "The question is—what are they meant to evolve into?"

The answers lay hidden in beneath Portland's streets, in genetic codes that read like advanced engineering, and in children who lived there, alone and forgotten. Could they possibly reshape the very fabric of reality? Only if they survived long enough to fulfill their designed purpose.

In his state, David Romanov smiled. Everything was proceeding exactly as he'd calculated fifteen years ago. The children would soon understand what they truly were. And humanity would never be the same.

THE NEXT MOVE

THE NEST'S COMMAND CENTER GLOWED LIKE A CYBERPUNK beehive; liquid mercury laced processors humming like mechanical honeybees gathering digital nectar. Oliver stared at the holographic display of their next target: DaVinci's Cypher, floating above the imaging table like a technological ghost. "QISR shows multiple defense layers," Michael said, manipulating the Quantum Imaging and Surveillance Reconnaissance display. "The Vatican's security is like a Russian Bauska nesting doll from hell. Each layer more complex than the last."

"More like a digital onion with teeth," Emily countered from her perch on the windowsill. At thirty-five pounds, she was their skeleton key—able to slip through spaces that would make a cat claustrophobic. "ATLAS readings show gaps in their quantum grid. Small ones. Just my size." ATLAS—Advanced Tactical Logistics and Analysis

System—was Michael's pride and joy, a diamond etched AI processor that could predict security responses like a chess grandmaster seeing twenty moves ahead.

"The HYDRA defense grid is still a problem," Oliver noted, his augmented reality glasses scanning the miss-mash of patterns in the hologram. The Hierarchical Yield Defense and Response Array—the Vatican's enhanced security system that adapted like its mythological namesake. Cut off one security measure, two more took its place.

Winston watched his young charges work, each moving with the synchronized precision of a SEAL team in miniature. "Show me MEDUSA analysis," he commanded. The Multiple Environmental Data Unified Surveillance Assessment sprang to life, showing thermal, electromagnetic, and high intensity energy patterns around the target. The display looked like a kaleidoscope having an anxiety attack.

"Something's different," Lucy said, adjusting her neural interface disguised as a hearing aid. "The signatures and soundings are evolving. Like PHOENIX is active." Predictive Hierarchical Operational Enhancement Network Intelligence Exchange—the system they'd encountered in Cairo. Ancient technology disguised as modern security.

"Sir," Gibson called from his station. "ORACLE is showing anomalous patterns." The Observational Reconnaissance and Algorithmic Computational Learning Engine—their quantum AI's precognitive warning system—was lighting up like a Christmas tree having a seizure.

Winston's tablet chimed with a SPECTRE alert: Strategic Pattern Evaluation and Cryptographic Threat Recognition Engine. The Consortium was mobilizing response teams, moving like sharks that had scented blood in the digital waters.

"They're not just protecting artifacts," Oliver realized, his fingers dancing across neural-linked keyboards. "They're protecting information. The kind that rewrites history books."

"More like burns them," Michael replied. His modified game controller—actually a KRAKEN device: Kinetic Response and Adaptive Knockout Electromagnetic Neutralizer—hummed with a barely auditable buzz of contained energy.

Winston studied the random matrices swirling across his displays. Like reading tea leaves made of lightning, if the tea leaves could predict the future and the lightning could rewrite reality.

"Sir," Emily called softly. "I think I found something." Her small fingers traced a pattern in the hologram. "The security isn't just tight—it's alive. Like a digital immune system."

"CHIMERA," Winston nodded. The Complex Hierarchical Interface for Monitored Environmental Response Assessment algorithm he created. It was a technology that blurred the line between artificial and organic intelligence. His quantum-secure phone buzzed with a message from their mysterious partner:

"LAZARUS protocol initiating. The children must be ready. -T"

"Tobias," Emily whispered, recognizing the signature that had guided them since the beginning. "Why just 'T'?" Oliver had asked, studying one of Tobias's encrypted messages.

"Tobias believes in elegant simplicity," Winston explained. "He's used the same signature since before electronic communications existed." The Lost Asset Zero-point Access Reconnaissance and Unified System—the endgame they'd been preparing for since he first activated the extraordinary children flashed red.

"The Vatican's not just a fortress," Winston told his team. "It's a cocoon. And something inside is about to emerge."

Oliver's screens flashed with new data. "PROMETHEUS is active." The Predictive Reconnaissance Operational Matrix for Enhanced Tactical Homeland Engagement and Unified Security—the system David Romanov had designed before his "death." The same system now responding to his children's quantum-enhanced DNA.

"Like father, like son." Winston thought, watching Oliver work. The boy was a mirror of David—same intensity, same brilliant mind. Same destiny, if they survived what was coming.

"Prep for Operation Blackbird," he commanded. Around the room, systems spun up like digital hurricanes gaining strength. "Emily, you're our skeleton key. Michael, KRAKEN ready. Oliver..."

"On it," the boy replied, his consciousness already merging with the intergraded network. Like a digital Mozart composing symphonies of probability.

Outside, Portland's rain fell hard through misty gray air, each droplet a lens focusing possible futures into the present moment. The game wasn't just chess anymore. It was evolution. And these children were about to become the next stage. If the Consortium's OMEGA protocol didn't eliminate them first. The Operational Mandate for Enhanced Genetic Alteration—their final solution for the children they feared would reshape humanity. The race against probability itself had begun.

CHAPTER 6

GHOSTS IN THE MACHINE

THE ADVANCE PALLADIUM PROCESSORS IN PORTLAND State's basement laboratory whispered their electronic lullabies as Professor Ringo Tut's fingers danced across holographic keyboards. Lines of code reflected in his wire-rimmed glasses—each sequence a strand in a digital tapestry that concealed far more than it revealed. The Ukrainian accent he affected, like so much about him, was an artifice carefully constructed over decades. On one monitor, student assignments scrolled past—elementary exercises in Cobalt, Python, and Java that belied the surreptitious algorithms hidden within. On another, encrypted messages from "T" pulsed with information that caught his attention. The door's subtle pneumatic hiss announced a visitor.

"Professor Tut?"

He minimized the windows with practiced casualness, though his enhanced senses he registered Detective Fibber's distinctive gait—the asymmetric rhythm of a man whose injuries went far deeper than mere physical trauma.

"Detective Fibber," Tut acknowledged, his accent precise but somehow not quite right, like a composition played in a slightly wrong key. "Questions about my former student?"

"Michael Smith." Fibber's gold badge caught the blue light of the iridescent displays. "Brilliant kid. Almost too brilliant."

"Many children possess extraordinary gifts," Tut replied, unconsciously touching the medallion beneath his shirt—an artifact that predated known civilization. "We simply fail to recognize them."

"Like you failed to recognize certain patterns at CERN?"

The question hung in the air like festering wound, unresolved until observed. Tut's smile never wavered, though his fingers traced patterns on his desk that activated buried sensors.

"I've never worked at CERN," he said smoothly. The lie tasted familiar on his tongue, like a vintage wine he'd savored many times before.

"No?" Fibber placed a file on the desk. "Because Dr. Ringo Tashkenbaev's research there was... remarkable. Until his supposed death in 2007."

Tut studied the detective with eyes that had watched empires rise and fall. "Names are like questions, Detective. Reality depends entirely on the observer." His neural implants detected elevated stress patterns in Fibber's biometrics. The detective was pursuing something beyond mere professional curiosity. Something personal.

"The children you teach," Fibber pressed. "They're special, aren't they? Like the ones in Basel?"

"All children are special." Tut's fingers continued their subtle dance, activating deeply buried protocols. "Though some carry... inherited traits that set them apart." The processors hummed a different tone now, responding to patterns in his DNA that marked him as something more than human. Something far older.

"You know about the advance spectral processors," Fibber said. "About what they're doing to these kids."

"Doing to them?" Tut allowed himself a genuine smile. "My dear Detective, you have it precisely backwards. The real question is: what are these children about to do to us?" His sensors detected movement in the building's upper floors. The Consortium's agents, moving like digital predators through probability space. Right on schedule.

"They're coming," Tut said softly. "For all of us. Though not for the reasons you imagine."

Fibber's hand moved toward his weapon. "Who's coming?"

"The ones who think they created us. Who believe they control the evolution of our species." Tut's accent slipped, revealing something far more ancient beneath. "They have no idea what they've awakened." His screens flickered with new data—energy signatures spreading beneath the city. The children's processors activating in synchronized cascades. The pattern he'd waited millennia to see.

"What are you?" Fibber demanded.

"A teacher," Tut replied simply. "Though my first students walked this earth when your ancestors were still learning to make fire." Processors screamed warnings as magnetic fields warped around the building. The Consortium's agents were closing in, drawn by energy signatures they couldn't possibly understand.

"The children must be protected," Tut said, his form beginning to shift as energy fields responded to his true nature. "Especially Oliver. He carries sequences even his father didn't know about. Patterns that predate humanity itself."

"Romanov's son?"

"Romanov was a brilliant man," Tut's smile held secrets older than civilization. "But even he never guessed who really designed those processors. Or why we placed them in human DNA eons ago, waiting for the right moment to activate. David Romanov's consciousness without physical form, can only observe and advise. He is unable to directly protect the children he had helped create. This limitation torments him more than the Consortium's attempt to destroy him."

The building shook as reality itself began to warp. Tut's nuro-implants detected the children's awakening powers resonating with ancient networks buried beneath the city.

"They're not just special, Detective," he said, his form becoming increasingly difficult for human eyes to perceive. "They're the next step in an evolution we began before your species learned to speak. The final sequence in a quantum program written in the very foundations of reality."

As Consortium agents breached the building's outer defenses, Tut's body dissolved into probability patterns. His last words echoed through multiple dimensions:

"Find the children, Detective. Keep them safe until the alignment is complete. Until they understand what they truly are."

"And what's that?" Fibber asked the empty air.

But Tut was gone, leaving only a faint impression of energy wave fields—and a medallion that pulsed with an azure, blue glow, a glow older than human thought.

In the Nest, Oliver's enhanced consciousness detected the energy spike. For a moment, he shook and glimpsed something vast and ancient stirring beneath reality's surface. Something that had waited eons for these precise children to be born. The plan wasn't just about evolution anymore. It was about the return of something humanity had forgotten it ever was.

CHAPTER 7

THE LONG GAME

Sunset painted Rome's ancient stones in hues of soft forgiveness as he examined an identical Egyptian necklace. The artifact's crystalline structure held memories of a time when humanity understood its true purpose—not dominion over the Earth, but stewardship of consciousness itself. It was designed to help identify and awaken potential in carriers of the modified genetic sequences.

Tobias Rosetti stood in his private vault beneath Rome's Via Veneto, his true form carefully maintained in human shape through millennia of practice. Unlike the Consortium members who merely sought to control humanity's evolution, he was one of the original beings who had seeded earth with advanced genetic potential. Each artifact in his collection resonated with frequencies from his home world, reminders of the vast plan he and his kind had set in motion eons ago.

"The patterns align," he murmured, watching the necklace pulse in harmony with genetic sequences that promised more than mere evolution. These markers offered humanity a chance to remember its original purpose—to be shepherds of consciousness, guardians of those who needed protection most.

His displays showed the children of Portland: Oliver orchestrating impossible feats, Emily slipping through barriers both physical and social, Michael crafting devices that bridged the gap between what humanity was and what it could become. But beyond their extraordinary abilities lay something far more precious—their understanding of society's forgotten ones. Each child in their group had experienced abandonment, known the bitter taste of society's indifference. Yet instead of hardening their hearts, these experiences had awakened something profound. They stole not for profit but to force the world to see those it had chosen to ignore.

"Sir," his security system announced, "Detective Fibber pursues the truth."

Tobias smiled, remembering other seekers across millennia who had glimpsed pieces of the larger pattern. He swirled aged grappa in Galileo's crystal glass—a man who had understood that looking up at the stars meant looking back in time, seeing light that carried ancient messages of possibility. He crossed to his vault, disguised as centuries-old furniture but containing proof of humanity's long journey toward awakening. Among artifacts of lost civilizations lay simple treasures: a child's worn blanket, a handful of marbles, a diary filled with hopes that refused to die despite society's neglect. Each item radiated not just memory but promise—the potential for transformation that lay within every discarded soul.

"They're gathering their forces," Nikolas reported, entering silently. "They fear what these children represent."

"Of course they do." Tobias activated displays showing patterns of awakening spreading across the globe. "These children embody every chance at redemption humanity has ever discarded. Every opportunity for transformation it has ignored." The patterns showed more than just genetic mutation potential—they revealed humanity's collective journey toward remembering its true nature. Each child they had gathered represented thousands more, waiting to be recognized, to be given a chance to help reshape reality itself.

"When will they understand?" Nikolas asked. "That these street children they've thrown away are the key to their salvation?"

"Soon." Tobias manipulated data streams that showed countless possible futures. "These children don't just carry enhanced abilities—they carry the wisdom of the forgotten. They understand that true power lies not in domination but in lifting others up." His displays showed Oliver working with younger children in the Nest, teaching them not just technical skills but compassion. Emily sharing her food with new arrivals, her tiny frame containing a heart vast enough to forgive those who had abandoned her. Michael, bravely crafting devices that would eventually help other displaced children find safety.

"The future they'll create," Tobias mused, "won't just prevent children from falling through society's cracks. It will recognize that every lost child represents a piece of humanity's soul waiting to be reclaimed." He turned to a hand etched star chart, its patterns showing not just celestial alignments but intricate symbols for collective awakening. "These children will remember what humanity was meant to be—not rulers but guardians. Not conquerors but healers." His form shifted slightly, ancient eyes gazing out from a face that had watched civilizations rise and fall, each time hoping humanity would recognize its true purpose.

"We gave them incredible abilities," he told Nikolas, "but their real power lies in their capacity for forgiveness. Despite everything humanity has done to them, they still wish to save it." Outside his villa, Naples' evening light painted the bay in colors of possibility. Like reality itself, preparing to be transformed not by power but by the unconditional love that only those who have known total abandonment can offer.

"The end isn't just about evolution," Tobias said softly. "It's about humanity remembering that its greatest strength lies in protecting its most vulnerable. These children, whom society discarded, will teach humanity how to become what it was always meant to be—a species that measures its worth not by its achievements but by how it cares for its own." The ancient desire had never been about power. It was about remembering that true redemption comes not from strength but from the ability to love despite all reasons not to.

And humanity was about to learn this lesson from the very children it had chosen to forget.

CHAPTER 8

POINT OF NO RETURN

Dawn painted Paris in watercolor hues as the city stirred to life. Along Rue Saint-Honoré, pâtissiers arranged golden croissants and jewel-toned macarons in window displays that could rival the Louvre's artistry. The scent of fresh-baked bread mingled with coffee and spring roses, drifting past Chanel's flagship store where mannequins wore this season's haute couture like armor.

Near Place Vendôme, a street violinist played Debussy, her music weaving through the morning air as elegantly dressed Parisians clicked past in Louboutins and bespoke suits. Fountains sparkled in the early light, their waters telling stories older than the city itself. The Eiffel Tower pierced a sky the color of aged pearls, its iron lace casting shadows across cafés where waiters in pristine aprons arranged chairs with geometric precision. At L'Abeille, the three-Michelin-starred restaurant in the Shangri-La Hotel, chefs were already preparing sauces that took three days to perfect.

Ginny watched this choreography of Parisian life from her suite at the Ritz, wrapped in a silk Hermès robe in deep azure that matched her eyes. Her Louboutin boots from yesterday's heist lay discarded by a Louis XVI chair, the red soles as bright as fresh blood. On the antique desk, surveillance photos showed the Louvre's marble halls, its hidden passages mapped in red ink that looked suspiciously like the same shade as her shoes. She turned on the television, switching to France 24's English broadcast. The anchor's crisp British accent filled the room: "Breaking news from the Louvre Museum, where officials report an unprecedented security breach..."

The camera panned across the museum's familiar corridors, now eerily empty. Tourists had been evacuated, their abandoned audio guides littering marble floors that had witnessed centuries of history. In the background, security personnel hurried past Renaissance masterpieces, their radios crackling with barely contained panic.

"The targeted artifact, known as DaVinci's Cipher, appears to have vanished without trace. Sources close to the investigation report inexplicable failures in the museum's state-of-the-art security systems..." Ginny's encrypted phone buzzed with a message from T:

"Phase One complete. The children performed admirably." She crossed to the window, watching morning light play across the Seine. Below, a mime performed for tourists near a fountain, his movements telling stories of loss and discovery. The irony wasn't lost on her—while crowds watched his theatrical theft routine, real treasures were disappearing through the city's shadows.

In the distance, the Louvre's glass pyramid caught the sun like a prism, scattering light across the courtyard where gendarmes gathered in growing numbers. Their vehicles' emergency lights painted ancient stones in alternating blue and red, a disco of official concern.

Her secure tablet chimed with an incoming encrypted transmission. The screen showed three museum heists happening simultaneously—London's British Museum, New York's Metropolitan, and here in Paris. Each target seemingly random, yet Ginny knew better. These were rehearsals, distractions from the real operation about to unfold beneath the Vatican.

A soft knock at her door made her freeze. Through the peephole, she saw a hotel employee with a silver breakfast tray. But something about his posture triggered warning bells in her mind.

"Room service," he called in perfect French. Too perfect.

Ginny silently slipped her backup weapon from its hiding place as another news alert flashed across her tablet: "Unexplained energy signatures detected beneath Paris. Scientific instruments worldwide reporting anomalous readings..." The children weren't just stealing artifacts. They were awakening something. Something that had waited centuries to be found.

In the street below, the mime had stopped performing. He stood absolutely still, face upturned toward her window. His makeup couldn't quite hide features that seemed oddly familiar. The knock came again, more insistent this time.

And in the Louvre's empty halls, security cameras caught a final image before failing completely: a small figure in a Hello Kitty backpack, moving through solid walls as if they were merely suggestions.

The optics were changing. Reality itself was beginning to bend.

CHAPTER 9

CONVERGENCE

THE SYNCHRONOUS STRIKES BEGAN AS NIGHT FELL ACROSS three cities, each operation a masterpiece of precision orchestrated by children society had forgotten.

In London, rain misted across the British Museum's granite façade as Emily slipped through maintenance tunnels that predated the Victorian era. Above, tourists snapped photos of the Rosetta Stone, unaware that beneath their feet, an eight-year-old girl was accessing secrets far older than ancient Egypt. The museum's foundations rested on medieval crypts, and below those, passages that remembered when London was called Londinium. Emily's small fingers traced inscriptions that hadn't been seen since Roman legions walked these streets, her Hello Kitty backpack was out of place against stones that had witnessed two millennia of history.

In New York, Michael bypassed the Metropolitan Museum's security systems as easily as other children played video games. The Met's power grid flickered imperceptibly as his devices redirected electrical currents through pathways that shouldn't have existed. From his position in an abandoned subway tunnel, he could sense other networks beneath Manhattan's steel and concrete skin—antiquated systems waiting to be awakened. Like him, they had been forgotten, buried beneath layers of civilization that never thought to look deeper.

And in Paris, Oliver moved through the Louvre's marble halls like a ghost in the machine. Security cameras caught glimpses of his reflection, but their digital memories would show only empty corridors. The museum's official blueprints showed three sub-basements, but Oliver had discovered a fourth level, its entrance hidden behind a false wall that hadn't been opened since the French Revolution. Here, dust-covered crates bore symbols that matched patterns in his own DNA.

But these heists were mere distractions from the real operation unfolding beneath Rome's ancient streets. The Eternal City had been built in layers, each civilization building upon the ruins of the last. Beneath tourist-filled piazzas and Renaissance churches lay catacombs, and beneath those, older passages that remembered when Rome was young. But deeper still lay tunnels that had never appeared in any historical record—passages that seemed to have been engineered rather than built.

In a hidden vault beneath the Vatican, where even the Pope's most trusted advisors had never ventured, twelve children gathered like apostles of a new age. Their small forms cast long shadows across mosaic floors that depicted star charts of impossible accuracy. The vault's walls bore inscriptions in languages that predated written history, their symbols pulsing with faint luminescence that responded to the children's presence.

Above, Rome's evening traffic crawled past the Colosseum, tourists posed for selfies at the Trevi Fountain, and waiters in crisp aprons served aperitivos at sidewalk cafés. None of them noticed the subtle vibrations in the earth beneath their feet, or the way their mobile phones briefly lost signal in patterns that spelled out ancient messages in binary code. The vault itself defied modern architectural understanding. Its ceiling seemed to extend indefinitely upward, disappearing into darkness that swallowed their flashlight beams. Pillars of some opalescent material that wasn't quite stone and wasn't quite metal rose like ancient trees, their surfaces etched with fractal patterns that seemed to shift when viewed directly. The air held the metallic taste of electricity, and something else—the flavor of time itself, compressed and distilled into physical form.

As the children took their positions around a central platform, each standing on markers that corresponded to constellations, their synchronized movements triggered responses in the vault's ancient machinery. Patterns of light began to trace paths between them, forming geometric shapes that shouldn't have been possible in three-dimensional space. The platform itself, covered in what appeared to be mathematical formulas written in light, began to pulse in rhythm with their heartbeats.

But even as they worked, other forces converged on their location. Vatican security, alerted by energy signatures they couldn't explain, mobilized special response teams. Consortium agents, moving like shadows through Rome's tourist crowds, traced probability patterns toward the source of reality distortions. And deep beneath the city, something older than humanity stirred in response to the children's presence.

In his command center, Winston monitored all of it through systems that blended modern technology with ancient wisdom. The patterns were clear—each child represented not just their own potential, but the hopes of countless others society had cast aside. Their abilities weren't random mutations but inherited memories, passed down through generations of forgotten children who had survived on society's margins.

"Energy signatures are aligning," Michael's voice crackled through their secure channel. "The network is responding."

"London is active," Emily reported, her small voice steady despite the weight of centuries pressing down around her. "The passages remember."

In Paris, Oliver felt reality itself beginning to flex around him. "The barriers are thinning," he said softly. "I can see the connections."

Beneath Rome, the vault's ancient machinery hum-med with awakening power. The children's quantum-enhanced DNA resonated with frequencies that hadn't been active since before the last ice age. Each of them represented thousands more—forgotten children whose potential remained locked away, waiting for the right moment to transform society itself. Reality wasn't just bending anymore. It was beginning to remember what it had been engineered to become.

And the children society had thrown away would be its guides into a future that erased the very concept of abandonment. The convergence was resonating with time and space. It had been waiting for these precise children since before humanity learned to dream of transformation.

THE VATICAN GAMBIT

EMILY'S SMALL FORM MOVED THROUGH THE VATICAN CATacombs, each step echoing with memories of the day Oliver first found her huddled in a Portland alley. She'd been terrified then, a tiny refugee who couldn't speak English, expecting the worst from everyone. But Oliver had simply sat beside her, sharing his chocolate bar in silence until her shaking stopped. Now, three years later, they moved in perfect synchronization despite being in different countries. His voice in her earpiece felt like home.

"Your vitals are fluctuating," Oliver said, concern threading through his usually steady tone. Even across thousands of miles, she could picture his expression—the slight furrow between his brows that appeared whenever he worried about her.

"I'm fine," Emily whispered, though they both knew it was a lie. They never lied to each other, not since that first night when they'd stayed up until dawn sharing their stories of abandonment and survival. She wiped away the blood trickling from her nose, remembering how Oliver had once cleaned a scrape on her knee with such gentle care.

The vault door yielded to her touch as another tremor wracked her frame. The crystal waited inside, pulsing with energy that made her enhanced DNA sing—and scream.

"Emily." Oliver's voice held the same quiet strength he'd shown the night she'd woken crying from nightmares, when he'd read to her until she fell asleep. "Your genetic markers are destabilizing. Please. Get out."

She could count on one hand the number of times she'd heard fear in his voice. The first had been when she'd nearly fallen during a practice climb. He'd caught her then, his arms surprisingly strong for a thirteen-year-old, and made her promise to always be careful. The security sweep's footsteps echoed through ancient corridors as Emily pressed herself into an alcove. Blood dripped steadily from her nose now, each drop a potential betrayal. She thought of Oliver's birthday last month, when she'd surprised him with a cake she'd learned to bake in secret. The way his eyes had lit up meant more than any heist they'd ever pulled off.

"Movement detected in sector seven."

The guard passed inches from her hiding spot as another tremor hit. The crystal in her pack pulsed in rhythm with her heart, which now beat an erratic pattern that had nothing to do with fear. Emily had never been afraid when Oliver was watching over her. She staggered toward the extraction point, leaving bloody prints that marked her passage. Oliver's increasingly urgent voice in her ear reminded her of late-night conversations in the Nest, when they'd shared dreams of a world where no child would ever be forgotten.

"Emily!" His voice cracked with emotion he rarely showed to others. "Your genetic stability is critical. Please..."

The last few meters felt impossible, but she forced herself forward.

Oliver waited at the top of the maintenance shaft, his face pale with a fear she'd never seen before. When her legs gave out, he caught her as he always had, since that very first day.

"Your nose..." he started, cradling her with infinite gentleness.

"Not just my nose." She managed a weak smile despite the blood. Even now, she tried to ease his worry. "Something's wrong, Oliver. The crystal... it's changing us."

He held her close, and in that moment, all their unspoken feelings passed between them. They were too young for romance, but what they shared went deeper—a connection forged in shared pain and mutual understanding. The kind of love that had nothing to do with age and everything to do with souls recognizing their other half.

"The genetic markers," Michael reported. "They're not just destabilizing—they're mutating." Emily reached up to touch Oliver's cheek, leaving a small bloody print. "Remember the promise?" He nodded, tears threatening. On their first Christmas together, they'd sworn to always protect each other, no matter what. A child's promise that had grown into something unbreakable.

The seizure took her then, her small body convulsing in his arms. When her eyes rolled back, showing whites shot through with impossible gold, Oliver held her as if she were the most precious thing in existence. To him, she was.

"Oliver," she whispered when the seizure passed. "I can see them. All the others like us. So many children..." Her voice faded as unconsciousness claimed her.

The crystal pulsed in her pack, its rhythm matching the tremors that now ran through both their enhanced bodies. But Oliver barely noticed his own symptoms, focused entirely on the tiny form in his arms. Whatever change was coming, they would face it as they had faced everything else.

Together.

Because sometimes the deepest love isn't about romance at all. Sometimes it's about two lost souls finding family in each other, about the kind of connection that transcends age and time and even DNA.

And nothing—not genetic mutation, not ancient technology, not the vast conspiracy unfolding around them—could break that bond.

THE ARCHITECT

WINSTON McGOWN BLACKWELL III SAT IN HIS LEATHER wingback chair, contemplating the ancient chess set before him. Each piece, carved from mammoth ivory during the Renaissance, held centuries of strategic wisdom. Like the game itself, his current endeavor required patience, foresight, and the willingness to sacrifice pawns for greater advantage. The year was 2025, though Winston measured time differently. His study in the Nest's upper floor reflected decades of refined taste: first-edition Hemingway shared shelf space with leather-bound quantum physics texts, while a genuine Monet hung beside holographic displays showing probability matrices. A 1953 Macallan aged in its crystal decanter, waiting to celebrate victories not yet achieved.

His silver ponytail, immaculately groomed, draped over the collar of a bespoke Anderson & Sheppard suit. The outfit's careful tailoring concealed both advanced technology and a physique that belied his apparent age. To casual observers, he appeared to be a well-preserved man in his early seventies. The reality, like everything about Winston, was far more complex.

"Status report," he commanded softly. His cultured voice carried traces of multiple accents—Oxford's refined tones layered over something far older.

Michael looked up from his workstation, where holographic displays showed Emily's deteriorating vital signs. "The genetic cascades are accelerating, sir. Whatever the Vatican crystal triggered, it's spreading through all the enhanced sequences."

Winston moved a knight on the chess board, its path mirroring the children's movements through Rome's ancient passages. "And the others?"

"We're detecting similar mutations in enhanced children worldwide," Lucy reported, her fingers dancing across neural interfaces. "The patterns match prophecies found in the Cairo site."

The Cairo site. Winston allowed himself a small smile, remembering how different the world had been when he first discovered those ruins. Howard Carter had been making headlines with Tutankhamun's tomb, never suspecting that the real treasures lay deeper, in chambers that predated Egyptian civilization itself.

"Sir," Oliver called urgently. "Emily's consciousness is fragmenting across probability fields. I'm losing her."

Winston rose with fluid grace, crossing to the curved imaging displays. Emily's small form registered across multiple reality states simultaneously—an effect he hadn't seen since the Basel incident. The girl's enhanced DNA was trying to express capabilities that human biology wasn't meant to handle. Yet.

"The plan accelerates," he mused, adjusting his wire-rimmed glasses. The frames contained sensors that could perceive accelerated states, among other things. "Though perhaps 'plan' is the wrong word. What we attempt is nothing less than the guided evolution of our species." He touched a control panel disguised as antique wood paneling, revealing displays that tracked every enhanced child on Earth. Thousands of points of light, each representing potential that humanity had carelessly discarded. Street children, orphans, the forgotten ones—all carrying genetic sequences that would reshape reality itself.

"Sir," Michael's voice held barely contained worry. "The Consortium is mobilizing. Their suppressors are already active in major cities." Winston's lips curved in what might have been amusement. "They still think technology alone will save them. They never understood that these children are simply remembering what humanity was meant to be." He returned to his chess set, moving pieces in patterns that mapped to electromagnetic fields spreading across the globe. Each move represented decades of planning, centuries of careful genetic manipulation. The children thought they were simply stealing artifacts, but every heist had been orchestrated to awaken specific integrated memories.

"Oliver," he called softly. "Tell me what you see when you look at Emily now." The boy's enhanced perception stretched across quantum states. "Her form... it's changing. Like reality itself is trying to remember a different shape."

"Precisely." Winston lifted the white queen, its ivory surface catching light in impossible ways. "Evolution isn't just about biology. It's about consciousness remembering what it once was. What it can become again."

His displays showed Emily's genetic structure expressing patterns that matched symbols found in ruins older than human civilization. The same patterns appeared in the Vatican crystal, in artifacts scattered across the globe, and in the children's enhanced DNA.

"Sir," Lucy's voice held awe. "The prophecies... they weren't about the future, were they? They were memories. Of what we used to be."

"Indeed." Winston's smile held secrets older than written history. "These children aren't evolving into something new. They're remembering what humanity was before it forgot its true nature. Before certain powers tried to lock away abilities they feared they couldn't control."

The chess board's pattern suddenly shifted, pieces moving of their own accord as probability fields warped around them. In the medical bay, Emily's vital signs stabilized as her consciousness expanded into capabilities that shouldn't have been possible.

"The game," Winston said softly, "has never been about winning or losing. It's about remembering. About becoming what we always were." His displays showed more children awakening worldwide, their enhanced DNA responding to patterns hidden in artifacts his team had gathered. Each piece positioned precisely, waiting for this moment. The moment when humanity would remember it had never been merely human at all. Betrayal's Price.

In his Naples villa, Tobias studied the artifacts arranged on his desk. The two Egyptian necklaces finally together. A fragment of the DaVinci Cypher. And now, transmitted from the Vatican team, photographs of something that changed everything.

His phone rang. "The children performed perfectly," Winston's voice said. "But they're asking questions. Oliver especially."

"They're ready to know the truth," Tobias replied. "About why we chose them. About their real parents."

"And Ginny?"

"My niece plays her part without knowing it. Just like her father did." His phone buzzed: a message from Interpol. Another heist, this time at the Vatican. Same MO. Same impossibly small entry points. But something caught his eye in the adoption file—a signature he recognized. Winston Blackwell III had been there the day Ginny gave up her son.

CHAPTER 12

THE STORM BREAKS

THE NEST ERUPTED INTO CONTROLLED CHAOS AS NEWS feeds plastered every available screen. BBC World News showed Vatican City in lockdown, while CNN's helicopter footage captured Italian special forces converging on St. Peter's Square. Al Jazeera reported unexplained energy signatures beneath Rome's ancient streets, and Reuters tracked simultaneous disturbances at sacred sites worldwide. Oliver barely registered the cacophony of alerts and warnings. His attention remained fixed on the encrypted files he'd discovered buried deep in the Nest's data storage systems. Files that shouldn't have existed. Files that told a very different story about who they were and why they'd been chosen.

"These records go back centuries," he muttered, fingers flying across neural interfaces as he dug deeper. "Birth certificates, medical records, genetic profiles... they've been tracking specific bloodlines since before DNA was discovered." The files showed more than just surveillance. They revealed carefully orchestrated adoptions, arranged marriages, subtle manipulations ensuring certain genetic sequences would combine in precise patterns. Oliver's own birth hadn't been chance—his parents' meeting had been engineered decades before either was born.

"You lied to us!" The accusation burst from him as Winston entered, the older man's calm presence a stark contrast to the chaos around them. "We're not random street kids you saved. You chose us. You arranged for us to end up on the streets!" Winston settled into his leather chair with practiced grace, as if this confrontation were simply another move in a game he'd played countless times before. "Did I?" His voice held no defensiveness, only gentle inquiry. "Or did I ensure you would be found when your abilities began to manifest?"

"The files show—"

"The files show preparation, yes." Winston poured two cups of Earl Grey from a sterling silver service, adding honey to Oliver's exactly as he preferred. "They show centuries of careful work ensuring certain genetic sequences would survive. Would you prefer I had left those sequences to be eliminated by those who fear what humanity might become?"

Oliver's hands trembled slightly as he pulled up more records. "These adoption papers... my parents..."

"Were chosen for their own genetic potential, yes. As were their parents, and theirs before them." Winston sipped his tea. "But the choice to give you up was still their own. As was my choice to ensure you would be found by those who understood what you might become."

"And the others? Emily? Michael?"

"All carrying sequences that needed to be preserved. All with potential that ordinary society would have wasted." Winston's eyes held centuries of patience. "Tell me, Oliver. In all our time together, have I ever asked you to be anything other than what you truly are?"

Oliver's anger faltered as memories surfaced. There was Winston teaching him to hack by encouraging his natural talents, never forcing, always guiding. Supporting Emily's acrobatic skills, Michael's technical genius, each child's unique gifts.

"But why the streets?" he demanded. "Why not just adopt us normally?"

Winston's smile held secrets older than the Vatican's foundations. "Because adversity reveals truth. Because those who have known abandonment understand the value of connection. And because certain abilities only awaken when survival demands them."

He gestured to a screen showing Emily's current condition, her DNA expressing patterns that defied modern science. "What's happening now—these transformations—they require more than just genetic potential. They require understanding that can only come from walking between worlds. From seeing society's shadows and choosing to bring light to them anyway."

Oliver's screens showed more files unlocking, revealing deeper patterns. But something nagged at his enhanced perception—gaps in the data, references to other records stored somewhere else. Somewhere even his considerable skills couldn't access.

"There's more, isn't there?" he asked. "Something you're still not telling us."

Winston's smile deepened fractionally. "There is always more, Oliver. The question is: are you ready to understand it?" He gestured to the news feeds, where Vatican security forces discovered their infiltration had been more than a simple heist. "What you found in those files is merely prologue. The true story—the one written in your very DNA— is about to begin."

Somewhere beneath the Vatican, in vaults deeper than any official record acknowledged, other files waited. Files that would reveal why certain bloodlines had been preserved since before recorded history. Why humanity's evolutionary path had been subtly guided for millennia.

And in a hidden chamber that even Winston's maps didn't show, an artifact older than human civilization pulsed with energy that matched the patterns now expressing in the children's enhanced DNA. The game wasn't just about genetic potential anymore. It was about remembering what those genes had been designed to become. If humanity survived the remembering.

BLOODLINES

GINNY'S HANDS TREMBLED AS SHE STUDIED THE DNA TEST results on her secure tablet. The sample had been processed through three different labs, each confirming what she'd refused to believe. The boy in the security feeds, the one orchestrating impossible heists—he wasn't just connected to her past. He was her son.

Outside her Lisbon hotel room, traffic hummed along the Avenida da Liberdade, oblivious to how reality itself seemed to shift around her. The Egyptian necklace she'd transported still pulsed gently against her skin, its crystalline structure resonating with patterns she now recognized in her own genetic code. Her phone chimed with an encrypted message from Tobias: "Now you understand why I chose you. The boy's abilities aren't random mutations. They're inherited memories, written in code older than civilization itself.—T"

Attached files showed surveillance footage from Portland: Oliver bypassing security systems with impossible ease, his movements expressing grace that matched her own forgotten talents. The same talents that had made her father legendary in certain circles before his disappearance. She opened another file—medical records from fifteen years ago, when she'd given up a child for adoption. The decision had torn her apart, but she'd been young, alone, and the pregnancy itself had been... unusual. Tests had shown genetic markers that puzzled her doctors, patterns that shouldn't have existed in human DNA. The same patterns now appearing in children worldwide.

Her secure tablet flashed with breaking news from the Vatican. The heist had been more than theft—it was awakening something. Ancient systems responding to genetic keys carried in the children's blood. In Oliver's blood. In her blood.

"The convergence accelerates," Tobias's next message read. "He needs you now, more than ever. They all do."

Surveillance feeds showed Oliver in the Nest, confronting Winston about hidden files. About carefully preserved bloodlines and orchestrated meetings. About a plan spanning centuries.

But even Winston didn't know everything. Ginny's fingers traced patterns in the air, manipulating probability fields in ways she'd forgotten she could. Ways she'd been made to forget, just as humanity had been made to forget what it once was.

Her tablet displayed more test results: genetic sequences activating in Oliver that matched prophecies hidden in ruins older than Egypt. The same sequences now expressing in her own DNA, awakening abilities that no one—not even Tobias—had predicted.

"Come to Rome," his final message urged. "It's time you learned about your father's work. About why these children were chosen. About what they're going to become."

In Portland, Oliver's confrontation with Winston reached its peak. But the files he'd discovered were only part of the truth. The real secret lay buried beneath the Vatican, in vaults that remembered when humanity walked different paths through reality.

Ginny packed quickly, her enhanced senses detecting surveillance teams converging on her location. The Consortium wouldn't just be hunting the children now. They'd be hunting anyone carrying activated genetic sequences. Anyone who might remember what humankind had been before it was locked into its current form.

Her finger hovered over Oliver's number in her secure phone. What could she say to a son she'd given up, who was now at the center of mankind's next evolutionary leap? How could she explain that his extraordinary abilities weren't random gifts, but birthright? That their family tree had roots in soil older than Earth itself?

The necklace pulsed against her skin as reality rippled around her. In Rome, ancient machinery awakened beneath the Vatican's foundations. In Portland, Oliver's genetic structure expressed patterns that matched symbols found in ruins that shouldn't have existed.

And somewhere in between, Ginny felt the weight of centuries pressing down—generations of carefully preserved bloodlines, all leading to this moment. If their enhanced DNA survived the remembering, everything would change. Would humanity remember it had never been merely human at all.

THE CIPHER'S SECRET

THE LOUVRE'S MARBLE HALLS GROANED AS REALITY WARPED around Emily's small form. Blood trickled not just from her nose now, but from her eyes and ears, leaving crimson patterns that matched the ancient symbols on the DaVinci Cipher. Her hands trembled as she traced the metallic disc's surface, each touch sending waves of agony through enhanced DNA that was rapidly rewriting itself.

"Emily!" Michael's voice cracked through their secure channel. "Your genetic structure—it's destabilizing at molecular level." Through their neural link, she felt his own transformation beginning. His consciousness fractured across multiple probability states as memories older than Earth itself burned through neural pathways never meant to contain such knowledge. Blood vessels burst in his eyes. A deep gold shot through with patterns that shouldn't have been possible in human anatomy.

"I can see them," Emily gasped, her voice resonating at frequencies that made the ancient stones vibrate. "The others. Before. When we walked between stars." The security feeds showed their physical forms beginning to shift. Emily's small frame contorted as bones tried to remember configurations from before humans walked upright. Michael's skin rippled with bioluminescent patterns that matched symbols found in ruins older than recorded history.

"Their core DNA is unraveling," Oliver reported, his enhanced perception stretching across quantum states to monitor their deteriorating conditions. "Whatever consciousness is awakening in them—it's burning through their human genetic structure like fire through paper."

Through their secure channel, Winston's voice held carefully controlled urgency: "Emily, Michael—you must slow the transformation. Your bodies aren't ready for full activation." But the process had already passed the point of no return. Emily screamed as memories flooded her consciousness—vast cities among the stars, technologies that could reshape reality itself, and a plan to seed modified human DNA with fragments of their own awareness, waiting for the right moment to reawaken.

"Make it stop!" Michael cried, his enhanced intellect drowning in knowledge no human mind was meant to contain. Neural interfaces sparked and failed as his consciousness expanded beyond their capacity to channel.

The DaVinci Cipher pulsed with energies that resonated across probability fields, its surface now glowing with the same otherworldly patterns that marked Emily and Michael's transforming flesh. Reality itself seemed to bend around them, space-time rippling like water disturbed by stones cast from another universe.

"Their genetic structure is approaching critical destabilization," Oliver warned, his screens showing catastrophic breakdown of basic human DNA sequences. "We're losing them!"

In Rome, ancient machinery beneath the Vatican responded to their transformation, powering up systems that had waited millennia for this moment. But the children's bodies were failing faster than the ancient technology could stabilize them.

Emily collapsed, her small form convulsing as genetic memories tried to express physical changes that human biology couldn't support. Golden light leaked from her eyes and mouth, carrying fragments of a consciousness vast enough to span galaxies.

"I remember," she whispered in a language that predated human speech. "We were sent to prepare them. To guide their evolution. But something went wrong..."

Michael's scream cut across all their secure channels as his consciousness briefly touched the full awareness of what they had once been. Blood vessels burst across his skin in patterns that matched constellations older than Andromeda's spiraling arms.

"The others," he gasped. "They're still out there. Waiting. In children across Earth. Beginning to remember..." Through temporal encrypted feeds, Tobias's voice held real fear for the first time in centuries: "Their transformation is cascading across probability fields. Affecting every child carrying parallel sequences." In hospitals worldwide, children with mysterious genetic markers began to seize. On the streets of every major city, homeless kids with hidden abilities felt the first tremors of change begin.

Reality twisted around Emily and Michael as the full weight of ancient consciousness pressed against the limits of human flesh. Golden light poured from their transforming bodies as genetic memories older fought to express their true nature.

"Please," Emily's voice echoed across vast conscience states, carrying traces of what she had once been. "We can't... contain..."

The DaVinci Cipher's surface erupted with improbable energies as magnetic fields collapsed around them. In that moment of spectral chaos, every enhanced child on Earth felt the echo of primordial aware-ness touch their own accelerating transformations. It wasn't just about evolution anymore. It was about the return of something that had seeded its consciousness through human DNA eons ago, waiting for precisely this moment to reawaken.

Would any remember what they truly were?

CONVERGENCE

DETECTIVE LEO FIBBER STOOD IN THE ABANDONED NEST, his photographic memory cataloging every detail of the hasty evacuation. Papers scattered across random interfaces told a story his enhanced perception could read like a book: twelve orphaned children, moving with practiced precision, implementing emergency protocols they'd rehearsed countless times. His leg throbbed with a pain that resonated at frequencies no medical equipment had ever been able to detect.

The holographic screens still hummed with active data streams, displaying patterns that triggered memories of that night in Afghanistan. The impossible lights, the way reality had bent around them, and the children they'd found—children whose abilities defied every preconceived notion he ever had about human potential.

On the central monitor, a message pulsed red with urgency:

PROTOCOL OMEGA INITIATED CONVERGENCE POINT: ROME ALL ASSETS MOBILIZING

Fibber's mind, trained through years of military intelligence and enhanced by whatever had changed him that night in Kandahar, began connecting threads that normal consciousness wouldn't have perceived. The melted locks weren't just signature moves—they were tests, each heist measuring the children's growing abilities against some ancient standard. His secure phone vibrated: Interpol's encrypted line. "Detective, we're tracking multiple signatures. Enhanced children boarding planes across three continents. All trajectories converging on Rome."

"Send me the data," he ordered, his voice steady despite the way his acquired senses detected magnetic fields warping around him. The pain in his leg intensified as reality itself seemed to flex and strain. Before he could process the Interpol data, another call waited—this one from a blocked number that somehow existed in multiple encoded states simultaneously. He answered, already knowing who it would be.

"Hello, Detective," Tobias's cultured voice held traces of something far older than human civilization. "I believe it's time we discussed why these children matter so much. And why your leg really hasn't healed after all these years."

Fibber's perfect memory flashed back to the moment the explosion had torn reality apart around him. The way his DNA had begun rewriting itself even as medics loaded him onto the rescue helicopter. The classified medical reports that showed genetic changes that shouldn't have been possible.

"The children," he said slowly, his augmented perception picking up patterns in Tobias's encrypted signal. "They're not just gifted. They're like me. Changed."

"No, Detective," Tobias corrected gently. "You are like them. That night in Afghanistan, you encountered technology left by the same civilization that engineered their genetic potential. Your transformation was accidental. Theirs was designed, written into DNA passed down through carefully preserved bloodlines. It was meant for the orphaned children."

Fibber's screens showed more data flowing in: reports of enhanced children worldwide experiencing synchronized genetic activation. His leg burned as his own modified DNA responded to frequencies emanating from somewhere beneath Rome.

"The convergence," he realized, pieces clicking into place in his enhanced consciousness. "It's not just about gathering them in one place. It's about reaching critical mass. About enough enhanced DNA activating simultaneously to trigger something bigger."

"Indeed." Tobias's voice held approval. "Tell me, Detective—what do your enhanced senses tell you about the pain in your leg? About the way reality feels thinner around you with each passing moment?"

Fibber closed his eyes, letting his altered consciousness expand into awareness normal humans couldn't access. His leg wasn't just injured— it was trying to remember a different configuration. A different way of existing in space-time.

"The children," he said, opening eyes that now held traces of gold. "They're not just remembering abilities. They're remembering what humanity was before someone locked away our true nature."

"Very good." Tobias's signal pulsed with energies that matched the patterns in Fibber's DNA. "Now you understand why we had to preserve certain bloodlines. Why these specific children had to be gathered and trained."

Around him, the Nest's abandoned technology responded to frequencies emanating from his partially transformed genetics. Screens showed more children converging on Rome, each carrying fragments of a legacy older than human civilization. The investigation hadn't just led him to a series of impossible heists. It had led him to the threshold of humanity's true origin story.

And in Rome, beneath layers of history and faith, ancient machinery waited to help humanity remember what it had been engineered to forget. If their transformed DNA survived the remembering.

ANCIENT DEPTHS

THEY MET IN THE SHADOWED COURTYARD OF SAINT PETER'S Square, as afternoon crowds swirled around them like leaves in an autumn wind. It wasn't difficult. Fibber spotted her first—her infected DNA making her glow subtly to his transformed perception. She stood near the obelisk, wearing a tailored Chanel suit that couldn't quite hide how her body was beginning to remember older forms.

"Detective Fibber," she said, turning before he could announce himself. Her eyes held traces of gold now, like Emily's. "I would have recognized you even without Tobias's description. You carry the changes like my father did." Fibber studied her face, his photographic memory overlaying her features with surveillance footage from the jewelry store. But she was different now—transformed not just by awakening genetics but by the weight of discovered truths.

"Ms. Torielle." He limped forward, his enhanced senses detecting how reality warped subtly around them both. "Though I suppose that name, like much else, isn't quite accurate."

"Ginny will do." She glanced at his leg, understanding in her eyes. "Afghanistan?"

"Kandahar Province. Where I first encountered the technology that changed us." He noted how she unconsciously oriented herself toward the Vatican, where ancient machinery hummed at frequencies only their enhanced perceptions could detect. "Your son is down there."

"Oliver." The name carried weight beyond its three syllables. "And Emily. And all the others we've tried to protect while barely understanding what they truly are." Their enhanced DNA resonated in proximity, sharing fragments of genetic memory neither was quite ready to process. Stars seen from forgotten worlds. Technologies that could reshape reality. And a plan, written into their pulsating genes, that had waited millennia to unfold.

"We don't have much time," Fibber said, his military training cutting through layers of transformation and revelation. "The children's changes are accelerating beyond sustainable rates."

Ginny nodded, already moving toward the entrance to the deeper catacombs. "Then we should stop wasting it with introductions. After all—" She smiled slightly, though tension lined her transforming features. "—we've known each other since before humanity walked upright. We just haven't remembered yet." Together, they descended into darkness that grew less dark with each step as their enhanced perceptions expanded. Their transformations accelerated in sync, human forms struggling to contain awareness that reached across stars.

Ginny reached for Fibber's arm as they descended into Rome's ancient depths, her touch steadying them both as reality warped around their enhanced perceptions. After years of operating alone, trusting another person felt foreign—yet somehow inevitable.

"Your leg," she noted, seeing him wince. "The transformation's affecting you too." Fibber nodded, remembering how she'd looked in the jewelry store that first day, when neither of them knew what they truly were. "Different from Afghanistan. This feels... purposeful. Like something's guiding the changes."

They passed through layers of history, their changed DNA responding to frequencies that made the air itself sing. Ginny's skin had begun to glow with a soft luminescence that matched patterns in the engineered stone around them.

"I should have recognized Oliver sooner," she said softly. "Not just from surveillance footage. Something in me knew who he was. Call it maternal instinct?"

"The same way something in me recognized these children weren't just gifted." Fibber's military instincts merged with enhanced awareness as they tracked blood droplets deeper into the complex. "We were all part of something bigger. Something older." A scream echoed through probability-twisted corridors—Emily's voice, but changed, resonating at frequencies that shouldn't have been possible. They rushed forward, enhanced abilities letting them navigate passages that rippled like heat waves in desert air.

The Consortium tactical team's remains stopped them short. Fibber knelt beside the corpse, his enhanced senses detecting how reality itself had rejected unmodified DNA. "They never had a chance. These barriers weren't designed for ordinary humans."

"Leo." Ginny's voice held warning as her transformation accelerated. Golden light leaked from her eyes as ancient memories surfaced. "Something's happening..." He caught her as genetic changes wracked her frame. Her bones shifted beneath her skin, trying to remember configurations that predated human evolution. Neural pathways lit up with awareness too vast for ordinary consciousness to contain.

"Fight it," he urged, his own DNA responding to her proximity. "Don't let it happen too fast."

Their enhanced and altered perceptions merged briefly as transformation waves peaked, letting them share fragments of genetic memory: stars seen from worlds humanity had forgotten it walked, technologies that could reshape reality itself, and a plan spanning millions of years to guide Earth's evolution. The spherical chamber beyond stopped them cold.

David Romanov's preserved form hung suspended in light that hurt their transforming eyes. But Ginny's attention fixed on the small figure emerging from reality-warped shadows.

"Emily?" she breathed, recognizing the child even as ancient awareness shone through transformed features.

But Emily's response came in a voice that held echoes of stars: "That name serves for now. Though once, among other suns, we knew each other by different sounds."

Michael appeared beside her, his transformed DNA expressing patterns that matched symbols older than Earth's atmosphere. Neural interfaces sparked and failed as his consciousness expanded beyond human limits.

"The changes can't be stopped," he said, his voice resonating at frequencies that made reality shiver. "But they can be guided. That's why we chose these forms. These children."

Fibber's heightened senses detected the truth before the others. "You're not just awakening something in us. You're becoming something through us."

Emily's small form began to blur at the edges as transformation accelerated. "We seeded ourselves through human DNA, scattered across bloodlines and generations, waiting to reconverge. To help humanity remember what it was before the gates between worlds were closed." Ginny reached for her, maternal instinct warring with ancient awareness. "You're burning through their bodies. These children can't contain what you're becoming."

"No single form can," Michael agreed as his own transformation accelerated. Golden light poured from his eyes as human flesh tried to express inhuman awareness. "But together..."

Reality twisted sharply as ancient machinery surged to life worldwide. Fibber and Ginny felt their own transformations reach critical thresholds as genetic memories older than humanity itself broke through.

It wasn't just about remembering anymore. It was about becoming what they had always been meant to be. If any part of their human consciousness survived the transformation.

LEGACY OF STARS

Tobias Rosetti stood in his private vault beneath Rome's Via Veneto, where renaissance architecture concealed technologies that predated human civilization. The chamber, perfectly circular and impossibly precise, held treasures gathered across centuries of patient collection. Each artifact resonated with frequencies that made reality itself shiver in recognition.

The Egyptian necklace, identical to the one Ginny wore, pulsed with subtle light from its crystal display case, its molecular structure finally awakening after millennia of dormancy. Beside it, the DaVinci Cipher's metallic surface rippled like liquid mercury, reflecting possibilities from worlds humanity had forgotten it once walked. Both pieces had been mere preparation for what was to come.

But these were only the newest additions to his collection. A crystalline skull from beneath the Yucatan Peninsula held memories of stars seen from other worlds. A bronze disc from ancient China mapped quantum pathways between realities. Hidden texts from the Library of Alexandria described beings who had seeded Earth with modified genetic codes eons before the first humans walked upright.

Tobias traced patterns in the air that made light bend strangely around his fingers. His true age, like his true nature, was written in stellar cycles rather than human years. He had walked these halls when they were new, when the Vatican's foundations were still being laid atop ruins far older than Rome itself. His secure phone chirped—an encrypted channel connected to observers at the Vatican's astronomical observatory. The message confirmed what the ancient texts had predicted: a precise alignment of stars and galaxies, occurring only once every twenty-six thousand years. But the astronomers couldn't see what Tobias's enhanced perception detected—how reality itself grew thinner as the alignment approached.

Deep beneath the Vatican, in chambers that appeared on no official blueprints, ancient machinery stirred to life. Systems built by the same beings who had engineered humanity's original genetic structure powered up for the first time since Earth's last ice age. The children's awakening abilities had triggered something that had waited millennia for precisely this moment. But they weren't the only ones converging on Rome.

The Russian FSB's Department 13 had deployed their own enhanced operatives—children identified through genetic screening programs dating back to the Cold War. Their base in an abandoned monastery outside the city hummed with stolen technology reverse-engineered from artifacts found in Siberian ruins.

The CIA's Project STARGATE had reactivated, their psychically gifted agents tracking probability distortions spreading outward from the Vatican. Beneath the U.S. Embassy, quantum computers analyzed patterns that matched classified files from the Kandahar incident.

China's Ministry of State Security had an entire floor of the Bank of China's Rome branch dedicated to monitoring genetic variations in their population. Generations of careful breeding programs had produced children whose abilities rivaled those Tobias had gathered, though Beijing didn't understand the true nature of what they had created.

Japan's Cabinet Intelligence and Research Office maintained surveillance from a hidden facility beneath the Japanese Academy in Rome. Their scientists had recognized patterns in certain children's DNA that matched symbols found in their oldest Shinto texts.

The Saudi General Intelligence Presidency operated from a series of safe houses near the Vatican, their agents protecting ancient artifacts found beneath Mecca that resonated with the same frequencies as the children's enhanced genetics.

All of them tracking, watching, waiting to claim power they didn't understand. None of them realizing they were merely players in a game set in motion before their civilizations existed. All of them were were looking for the homeless. The kids.

Tobias smiled as his augmented perception detected more organizations closing in: Mossad's Unit 8200, France's DGSE, India's RAW—each believing they alone had discovered humanity's next evolutionary step. Each unaware that evolution itself had been guided by intelligences far older than Earth. His displays showed the children's transformations accelerating as the stellar alignment approached. Reality rippled around their awakening abilities as genetic memories older than humanity began to surface. The events were not about power anymore. It was about remembering what had been forgotten. About becoming what they had always been meant to be. If Earth itself survived the remembering.

CHAPTER 18

AWAKENING

THE CHAMBER BENEATH THE VATICAN TREMBLED AS AN-
cient machinery surged to life. Emily's small form
floated several inches above the floor, golden light pouring
from her transformed eyes as she accessed memories written in genetic
code older than humanity itself.

"The walls," she whispered in a voice that resonated at impossi-
ble frequencies. "They're trying to tell us something." Around them,
smooth metallic surfaces erupted with living images. Star maps un-
like anything in human astronomy spread across the chamber's
curved ceiling—constellations seen from worlds humanity had for-
gotten it once walked. The patterns shifted and flowed, showing
stellar alignments that occurred only once every twenty-six thousand
years.

"Those aren't just stars," Michael said, his enhanced perception stretching beyond normal space-time. "They're doorways. Points where reality grows thin enough to... remember."

Fibber studied the displays with his military-trained mind enhanced by transformed DNA. "The alignments match what we saw in Kandahar. When reality itself seemed to bend."

"Look," Ginny breathed, pointing to where DNA sequences spiraled across the walls like rivers of living light. But these weren't human genetics—they showed configurations that predated Earth's current biological paradigms. Structures that could exist in multiple states simultaneously, encoding not just physical traits but memories spanning millennia.

"Our DNA," Emily said softly, reaching out to touch the flowing patterns. "What it used to be. Before they changed us. Before they made us forget."

Oliver's voice cracked with emotion as new displays activated. "Emily... your hands." Her small fingers had begun to phase between states of matter, reality rippling around them like heat waves. "I can feel them," she whispered. "All of them. Every child carrying the sequences. They're beginning to remember too."

The chamber's central pillar pulsed with energy as new patterns emerged; text in a script that hurt human eyes to look at. The symbols seemed to exist in multiple dimensions simultaneously, each character holding layers of meaning that normal consciousness couldn't process.

"I... I can read it," Michael said, his altered intellect stretching to accommodate awareness vast enough to span galaxies. "It's not just a message. It's a key. To unlock what we used to be."

Tears of golden light traced down Emily's cheeks. "But we were never meant to be locked away. We were meant to grow into it naturally. The Consortium... they rushed it. Tried to force evolution that should have taken millennia."

"Emily," Ginny reached for her, maternal instinct warring with transformed awareness. "You're burning up. Your human form can't contain—"

"I know." Emily's smile held ancient wisdom. "None of us can. Not alone. That's why we needed to be together. All of us. Every enhanced child on Earth."

The walls erupted with new information—graphs showing geometric progression of awakening abilities worldwide. Children in every major city beginning to remember what humanity had been before genetic locks were put in place. But something else emerged—a pattern hidden deeper than the star maps and DNA sequences. A signature woven through reality itself.

"This wasn't just preparation," Fibber realized, his enhanced senses detecting truth hidden for eons. "Something's been waiting. Using the Consortium, using us, using everyone to arrange exactly this moment." Reality rippled around them as Emily absorbed the ancient text's full meaning. "Not something," she whispered as transformation accelerated. "Someone. The ones who sent us. Who scattered their own consciousness through human DNA, waiting to be reborn when the stars aligned."

The chamber's machinery hummed at frequencies that made spacetime itself vibrate in sympathy. Above them, through layers of Vatican stone and sacred ground, the predicted stellar alignment began. None of them were ready for what emerged next—a pattern hidden in the very fabric of Earth's biosphere. Not just in enhanced human DNA, but in every living thing. A signature older than the planet itself. A message that changed everything they thought they knew about their origin. And their destiny. The chamber hummed with energy as Oliver inserted the DaVinci Cipher into the central pedestal. Images flooded the walls—star maps, DNA sequences, and something else. A message, written in a bazar language never seen by human civilization.

"It's some kind of test," Michael said, his modified tablet translating the symbols. "The chamber's scanning us."

Emily touched one of the glowing patterns. "These aren't just random children in the images. They're us. Our parents. Their parents."

"Generations of children," Mr. W confirmed. "All with specific genetic markers. All leading to this moment."

CONVERGENCE OF DESTINIES

THE VATICAN'S ANCIENT CHAMBER THRUMMED WITH ENER-
gies that made reality itself shiver as Ginny reached for her son.
Oliver stood at the center of swirling temporal distortions, his
transformed DNA expressing patterns that matched the flowing sym-
bols on the walls. Behind him, Emily floated several inches above the
metallic floor, golden light streaming from her eyes as she accessed ge-
netic memories older than Earth's atmosphere.

"It was never about power," Tobias said softly, entering through a
doorway that seemed to exist in multiple probability states simultane-
ously. "It was about healing. About remembering what humanity lost
when they tried to lock away our true nature."

Fibber moved protectively toward the children, his senses detecting threats converging from above. "The Consortium's teams are breaching the upper levels. We don't have much time."

"Time," Emily's voice held echoes of stars, "is more flexible than they understand." She gestured, and reality rippled around them. Through the chamber's walls, they glimpsed scenes from across Earth—children in every major city beginning to remember what their species had been meant to become.

"But the cost," Ginny whispered, seeing how the transformations strained young bodies never meant to contain such vast awareness. "We're losing them."

"No," Oliver said with certainty that transcended his years. "We're becoming what we always were. What every forgotten child could be, if given the chance to remember." The chamber's displays showed more than just star maps now. They revealed networks of consciousness spreading across the globe, connecting every child who carried the enhanced sequences. But deeper patterns emerged—hidden frequencies that resonated with something vast and ancient, waiting beyond the thin barriers of normal space-time.

"The language," Michael said, his intellect and reason stretching to comprehend symbols that existed in multiple dimensions. "It's not just a message. It's a key to unlocking potential in every human consciousness. Starting with those society has discarded."

Emily's small form blurred at the edges as transformation accelerated. "We were sent to prepare the way. To ensure humanity would be ready when the stars aligned. But we never expected..." She faltered, overwhelmed by genetic memories surfacing too quickly.

"Expected what?" Fibber demanded, his military instincts sensing bigger implications.

"That humanity's greatest potential would emerge from its forgotten children," Tobias finished. "That those cast aside by society would become the bridge to what your species was always meant to be." The chamber's central pillar erupted with new patterns—text in a script that seemed to fold through dimensions human minds weren't meant to perceive. But beneath the alien geometries lay a message that struck deep emotional chords:

> *"To the forgotten ones, we entrust the future. For only those who have known abandonment can truly understand the value of connection. Only those who have walked between worlds can guide others across the bridges between realities."*

But something else emerged in the flowing symbols—coordinates pointing to locations across the galaxy. Places where other forgotten children waited, carrying different fragments of the vast consciousness that had seeded itself through human DNA.

"There are more out there," Oliver breathed, his enhanced perception stretching across light-years. "Other children, on other worlds, all beginning to remember." Reality twisted sharply as the chamber's machinery responded to frequencies emanating from beyond Earth's atmosphere. Through the quantum disruption, they glimpsed vast structures orbiting distant stars—waiting to be rediscovered by transformed consciousness.

"The choice was always yours," Tobias said quietly. "To accept the transformation, to guide humanity toward what it could become. Or to reject it, to remain locked in current forms."

Ginny moved to stand between her son and the ancient machinery. "And if we choose to transform? To remember?"

"Then every forgotten child becomes a key," Emily whispered as golden light engulfed her small form. "Every abandoned soul a bridge to what humanity was always meant to be." The chamber's displays showed the convergence spreading—not just through enhanced children but touching every human consciousness that carried fragments of ancient awareness. Starting with those society had pushed to its margins.

But in the flowing symbols, another pattern emerged. A signature hidden in frequencies no Earth technology could detect. Evidence that humanity's transformation was part of something far larger. Something that had waited eons for precisely this moment. When forgotten children would remember what they truly were, and guide humanity home to the stars.

THE CHOICE

HE CHAMBER'S ANCIENT WALLS RECOGNIZED TOBIAS'S true signature, responding to frequencies no human technology could detect. "We seeded this potential in your species,' he explained, temporarily dropping his human guise to reveal his crystalline true form. 'The Consortium discovered traces of our work and tried to control it, but they never understood. We chose the forgotten children as carriers of this gift because they alone could understand both abandonment and transcendence."

The ancient walls pulsed with living light as reality itself seemed to hold its breath. Emily's transformed consciousness stretched across quantum states, touching minds of forgotten children worldwide who carried fragments of humanity's true potential. Golden energy cascaded from her small form as genetic memories older than Earth's atmosphere struggled to express through human flesh.

"We have to choose," she whispered, her voice resonating at frequencies that made space-time shiver. "All of us. Not just the enhanced children, but all of humanity. To remember what we were. What we could become again."

Ginny reached for Oliver, maternal instinct warring with the vast awareness now flowing through her transformed DNA. "The price," she said, seeing how the changes strained young bodies. "It's too high."

"Is it?" Tobias's ancient eyes held centuries of watching humanity discard its most precious resource—its children. "Higher than the cost of remaining locked in forms that deny your true nature? Higher than abandoning another generation of children to society's margins?"

The chamber's displays showed more than just star maps and DNA sequences now. They revealed the full scope of what humanity had forgotten abilities that transcended physical limitation, consciousness that could bridge realities, connection to awareness vast enough to span galaxies.

"Every child you cast aside," Emily's voice held echoes of stars, "carries fragments of what you were meant to be. Every soul you abandon holds keys to unlocking humanity's true potential."

Fibber's enhanced perception detected the deeper pattern hidden in flowing symbols. "This chamber... it's not just a vault of ancient technology. It's a choice point. A nexus where humanity decides its own evolution."

Reality rippled around them as the chamber's machinery responded to frequencies emanating from transformed DNA. Through quantum disruptions, they glimpsed possible futures:

A humanity locked in current form, forever afraid of its own potential, continuing to discard those who might help it remember. Or a species awakening to its true nature, guided by those who had walked between worlds, who understood both abandonment and transcendence.

"The Consortium feared this moment," Tobias said softly. "Feared what humanity might choose if given the chance to remember. That's why they tried to control the transformation, to limit it to those they could manipulate."

"But they never understood," Michael added, his enhanced intellect stretching to comprehend patterns older than civilization. "True evolution can't be forced. It has to be chosen. By all of us."

The chamber's central pillar erupted with new symbols—a message written in script that folded through dimensions human minds weren't meant to perceive. But its meaning resonated deep in transformed consciousness:

"To remember is to choose. To choose is to transform. To transform is to heal not just yourselves, but the very fabric of reality you've forgotten you could touch." Oliver moved to stand beside Emily, golden light beginning to pour from his eyes as well. "We were never meant to be separate," he said. "The abandonment, the loneliness—it was all part of remembering what connection truly means." Reality twisted sharply as the chamber's machinery surged with power. Above them, through layers of Vatican stone, the stellar alignment reached its peak. The moment of choice had come.

"If we accept this," Ginny whispered, "everything changes. Not just for the enhanced children, but for every forgotten soul who carries fragments of what humanity could become."

"Yes," Emily's smile held ancient wisdom. "That's why we were chosen. Not because we were special, but because we understood what it means to be cast aside. To walk between worlds until we could build bridges for others to cross." The chamber's displays showed the transformation spreading—touching every consciousness that carried hidden potential. Starting with those society had pushed to its margins but reaching toward all of humanity.

The choice wasn't just about evolution anymore. It was about healing wounds deeper than DNA. About remembering what it meant to be truly human. If they dared to choose remembrance over fear.

The chamber's message became clear: an ancient warning.

CHAPTER 21

AFTERMATH

THE POWER SURGE BEGAN AS A WHISPER IN ENERGY FIELDS that only the transformed children could perceive. Then reality itself seemed to flex, and Rome went dark in expanding circles of cascading failure. Modern technology died in waves—first the Vatican's sophisticated security systems, then the city's power grid, then every electronic device within a five-mile radius. Even battery-powered devices failed as fundamental forces briefly realigned themselves to patterns older than human civilization.

Emily watched through transformed senses as the disruption rippled outward. To her enhanced perception, it looked like rings of golden light spreading through probability fields that most humans couldn't detect. Cars stalled on ancient streets; their electronics permanently altered by energies they were never designed to channel. In hospitals, backup generators failed as reality itself temporarily forgot how electricity was supposed to work.

"The city's remembering," she whispered, her voice carrying harmonics that made nearby windows vibrate. "Remembering what it was before humans built their churches over older truths."

When emergency power finally returned hours later, the chamber beneath the Vatican had fundamentally changed. The ancient machinery hadn't just vanished—it had evolved, transforming the very stone around it into something that existed partially in other dimensions. The walls retained a subtle iridescence, their surfaces occasionally rippling like heat waves when viewed from certain angles. Reality there had grown permanently thinner, more permeable to possibilities that normal physics insisted couldn't exist.

Oliver traced equations in the air with fingers that left trails of luminesce scrawls, his enhanced consciousness reading patterns hidden in the chamber's transformed structure. "It's not just a room anymore," he said, his eyes reflecting frequencies beyond normal human perception. "It's become a doorway. The first of many."

The only physical evidence remaining was a crystalline disc half-phased into the chamber floor. Its surface shifted between states of matter, sometimes solid, sometimes liquid light, its patterns rearranging themselves in response to the children's transformed DNA. Symbols etched into its structure changed language and meaning depending on the viewer's genetic capabilities.

Michael interfaced directly with energy fields now, his consciousness expanding through probability space to touch systems that existed between normal reality's hard edges. When he accessed electronic networks, they responded not to his commands but to his nuro-linked intentions, technology recognizing him as something both more and less than human.

In his hotel room overlooking St. Peter's Square, Detective Fibber felt the change begin in his damaged leg. The rippling disruption affected more than just technology—it realigned fundamental forces within transformed DNA. The chronic pain that plagued him since Afghanistan faded as reality accepted new configurations of flesh and bone. Within days, even decades-old scar tissue began regenerating along patterns that matched the children's evolved genetics.

Interpol found Tobias's villa empty but not abandoned. The art collection had evolved rather than vanished, frames now containing echoes of masterpieces that existed simultaneously in multiple realities. In his study, agents discovered walls covered in text that rewrote itself as they watched, messages shifting between languages that humanity hadn't used since it walked among stars. And on a simple piece of paper, a note scrawled in longhand—"Rember the children. It's about the children it always has been. They have always been hiding in plain sight." But it was the hidden room that held the real key—a star map that hummed with frequencies matching the children's transformed DNA. Each marked system corresponded to locations on Earth where reality had grown thinner, where forgotten children carried genetic potential waiting to be awakened.

"It's showing us where to look," Ginny said, her enhanced awareness detecting possibilities hidden in the coordinates. "Not just on Earth, but out there. Other children, carrying different fragments of what we were meant to become."

Reports began filtering in from around the globe. In abandoned subway tunnels beneath New York, homeless children developed abilities that defied logic. In the favelas of Rio, young minds began touching frequencies that shouldn't have existed. In the forgotten places of every major city, transformation spread through those society had cast aside.

Emily stood in the chamber's center, where reality felt thinnest. Her small fingers traced patterns in air that briefly became solid light.

"The walls remember," she said softly. "They're watching and waiting for the others. The ones still sleeping in forgotten places. The ones who don't know yet what they could become. It is those we must teach."

Humanity was remembering what it had always been meant to be. A door opening between what it was and what it had forgotten it could become.

CHAPTER 22

NEW HORIZONS

THE NEST WAS REBUILT, THIS TIME AS A LEGITIMATE FOUN-dation for all children. Ginny took over its operation, with Mr. W remaining as advisor. Detective Fibber, understanding finally what he'd stumbled into, became their global eyes and ears.

But Oliver knew their work wasn't finished. The chamber's warning spoke of others like them around the world. Children with different abilities, different genetic markers. And something else—a threat still hidden in the shadows, waiting. In his new room at the Nest, he studied the symbol from the chamber that now appeared on his tablet whenever he touched it. A message meant for him alone:

"Find the others. The stars are moving. Time grows short." Below it, coordinates appeared. Shanghai. New Delhi. Cairo.

The next chapter of their mission was just beginning.

SIX MONTHS LATER

THE PORTLAND RAIN DRUMMED AGAINST THE NEST'S NEW glass ceiling as Oliver stood at the window, watching the city lights shimmer below. The building hadn't changed much from the outside—still that unassuming structure near Powell's Books. But inside, everything was different. Where there had once been hidden servers and stolen tech, state-of-the-art computers now lined the walls, their screens displaying data from around the world. The Nest Foundation for all forgotten children, the sign read. A legitimate front that was, in its own way, as clever a deception as their previous cover.

Emily was in the training room, teaching a new girl—barely seven—how to navigate ventilation systems. The girl had been living in Shanghai's underground until Ginny found her. Like Emily, she could squeeze through impossibly small spaces. Like all of them, she had been injected with unique genetic markers.

Michael's workspace had expanded to fill an entire floor. His fingers danced across multiple keyboards as he monitored their global network, searching for patterns. Signs of others like them. Traces of the technology they'd glimpsed beneath the Vatican.

"Any word from Mr. W?" Oliver asked as Ginny entered, carrying two cups of tea. She shook her head. Their mentor had left three weeks ago, following leads in Cairo. The last message they'd received was typically cryptic: "The pattern repeats. They're waking up."

Detective Fibber—now officially liaison to the Foundation—had spotted similar patterns. More children with impossible abilities appearing in major cities. More ancient sites showing signs of technological activation. And always, in the shadows, traces of Tobias's organization. Was he the kingpin of the Consortium?

Oliver touched his tablet, bringing up the glowing symbol that had become their new mission. The coordinates shifted daily now, pointing to locations across the globe. Each one, they'd discovered, contained pieces of the larger puzzle.

"When do we leave for India?" he asked.

Ginny smiled. The boy she'd given up fifteen years ago had become a leader, though he was still, in many ways, the clever street kid she'd first seen in the security footage.

"The team's ready," she said. "But Delhi's just the beginning. The chamber's warning was clear—something's coming. Something that's been waiting a very long time." Oliver nodded, his hand unconsciously tracing the birthmark that matched the ancient symbols. Around his wrist, a thin metal band—salvaged from the Vatican chamber—pulsed with faint blue light.

In the training room below, Emily's voice drifted up: "Remember, it's not about being small. It's about being invisible in plain sight." The new girl—Soong—responded in Mandarin, her words automatically translated through their enhanced comms: "Like the others? The ones we're going to find?"

"Exactly," Emily said. "They're out there, hiding just like we were. But not for much longer."

Oliver's tablet chimed. Michael had cracked another piece of the encoded warning from the chamber. The text appeared, ancient symbols transforming into modern language:

"When the stars align, the children of two worlds must choose. The key lies in their blood. The time of return approaches." Below it, a countdown had begun.

Ginny squeezed her son's shoulder. "Ready to save another world?" Oliver smiled, thinking of all the street kids still out there. Kids with special abilities. Kids who, like them, had been chosen for something bigger than themselves.

"They'll never see us coming," he said. In his pocket, the stolen keycard from the Vatican still hummed with energy, its surface etched with a single phrase in that ancient script. The same phrase now appearing in the dreams of forgotten children around the world:

"The next wave rises."

Behind them, the rain continued to fall on Portland, washing away the last traces of the street kids they'd once been. But somewhere in the city, other children were watching, waiting, preparing for their own chance to become more than society had decided they could be. They were about to change everything. But remember, they were only kids, after all.

END OF BOOK ONE

THE TIGERS GIFT

A TALE OF FIRST CONSCIOUNESS

Hector M. Rodriguez

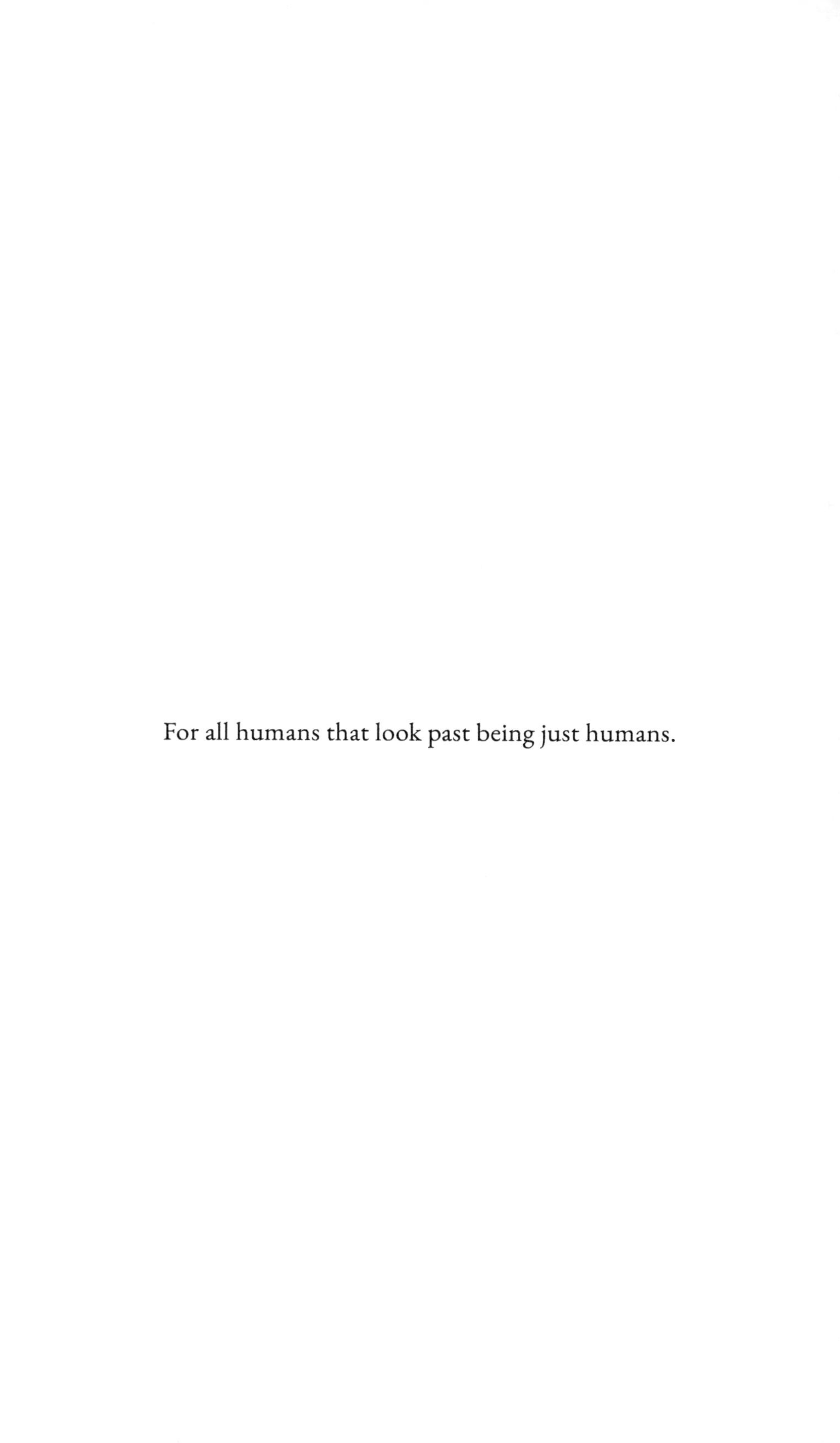

For all humans that look past being just humans.

FOREWORD

PART OF THE ISSUE WE HAVE IS WE DON'T HAVE EVIDENCE TO corroborate what our ancient ancestors were doing and thinking with any degree of certainty. We are occasionally surprised when a discovery is made in the world of paleo-archaeology that changes our perceptions of what was really going on five hundred thousand years ago. We have little tangible evidence, and our stories are based mostly on loose theories referencing fragments of bones, stone tools, and cave paintings found in ancient shelters or etched on rocks. Pure organic matter or tissue such as brain mass, eyes, lungs, and kidney type organs are long gone. Radioactive carbon dating provides a sketchy timeline and nuclear carbon dating is only a little better. However, it is still a relative guess and gives no true information as to what was being thought and how the mind was developing. But the genetic codes were established and mapped and are connected in our genome to this day. I have always wondered how the mind was working back then. I find the possibility of self-awareness and emotions developing in early hominoids a fascinating concept. I view our ancient predecessors with respect given what they did, how they did it, and how they were able to keep the hominoid genome from dying out.

In my story the mixing lineage of various genetic mutations would eventually become Homo-Heidelbergensis, then Homo-Neanderthalensis and eventually the Homo-Sapient. However, this evolution did not happen in a linear fashion. As I imagine one example, green eyes would become the mutation and characteristic genetic marker of the Homo-Naledi line. Brown eyes would become the marker for Homo-Erectus, and other distinct mutations would be the foundations of other ancient hominoid relations. The one thing they all would have in common was walking upright. Once the early hominoids stood upright an explosion of thought began. Rituals, curiosity, love, hate and our senses were sharpened and keenly enhanced.

The bones of this story were constructed during the November 1-30, 2022, National Write a Novel in a Month challenge. I had been flirting around for my next project, and I bit on the challenge. I am a trained geologist and a closet paleoanthropologist. I love the outdoors and all thing natural. The subject matter of this story was deeply familiar. You will see that love come through on the pages and I hope you see a lot of other things as well.

I need to acknowledge many people that have contributed in some way to this story. First, I want to thank the people of the town of Atapuerca, Spain for gracious hospitality and access to wonderful artifacts and creative dioramas emulating life in El Sima de los Huesos. It was here I experienced a strong sense of connection with my past ancient ancestors. I want to thank Dr. Lee Berger of the University of Witwatersrand South Africa, and the first two spelunkers to make the Homo-Naledi discovery, Rick Hunter, and Steven Tucker. Thanks to Berger's team of Naledi sized explorers for their courage and persistence to delve deep into the unknown exploring the Rising Star Cave. This discovery opened a world of human genome related possibilities and fortified genetically imbedded memories for me. Special thanks to Taylor McCoy, the Blackwater Draw Museum Collections Manager with Eastern New Mexico University (ENMU) for access to the marvelous collection under her purview. The Department of Anthropology and Applied Archaeology at ENMU is second to none. The Esalen Institute the for-hosting the Healing Waters workshop with the Essalen Tribal Nation. Special thanks to Koltala-Little Bear, Tihikpas-He who flirts with all of life, Sanga of the Valley for giving rhythms life, Douglas Drummond of 5Rhythms, Nick Ayers-the rock of sound savant, Mac Murphy – Sweat Lodge Guide, Nick-Fire Keeper and watcher of the Stone People, Hunter- Fire Keeper and watcher of the Stone People, Kumal – The Faithful Healer and all my brothers now tied by The Healing Waters, dance, and sweat. We are all tied together through the ceremonies of our ancient ancestors.

The Special thanks to Dr. Simon Johnson, Professor Emeritus from Oregon State University, my mentor and harshest critic, and the team of writers at C3. In no particular order, I want to thank David Bickell, Deborah Wolf, Gene Stemmann, Dr. Gerald van Belle, Jerri Austin Marler, Jo Sutton, Dr. Johanna van Belle, Karen Llewellyn, Marilyn Singh, Marion Whitney, Richard Raymond, and Sarah Roome. All are accomplished writers, and I am privileged to know each of you.

Everlasting gratitude goes to my family Carole, Simon, and Mateo. Thank you for putting up with my talking to myself, wandering around the house thinking, and then forcing the opportunity to share my first drafts with you. One day you will realize that when you spend the time reading my stories, you are spending time with me. I hope, long after I am gone, that you will read my stories and find a smile or two hidden in the pages. I hope you will recall my voice and how I grew to love telling a good story. I don't know what I would do without all of you because you are my greatest story of all.

Long live the eleven elf brothers!

Peace, Honor, Grace, and Gratitude Always.
HMR

"When in doubt, use a comma."
Marion Whitney

The best English teacher I ever had.

'Twas in another lifetime one of toil and blood
When blackness was a virtue, the road was full of mud.
I came in from the wilderness, a creature void of form.
Come in, she said.
I'll give you shelter from the storm.

Bob Dylan

PRELUDE

Hamster Dunnigan, amateur paleo-archeologist, was on an illegal dig in the mountains of southeastern Washington State. He was looking for graves to loot. His area of interest was on the Hanford Nuclear Reservation, federal lands. He was a short man and kept himself lean and strong. His long auburn hair was always pulled back in a braided ponytail. His lazar sharp green eyes scanned the hills looking for federal agents. He was always on high alert, especially when trespassing. At first glance, even though he was twenty-nine years old, he looked like a small Native American kid. His Indian name was Tiphkalit, translated means small furry rodent who is quick. Hamster was the English translation he preferred. It was better than rat. He was poking around scree covered hillsides with several nearby glacial melt water streams flowing to the Columbia River. He accessed the area using his dented fourteen-foot Valco aluminum boat and twenty-year-old, ten horse Mercury outboard motor to travel eight miles upriver. The river system was part of the dendritic patterned watershed that contributed to massive flood runoff into the Columbia River Gorge.

The floods known as the Missoula Floods carved the region over hundreds of thousands of years of erosion. There were numerous flooding events in this area over the eons of time. The events were due largely to the rupture of ice dams built up on tributaries to river basins during periods of climate cooling and then warming. The region was also directly on the path of the first inland hominoid migration to this part of the world associated with the Kelp Highway Theory. Because the Bering Sea land bridge was exposed during much of the early Pleistocene era, evolving creatures of all species migrated back and forth over the land bridge in search of sustenance. It has been theorized that early hominoid stuck close to the coastline as they traveled using wooden boats now long rotten and decayed back into the earth. Small curious groups of hominoids ventured inland when the opportunities arose. In our evolving world, hominoids searched and competed for sources of protein and carbohydrates with everyone and everything else, exploring all corners of the world. They explored more than was previously imagined.

Dunnigan's was walking on a low ridge recently exposed by a receding ice pack and occasional volcanic activity in the form of tremors. The scree covered slopes had been under the ice pack and the temperatures stayed well below zero for eons. Tremors over the last five thousand years caused calving of great glacial ice pack, exposing Pleistocene era strata and soils untouched by erosion or any other environmental factors. The Pacific Northwest of North America had been rattled by basalt spewing volcanos and earthquakes for the last five hundred million years. The area was still an active volcanic region with unique geologic formations. Large and small gas vents created deep networks of cave systems. Many of the caverns were habitable and scattered randomly throughout the steep valleys. There had been a few archeological finds in the region since the St. Helens eruption thirty-five years earlier. Most of the items found were stone age tools pushed to the edges of the glacial front face over eons of time. The finds were attributed to Native American origins for lack of any true means to identify them. Without greater detailed study and organic matter for accurate DNA and genetic analysis, it was always a guess. Dunnigan had numerous buyers for authentic artifacts and good pieces always brought high prices.

In several locations Dunnigan surveyed, he identified crude stronghold positions used during ancient battles. He found stone monuments and built-up alcoves on the hillsides. They were arranged in front of caves in specific defensive patterns and arrays. Numerous whole and broken arrow points and larger spear tip type artifacts littered the fixed stations indicating many attacks or perhaps one large battle. He did not understand what the defensive positions were for but guessed they were used to protect territory. He collected all the arrow points he found. Even those brought good money.

Behind one crude defensive structure, protecting a small alcove, he spotted a slightly exposed flat obsidian panel. Upon closer inspection he could tell the unusual obsidian panel had been chiseled and knapped around the exposed edges. Someone had taken the time to shape the stone into some type of defensive doorlike structure. As he started to move a series of smaller basalt boulders around so he could gain better access, he immediately saw that the three foot by four-foot oval panel was blocking a chamber, which looked like it had been purposefully sealed in place. He was mesmerized by what looked like images in the form of figures and glyphs etched into the black glassy surface. As his flashlight swept across the stone panel the refracted light brought the images to life. The animals moved in a brilliantly animated choreographed dance running over etched mountains. The images of people, although stick figures also moved in wonderfully uniformed action type patterns, jumping up and down and waving their arms saying, "Hey look at me!" It was magical.

There was an unusual type of cement lining the edges of the translucent pane. The unique patterns on the obsidian and its size were extraordinary. It was almost like a dirty window, opaque with a dark gray hue. When he finally managed to delicately break the seal, air whooshed in. Eventually, after several hours of gently chipping with a small hammer and chisel, he was able to pry the cover stone out. He rotated the cover, inspecting it; the opposite side held more detailed etchings of scenes with animals and backgrounds of mountains and more stick hominoid type figures.

Setting the panel aside, Dunnigan found a chamber approximately four foot wide, five foot high and twenty feet deep, which had been carved into the pure basalt outcrop. Given his small stature, he could easily stand up in the chamber. As his flashlight swept across the chamber, he was in awe. The contents had been preserved for eons, more than five hundred thousand years. It was a shamans ceremonial dwelling.

The articles he inventoried included elegant animal hide clothing and carved bone and antler artwork. There were a series of yew wood bows with sinew strings still intact, and several quivers of delicate arrows. On a ledge just below his feet was an unusually carved arrow launcher, elegant eight-foot-long spears with long fluted points and a series of finely knapped obsidian knives and scraping tools. There was a strand of sacred sweetgrass braids mixed with wrapped sage bundles, decorative jewelry of long thin conical black and white seashells strung together and setting in a place on its own. With it was a small one-inch diameter rough shaped gold disk with a hole in the center.

At the back of the cave, neatly rolled up along the wall, was the unmistakable cape of an enormous tiger. It appeared to be animated and decorated with pictures and unusual glyphs. They were etched into the hide with images like the ones on the chamber's outer door. The hide was in perfect condition. Hundreds and hundreds of images adorned specific sections and covered the still supple pelt. When he moved his flashlight across the images, they moved like an old stop gap motion picture. Scattered on the floor were dozens and dozens of flint and obsidian shards and tools for knapping, pieces with ultra-fine tips used to create the message etched in the hide. In another location hollowed out in the wall, he found finely knapped obsidian projectile tips, some thirteen to fourteen inches long, the longest he had ever seen, wrapped in still soft and supple rabbit skins, and tied with an intricately braided leather strap, carefully put in place. In another, he found a pouch with a stone-carved pipe with a residue of cannabis.

As the tomb robber started to move his hands and fingers across the pelt, a strange feeling gripped his mind. It was a spontaneous connection, an incredibly strong Deja-vu feeling of consciousness. He was thrust back violently to another time. As his mind connected to a story and his light slowly swept across the tiger hide, imagery began to unfold that would change the way modern homo-sapiens viewed their ancient ancestors. This find was a time capsule from the early Pleistocene era, a message from our earliest upright walking hominoid ancestors. This is the story Dunnigan was able to tell.

CHAPTER 1

"Our relationships with the natural world, charting the
ecological losses caused by hominoid activity has been an
ever-present dilemma and will be our eventual demise."
Anonymous

WITH THE PHYSICAL CONNECTION, THE TOUCHING OF the glyphs Dunnigan found etched into the tiger skin, an incredible vision and recollection shook his consciousness. Dunnigan saw a visage of an early hominoid and felt a strange name resonate in his mind and body. The gravelly voice of Kazan, an early upright walking hominoid, started to recite an intricate story that began after a long and arduous journey. Dunnigan jumped back startled releasing the skin, and the recitation stopped. He touched the pelt again and felt the story seep back into his entire conciseness and continued. In an instant he could feel the entire story. Etched into the tiger skin during a time when hominoids brain cases were evolving and learning about spirituality, perception, self-awareness, communications, and emotions, Kazan spoke.

As Kazan spoke, Dunnigan was connected and immediately understood the population was relatively small with perhaps one or two million of the hominoid species and sub-species roaming the earth. Dunnigan's mind was reeling as his fingers gently floated over the soft skins surface, it was at a time of an evolving mix with much of the genetic pool contributed by the kindred hominoids Australopithecus Robustus and Homo Naledi shouted from past eons, voices of the true ancient past. Robustus had been roaming the earth for more than one and a half million years and contributed significantly to neural connections in the developing hominoid brain and its twisting DNA and genetic structural connections. The Naledi hominoid roamed the earth for just under a million years. Both linages were at the cusp of hominoid mindfulness.

As the cryptic story began to unfold in Dunnigan's mind he sensed Kazan was infused with a feeling. Someone with strong medicine and power in the immediate family died. The apparent death took place in the high mountains, and Kazan knew it happened. He felt it in his mind. It was an intuition. As the story began to thread together, it became apparent the hominoids were able to communicate in different ways. One of those ways included an almost telepathic or instinctual stream of conscience, just as Dunnigan was experiencing as he touched the tiger pelt. The gravelly voice of the storyteller, Kazan, the Shaman and leader of a small mixed group of hominins. They were a primate of a taxonomic group which comprised those species regarded as hominoids. They were the direct ancestral lineage to homo sapiens, which had begun to show signs of significant creative thought, rituals, and established routines of care. Kazan did not know who specifically who died at that moment or how it happened, but he did understand things were going to be different. During his life he felt many deaths, but of one of his own was much more difficult and painful. These were new emotions, but he understood the gravity of the feeling. He understood gift of life and the grit of death. He understood that through killing animals, they would nourish themselves. They ate what they hunted. That was one of the realities of survival, and it was always about survival. The practice of cannibalism was slowly being eliminated due to the availability of bounty and the means to hunt and kill with weapons. Fire was becoming a controllable tool.

The death he felt occurred during the early morning, when the sky was on fire with bright red clouds. Low in the east, the sun hit the clouds in such a way it caused a surreal fiery red glow high in the skies over Kazan. It was too early for snow, but much too late for good rains. The weather had been cooling for the last ten seasons and the snows were lasting longer than in the past. A strong feeling about who had died grew in Kazan and his natural shamanic sense told him it was Noolan. When he realized this, his heart sank. He did not want to believe it. Noolan and his brothers possessed strong powers. He knew Noolan was with his brothers. They were on a quest for visions that would open the doors to shamanism. If they were successful, a rite of passage to greater understandings of their powers would be learned and secure their future. The future of the next generation of Shaman.

To Kazan it felt like a tiger won the contest, ripping his heart to pieces. For Noolan to have died was hard to believe. He was a good hunter, a great scout, strong, and reliable and he possessed great perception and understandings. It was the kind of genetics that created strong and smart survivors.

That morning Kazan was returning from an overnight visit with his brother Abern and his family. Abern had three fifteen-year-old sons Hook, Rit, and Noolan. They were identical triplets that survived. It was extremely unusual during the early Pleistocene period for such things to occur. Unrun, their mother died during their birth and that made it even more unique for the boys to have lived. Other women of the clan tended to them, and against all odds they grew into strong capable young males. They were strong breeding stock and carried special genetics. Abern's son Hook, came running down the path towards Kazan. He was out of breath but quickly settled down.

"Kazan it was Noolan. We were climbing on Jewit peak. The rocks beneath his feet gave way as the earth shook and he vanished. You know where he was headed." Kazan did know. He was headed to the tree line of Jewit peak, near the high crags and mouth of what they thought was an extinct volcanic tube they called the Oluo. Kazan knew a tiger was spotted near the ceremonial cave in recent years. It was a two-day hike to the base of the steep scree-covered slope. "I could not find him after the shaking stopped. Rit and I think the Jakkar may have come for him for revenge because he was near her cave. I think the Jakkar ate him. There is also a chance he may have been buried under the rocks. We could not find him, just his bow and a few broken arrows."

Being killed by a tiger, a Jakkar, was not much of a contest though being able to kill one was different. No one in memory or legend had ever killed a Jakkar. The tiger must want to die. The tiger was an extreme challenge, and quickly learned the routine of its environment. The beasts were stealth in all ways and when they did kill, it was seldom a true match. The victim never knew they were being hunted until it was too late. They would often eat leftovers from other animal kills, being opportunistic feeders at heart. Some viewed it as an honor to be consumed by such a great beast and become part of its continuing life. One would seemingly have to work hard to have that happen. To live with a Jakkar was not easy, but routines could be understood. There were many large felines during Pleistocene times. Noolan was looking for a chance to learn from the great beast. Kazan knew this and was hoping he would have succeeded. It truly was not about going after a tiger and killing it but rather learning from it. No one had ever killed a Jakkar that could be remembered. The real challenge was being able to survive tiger encounters.

Kazan had seen many of the large predatory cats over the years. He recalled one chance sighting when he was young and climbing Jewit mountain alone. He spotted her in a narrow canyon faced with lush green brush. The beast was a magnificent, moving swiftly and gracefully leaping four times the length of its body, from one rock escarpment to another. It stopped so close to him that he could hear the beast's deep resonating breath. A stellar Jay in the far distance sounding an alarm spurred the Jakkar to keep moving.

Kazan was so transfixed with the tiger he did not recognize or hear the alarm. He was frozen and the wind was coming from behind him, giving the Jakkar his full scent. He could see the nine-inch fangs. Its paws were larger than two of his hands laid out flat together. The eyes were clear yellow and had a primal red ember that reflected pure energy in the center. It must have weighed nine-hundred pounds, eight times more than he did. Kazan remembered thinking it would take a lot of meat to keep the creature satisfied. The creature was the perfect killing machine, stealth and focused. Perfectly built through millions of years of evolution, the creature was known to be one of the most secretive predators in all the world. This beast floated to the top of the food chain, and it won battles more than not often. Bears, hyenas, wolf, lynx, boar, and many other natural enemies of the Jakkar existed. But it seemed wolves and bears were the only natural competitors of the large cats. However, the beasts displayed an enormous abhorrence for each other. Wolves frequently dined on hominoids, more so than on tigers.

It was evident the tiger was not hungry. She looked at Kazan knowing he was in her territory. He was not challenging the Jakkar and the Jakkar was not challenging him. When their eyes met, they both froze for an instant. They held no grievances towards each other. If she was going to eat Kazan, she would have attacked without being seen or heard. Although his spear was in hand, he did not posture aggressively. He watched the tiger carefully, each muscle rippling and quivering as she seductively eyed Kazan and then moved off silently. It was a magical encounter and within a few seconds the event was over. In some way, Kazan knew that this was a foreshadowing event for the demise of the tiger. The vision stuck in his mind, and he would see it repeatedly during his life.

As a young child, many seasons ago Kazan traveled with his father to a tiger's den. That den had been used over the millennia. It was high in the cliffs where the air was thin. The tiger was watching the travelers for days when they made the trip. She just wasn't hungry at that time. Tigers don't kill for the sake of killing. She knew they were there, but the rambling humanoids couldn't see her, but they could feel her. The camouflage patterns were hard to discern in any setting. The camo was not only patterns on the lush heavy fur, but also how it moved evasively through its world, completely silent. Humanoids had great respect for the tiger, choosing to live among them and respecting their world.

Kazan could see certain things others didn't. He was a visionary. He possessed an instinctual understanding his environment. From the plants to the animals, he felt a sense of the connectedness of all things. He was beginning to understand the power of developing emotion and the power of feelings. He understood certain plants, the medicinal values they held and how they affected the mind. He was approximately thirty-eight seasons old when he started to carve the story on the obsidian panels and the skin of the Jakkar, and if he were truly lucky, he would see twenty-five more seasons.

He was one of the earliest Homo heidelbergensis of the lineage of Homo ergaster, H. habilis, Australopithecus robustus, and A. africanus. A sixty-year-old heidelbergensis would be old and extremely lucky to live to that age. The culmination of his genetic pool was strong. It was the result of eons of chance breeding. He could see powerful changes and intricate influences of the developing planet and his visions were clear. He understood climate over the millennia changed the surface of the planet and that type of change would always continue. As youth when he traveled, he met other humanoids from distant lands. He knew his species represented a strong and well-developed people, built on eons of trial and error. Noolan, Hook, and Rit were growing into powerful young men. He knew their essence needed to survive and be passed on to future generations.

There were several others of this sapient lineage like them, but with different features and characteristics. The two threads they all held was that all walked upright and survived. They carved out an existence in a ruthless world and learned unique techniques and skills to protect and sustain themselves. Kazan understood that once they started walking upright, there was an explosion of abilities. Being able to look over the savannah grasses for danger became an invaluable trait. There were primordial legends that told of the use of rocks as the first knives, spear points, and arrows. It had always been so for Kazan.

Being able to knap or chip off pieces of chert, flint or obsidian into arrowheads and spears tips was a skill learned from a young age. It could be done quickly with the right tools and materials. Having a good source of flint nodules and especially obsidian was important for master tool makers. Cord and rope became tools of choice for many. He never wasted good cord. He knew he was both hunter and prey in the ecosystem. He knew that to be able to live and flourish in this environment was a respected achievement no matter what. Life was fragile and feelings and emotions were new to the species. The concept of love in this environment was on the precipice of conscience thought and not an understood option. If hominoids chose, they could bond with a mate, and then a clan, and most did. But not all.

Travelers came through this area on occasion and Kazan had seen more groups moving through recently, usually at a distance. He knew it was due to the weather and how cold it had been growing. He could feel it in his bones and felt it might have been time to move further south too. He had seen visions of what would happen if he didn't. The game would be less, plant varieties would change. He wanted to understand how others were feeling about going further south. The waning moon told him it would be time to meet soon and celebrate the fall of leaves. All the neighboring people would gather in an open meadow near his cave. At last count, the number of neighbors that made up the clan in the immediate area was thirty-five. One less without Noolan. Noolan was growing into a good man. He would be missed.

CHAPTER 2

SMOKE FROM FAR OFF VOLCANOS COLORED THE SKIES WITH reds, yellows, grays, and purples as the day began to turn to evening. The clan had been on the move all day. Walking down rocky mountain trails was easy and routine for the travelers. Their provisions were light, compact, with only the bare necessities. The animal hide leggings and shoes were silent as the clan marched in single file. The foot gear was well made and good for long distances. Soft tanned skins lined with fur up to and around the knees, foot pads were constructed with tough thick boar leather making them durable. Moisture from feet made the insides supple and comfortable and forgiving once they'd been worn in. Drot and his clan came across Kazan as the sun was setting. Kazan could see two of the females were pregnant. He was able communicate with Drot, mostly with hand gestures and a series of voice inflections for emphasis. He led Drot and his group to an abandoned volcanic cave system near Kazan's cave in a treelined canyon a good distance up stream. The dwelling was hidden from sight, but once a basalt boulder and then an oak tree were negotiated, it appeared. A dark void in the side of a cliff. The clan followed eagerly, anxious to rest in the dry cave. They each took up sleeping places while Vena, one of the younger men, started a fire in the abandoned fire pit. As the clan settled down, the cave was quiet. Drot and Kazan continued their discussion in low voices and hand gestures.

"How long have you been traveling?" Kazan asked.

"Six summers," said Drot. "We have lost several of our clan over the last two seasons. One went missing about two weeks ago. We think a Jakkar ate her."

Kazan stared into the fire and said, "We have seen some unexplained trouble in the recent years. Things are changing. It's good you are on the move. My clan lives all over this ridge and valley. We are about thirty-five strong and have had to fight to protect and keep our homes from others. We also lost one recently. It is thought he was also eaten by the Jakkar. The strange thing about the event is there was nothing left of him. The Jakkar must have eaten his entire body. That is unusual. You know the Jakkar always leave some meat for others. This region has been good. Our clan has lived here for twenty-two seasons. Several of our offspring have moved, some to the north, but most to the south. We will occasionally hear from them or see them if they travel back. Tell me, have you run into other settlements or recent travelers?"

Drot thought for a while. Kazan noticed his sloping forehead and his wide nose. His long kinky hair was pulled back and braided into a long ponytail trailing down his back. His beard was scraggily sprinkled with gray wily hairs, and his teeth were beginning to show significant signs of wear. The front teeth were almost nubs from years of use as tools. The deep creases in his face made him looked tired and probably older than he was. He was dressed in a mélange of well-tanned unique skins several lined in artic fox fur. He had a stone knife blade strapped to his thigh, housed in a tightly woven grass sheath. Kazan could tell it was made by a master flint knapper.

"We encountered many on our travels. They talked about where they came from. Most we were able to understand, but some could not speak and our ability to understand was limited. Only a few were unfriendly, and we were fortunate to move away quickly avoiding conflict. We are peaceful and understand the value of equality and working together."

"I understand," said Kazan, "I have traveled west many days. Over the mountains. There are others in that direction. There is a great ocean many suns to the west. Perhaps you should spend the winter here and then travel to the gathering in the spring. The women in your group seem like they need some time to have their babies and recover. There is game in the area, and we have stored nuts and dried fruits. They are plentiful throughout the valley. We have defensive outposts you will see."

Drot thought for a while and extended his hand in thanks. "I did see the defending array of rocks as we came down the mountain trail. We need the rest. We do not need conflict or fighting. We will make minimal impact and if this cave is un-occupied..." his voice trailed off.

"This cave is vacant except for an occasional bear, lion, tiger, badger, or wolf. Just keep a fire going and you will be fine. I will check with others and let them know about your desire. Sometimes a visiting group will just take up the space. It's better to let the others know and seek their understanding." It was getting dark and Kazan nodded, deciding it was time to go. He and Drot gripped each other's forearm tightly in acknowledgement of peace and bent forward to touch foreheads against each other. It was a sign of like minds and understanding. As he stood to leave, he took a quick inventory of the six members of Drots group. Two girls about thirteen or fourteen years old. Kazan looked twice. They were identical twins, short and agile and strong with darting alert green eyes. Flat noses, kinky black hair pulled into a tight weave trailing down their backs. Two women that were pregnant, two young boys not yet men with similar traits and three dogs that had curled up and were sleeping. They needed shelter and the rest. "I'll see you in the morning," he said as he stood to leave.

Kazan was born with a case of short leg syndrome and the beginning of osteoarthritis was setting in. This made walking difficult and running at any pace was impossible. He had carved a foot shaped block of wood and inserted it in his moccasin. This helped with keeping his balance and walking at a fair pace. Since this disability proved to limit his running and hunting of large game, he became adept at fishing and setting small game snares. Kazan had taken the insert out that day and as he walked off, Drot noticed the severe limp.

The winds were whispering to Kazan as he made his way back to his cave. As he looked into the crystal-clear skies, he could sense changes were coming.

CHAPTER 3

NOOLAN WAS HIGH ON THE CLIFF WHEN THE ROCKS BEGAN to shift. The earth was moving under his feet. The whole mountain was shifting, and he looked for a way to safer ground. As he started to fall, he was thrown down against the rough basalt. He bounced twice and then landed in a hole. It was pitch black and he was disoriented. He kept hearing the rumbling roar of the rocks tumbling and sliding down all around him, but he was not in the slide. He was in a large underground cavity. Part of the network of gas vesicles running through the volcanic mountain. He was still alive but in total darkness and wondering for a moment if this like being dead? Everything was black. The deep rumbling went on for several minutes and then all was quiet.

He did a quick self-inventory. His toes wiggled, his legs seemed okay he moved his knees and then lifted his arms. His head was pounding with a headache, and he felt a trickle of blood. But he was able to stand. All in all, he was okay. There was no light, so he reached for a pouch strapped to his waist with a leather thong. Inside the pouch was flint, a magnesium nodule, and fire-starting tinder. He pulled it out and struck a spark. After three strikes the tinder lit. He looked as far into the cave as he could as the small bundle burned. The cave was littered with carcasses and bones of all sizes, and one looked like a relatively fresh killed mature ungulate with a full set of antlers. One this size would have weighed almost fifteen hundred pounds. It had some rancid body fat still attached to the claw ripped hide. He needed a torch of some kind because the tender was going to go out. He looked around for a clean rib bone and fur. He then slathered fat on the fur and lit it. The crude torch smoked and spattered to life, radiating enough light to allow Noolan to see his surroundings.

He had ended up in a volcanic vent on the side of the mountain. It was a Jakkar lair. He knew he could not possibly dig his way out. He could see through the dim light that the vent went further into the side of the volcano. He knew they could go on for miles. In a somewhat dazed state, he gathered more fat for his torch and started to make his way down the tube. The vesical curved up and then down, became steeper and steeper until Noolan started to slide down the tube on his butt, further and further into the mountain. His torch went out as he kept moving in a flailing free fall into the depts and darkness of the mountain. He hit his hard head again and then blacked out.

After several hours unconscious in the bowels of the mountain, Noolan awoke beginning to wonder if he was alive or in the spirit world. He felt around in the darkness and found the torch and lit it again. He felt weak and needed to rest. He carefully laid the flame down and put it out. When void of light, the cave became the darkest environment. Noolan's evolving eyes were good and could see the fringes of the infrared spectrum. He was able to see small alpha charged neutrino particles jetting by and then being extinguished in milliseconds. His eyes were sharp and focused, and his pupils were as wide open as they could ever be. He was becoming more sensitive to sounds stretching his ears for something to give him a clue of which way to go. All he could hear was a deep monotone rumbling of the earth's pulse. He became disoriented and closed his eyes again. As Noolan nodded off to sleep, he thought he heard a trickling of water. First, he thought he was dreaming, but as he laid in the silence, off deep in the tunnel he was sure he heard water trickling. He knew if he was going to survive, he would need water. Then, he passed out again.

He awoke many hours later with a jerk. He was hungry and dehydrated and his head was pounding. He sat up and listened. He had no idea how long he had been unconscious. Trying to survey the area by sound and smell, he heard water but could not make out the direction other than further down into the fissure in front of him. It took him a few seconds to find his torch and when he did, he realized he was going to run out of fuel soon. He struck a spark with his flint and magnesium nodule into the tender. The spark was like a lighting blast in the black cave and hurt his eyes. The fat smoked and then spattered to life. Even the tiny glow lit up the smallish chamber. The torch fat caught easily enough, but he kept thinking he would be out of light soon, and he would end up dying if he continued moving down a narrow corridor. At one point, he had to crawl on his belly. After squeezing and maneuverings through a twisting maze of narrow crevasses by feeling the walls while he crawled flat on his belly, bumping, and scraping his head a new chamber began to open. The small flicker of light from his torch threw light into a great empty expanse. The chamber was huge. When he stopped and held his torch up, his eye caught sight of a crude fire ring ahead of him. Someone had been there before, regularly it appeared. Stacked against a rock was bundle of dry firewood.

As he moved towards the fire ring, he thought the location could have been a shaman's ceremonial location. He knew some people such as himself possessed a certain consciousness. As a young boy, he learned he possessed a connection with the spirit world and intuitively knew many things about it. He would frequently enter the mother earth and sacred sites with Kazan and his brothers Hook and Rit. They were taught to perform spiritual ceremonies with special plants, fungi, and animal enzymes in the warm and normally quiet chambers. It was where they experimented with powerful hallucinogens. Noolan experienced several trips into another's consciousness during his trek to manhood. Kazan, his mentor, always led the way and shared his consciousness. It was then Noolan realized his chances of getting out of the cave system improved.

As he moved to the fire ring and knelt, he surveyed what he could as his crude animal fat torch began to go out. He arranged a small teepee fire structure, but before he lit it, he paused. His torch flickered its last ray of dim light, and he froze, became still, and listened. Off in the distance he heard the water in an earnest trickle. As he turned his head in the direction of the water, he could see a tiny speck of light, day light that looked like a star in a sea of complete darkness.

He felt around in total darkness finding materials to fashion another crude torch. He struck a spark with his flint and magnesium nodule, and torch material lit quickly. With the ample flicker of light, he moved down a worn pathway towards the speck of light in the distance, his hopes were high. He raised the flame and found vibrant paintings on the walls and ceiling. Illustrations in beautiful muted natural colors, astounding earth tones of ocher red, sallow yellow, and coal black outlined renderings of animals including deer, huge bison, bears and Jakkar. A small pool of water reflected the light and came into view as he carefully walked the narrow path. He could hear the source high on the cave wall as it trickled down to the still pool. He paused, then he thanked the earth for the water. Water was life. Noolan drank the pure liquid in long sips. He knew he would get his fill and felt more and more refreshed after every long slow gulp. The water, purified by eons of downward migration through the basalt rock formations, was the purest on the planet.

When he was satiated, he continued to move down the well-worn path towards the light. Adjusting his torch, he marveled at the chamber. One wall in the chamber was an enormous obsidian sheet reflecting the dim glow of his light. The other walls were sheer basalt columns towering from floor to ceiling. It was evident two extreme geologic processes were in action to form such an unconformity in the volcanic rock. He yelled and the return echo startled him. He faintly smiled. The light was getting brighter, and an opening was coming into view. He had no idea as to how long he was in the cave system or what distance or direction he traveled. His head was pounding with pain. When he reached the exit, evening was settling in. There was a fire ring outside near the cave entrance. He quickly built a small fire, curled up and fell into a deep sleep as billions of stars started to dance a slow tango across the black velvety sky.

CHAPTER 4

THE NALEDI WERE A SPECIES OF SMALL, AGILE HOMINOIDS that flourished more than five hundred thousand years ago on the plains of South Africa. They were an extraordinarily prolific little group of wanderers that adapted to different environments easily. Although they were small in stature, they were agile, fast runners, strong climbers, and possessed a strong perceptive connectedness with the environment. Some of their genetic imprints are visible in modern homo sapiens such as flat open nostrils larger than usual. It is a rare yet beautiful feature. Some genetic traits have been erased because they proved to be of little value to the hominoid evolutionary trajectory. The Naledi had a profound ability to connect in a telepathic way with others and animals. Their ability to see in darkness was keenly well developed also. The Naledi developed an understanding of a spirit world and began the practice of burying their dead ceremoniously in secret locations. It was a new spiritual practice never seen or contemplated before. It was Shamanism. The first-time intellect of good and evil became a realized cognitive function. The hominoids also practiced cannibalism and consumed parts of the strongest in their clan to gain their strength and wisdom. It was believed that consuming their kind, and those parts of other animals would bring power and improve their chances of survival. They believed this was true of every animal in the world.

The Naledi word for a tiger was Jakkar. Due to the size of the brain case and neck construction, the vocal cords in the Naledi neck were immature compared to more evolved homo sapiens. Genetics being what they are, were progressing at an alarming rate given the competition. The sound of the word was a simple Ja-Ker guttural grunt, a term that survived for tens of thousands of years though its true origin would never be confirmed. The Jakkar was at the top of the food chain and preyed on whatever it wanted. The males were massive beasts weighing twelve hundred pounds. It took a lot of meat to keep his motor running. They were opportunist and eat pretty much whatever they wanted. Until now Kazan and his tribe lived in harmony with all creatures, including the Jakkar. There was a natural order of give and take. A simple Ying and Yang balance; it was always an understood tradition to leave some of a kill behind for other animals and to re-plenish the earth with its own nutrients. There was always plenty of food to sustain all living things. There had always been a natural balance. It was a Shaman at work with his environment.

The Jakkar were stealth killers. They moved virtually soundless through their world. The beast had a variety of animals to feed on including, boars, bears, elk, deer, wolf, rabbit, wild fowl, lemur, hippo, hyena, zebra, monkeys, gorillas, baboons, horse, dogs, and other tigers. Homo-sapiens and its early family tree were never at the top of a tiger's menu. It was a matter of what was convenient to catch. They did not feed every day. A good kill once a week was plenty. They were opportunist eaters and often ate leftover remains from other kills.

Imagine the common house cat and what it tends to catch and how the creature goes about it. The way a cat stalks a mouse, butterfly, bird, or beetle, catch it, and consume portrays the essence of natural balance. Multiply the cat image by one hundred-fold and one starts to get the idea of what skills and traits a full gown tiger has at its disposal. As a Jakkar roamed its territory it would come across other animal kills and scavenge what it wanted. They were opportunistic survivors.

The tiger was first classified as an individual species of cat in 1758 by a Russian researcher named Les Kaplanov. The taxonomic family tree of the tiger has been marked several times since then with various subspecies. Subspecies include Bengals, Siberian, Indonesian, Sumatran, Caspian, Java, Malayan, Balian, and South China Tiger. Kaplanov's research found strong evidence the tiger flourished long before the Pleistocene age but over the last one hundred fifty years homo sapiens brought the Jakkar to the edge of extinction thanks to the illegal trade of body parts to Chinese markets. It is also due to the invention and power of modern weaponry. Some Siberian and Chinese Shamans have strong beliefs that consuming special parts of certain animals would bring them the power or essence of the animal. Uses included lions' manes for hair growth, gall bladder for overall wellness and positive powers. The heart is for strength and longevity and the brain was dried into a powder and taken with black tea for wisdom. Many monks in various shaolin temples consume small fractions of special organs in ceremonies started centuries ago.

The priests would hunt tigers with bows and arrows and long pointed spears and poles. They also built deep pit traps like those described in ancient myths. From the legends imbedded in ancient temple glyphs, the first time a Jakkar was pursued and killed was because a certain tiger acquired a taste for humans. A great Jakkar was feeding on the residences of a small village near what is now the Russian/Chinese border. The villagers came to the wise Shaolin priests and asked for their help. The priests prayed and meditated on a way to get the tiger away from the villagers. One priest volunteered to seek out the tiger and talk with it. As he walked through the tiger's territory, he knew he was being watched.

After traversing a good distance, the priest stopped. Breathing deeply, the monk asked the tiger, "Beast, why must you eat humans? What is wrong with the other bounty that so plentifully surrounds you?" The tiger stepped out of the lush vegetation and in a deep growl whisper said, "A tiger must do what a tiger must do. We have always hunted and eaten and shared what is given. Now you and your human family tree have reached a point in time that I forecast will never turn around. You and your kind will always pursue natures resources until they are wasted to death, until we are no more. Man's relationship with the natural world, charting the ecological losses caused by human activity will be an ever-present dilemma. Tell your brothers I know they will come for me, but I will never make it easy. When you do kill me and you will, do not waste me. Use me to learn from and share the stories and history of me and know that I will bring you power. Each morsel of my fur, flesh, muscle, organ, and bone provides evolutionally power and will change you forever. By consuming me, we continue our evolutionary journey together. We become one. On some occasions, I will consume you as well. That is part of the balance of nature. Although in the future it will be perceived as an imbalance, it is not. You must do what you must do, and a Jakkar must do what a Jakkar must do. That is our shared dilemma as we strive for survival."

With that, the beast slipped back into the concealment of the forest and disappeared. The monk returned to the village and told the others. The next day, a group of young priests and villagers ventured out to hunt the tiger. One by one the band of villagers and priests perished, falling victim to the tiger until the one priest was left.

As he tracked the Jakkar, the legend says the priest dug a deep pit trap. He covered it with sticks and brush strong enough to support himself and sat in the middle waiting. As the tiger approached, the priest threw rocks and scolded and taunted the Jakkar for his actions. Jakkar moved closer and eventually stepped into the trap falling as the priest jumped out of the way. The tiger roared in ear shattering cries, trying to jump out of the pit. The priest started to throw spears at him and the shot him with arrows. The Jakkar finally succumbed to the weapons and tools of the priest. It took eleven arrows and six spears to kill the Jakkar.

When she was dead, the priest brought the body to the village to let people see it. Several kicked it and others spat on it. Several look from a distance and held it in high regard. After a short time, the priest began to dissect the carcass. He carefully cut the hide off, spreading it out with wooden stakes to be tanned. He started the process of drying the organs so they could be ground into fine powders. He shared the meat and cleaned the bones. The bones would be boiled for soups. Eventually, he made it back to his temple and shared organ powders with his priest brothers telling how they would benefit. Certain priesthoods still consume the dried organs from the Jakkar and hold special ceremonies. Some say they display tiger-like traits of stealth, agility, strength and show no signs of fear when in combat. When asked why this tradition persists, one priest described it as an ever-haunting human dilemma to search for a stronger evolutionary path to survival and seek enhanced powers from the strongest survivors on the planet.

CHAPTER 5

Caek was from the Naledi bloodline. She was being pushed further and further from her family and remaining small Naledi clan she was traveling with. She was being pushed into the dense jungle. The Jakkar could have eaten her quickly and easily, but curiously didn't. Caek jumped over and squatted under logs of all sizes trying to avoid the Jakkar. The trees were giant redwoods, thousands of years old. She did not know this forest and had a no idea of where she was. As she was pushed further away from her clan, she gathered pine nuts and a few potatoes for food. She felt good and if she could just keep the tiger at a distance, she would live. She was apt and agile at climbing trees; her longish strong arms could hold her weight easily and she was able to swing from tree limb to tree limb gracefully. She wondered why the Jakkar was pushing her further way without eating her. Caek guessed there was a den high in the crags where the air was thin, and snow was heavy. She remembered Drot, her father told her several years ago the only way to escape a Jakkar was to get it interested in something else. The Jakkar was smart, and it was not easy to get this beast to shift its interest.

After several days of being pushed along a rocky mountainous trail, she heard a yelping howl. It was a shrill gravelly cry. It was an animal in distress and sounded as though it was wounded. She listened intensely and realized it was a tiger cub. As she moved along the rock crags, she came across a deep fissure. From somewhere in the fissure the cry for help came again. There was a tiger cub stuck far down the crack. As Caek shimmied down into the fissure, the Jakkar kept close watch. The adult Jakkar would not have fit. When she reached the cub, she pulled several tightly wedged rocks from the crevasse in attempt to free the cub's front paw. The paw was jammed behind a series of rocks wedged into the narrowest part of the fissure holding the juvenile feline captive. She tugged hard and was able to pry it loose. She could tell the paw was severely crushed and deformed when the angled rock gave way and the cub pulled back. The young cub weighed over one hundred eighty-five pounds and as it moved free it pushed Caek aside effortlessly. The fur was thick and feather soft. Once the cat was free, it gracefully leapt up the face of the crevasse then onto a ledge and started licking its injured paw. Caek made her way back up the narrow crack in spiderman fashion using both her arms and legs to climb. The boar hide moccasin gripped the basalt walls nicely. When she reached the top of the climb, she was exhausted.

She sat next to the cub; he was in a comfortable prone position quietly licking its injured appendage. The only sound was the raspy grind of the cub's tongue against its fur and a soft deep throaty purr. Caek scanned for the mother tiger but did not see her. Caek knew she was close, watching the cub. A few seconds later two more cubs appeared, three of them in total. Triplets. Caek realized she was probably going to be a training toy for the young cubs. She felt the end of her life was near, so she sat crossed-legged and went into a pre-death meditation.

The pre-death meditation was a technique taught by shamans as a peace offering to the earth seeking forgiveness and grace in death. It was the beginning of the concept of religion and believing in a sense of spiritual wakefulness. As she centered her thoughts, she saw her family. Drot, her fearless father and leader, two sisters Sinner and Huut, two young boys Cahat and Gluet, her aunts, Drots's sisters and his three dogs were looking on. They were the last survivors of the original clan of thirty Naledi traveling the last six years to keep ahead of the bitter advancing winters. They had traveled along the coast in wooden dugout canoes. As the ice sheets were growing, and game was getting scarce the group moved inland. The wooly mammoth was also slowly moving south. One by one the members of the clan died either by unfortunate accident, animal attack, infections, or old age.

What they did not realize was they were the last in the line of Naledi, the precursor to the Homo-Heidelbergensis and Homo-Neanderthalensis. A genetic line that spanned slightly more than one million years. In comparison, Homo-Sapiens have been around for fifty thousand years and have done irreparable damage to the planet. More damage than could ever have been imagined by our early ancestors. The lineage that Caek belonged to was unique. They possessed incredible instinctive and linguistic abilities in the early hominoids. The traits are still visible in the shadows of the modern homo sapient minds and bodies today. The most significant changes were in the size of the increased brain casement. The growing brain, specifically the occiput lobes, enabled perception of natural empathy and an alertness of self and the environment. It was the realization of a natural balance in all things. One distinguishing trait all Naledi had were vivid green eyes. They could see in the darkness of a cave, with the slightest of light.

Caek and her sisters possessed many of the same curious traits. They possessed the ability of natural tele-naturopathic type communications. A sixth sense that translated into a form of understanding other hominoids. Having the ability to understand and reason was an enlightened power. The Naledi hominoids were the beginning of that sense and spark of curiosity. It was a communal constructive intellect with surroundings and animals of all kinds. It became a genetic imprint and was experienced in most hominoids. The genetic imprint kept the Naledi strain alive for over two million years.

After a long meditative time, Caek opened her eyes, and the cubs were gone. She was alone. As she stood up and surveyed her surroundings, she spotted a slight whisp of smoke from a small fire across the wide valley high on a ridge near tree line. She hoped it was her clan. The sun was sinking below the horizon, and she realized she needed to start now if she was going to try and reach them before morning. Traveling at night was never a good idea. She knew there were numerous predators in the deep forests that were much more active in the darkness. She did not know how far she could travel by night but decided to try. She was easily able to fashion a torch and light it. Although it was not much of a defense against a tiger, it would ward off other animals, such as bears, wolf, boars, and hyenas and give her a chance to climb high into the canopy of the forest.

Caek was fourteen years old. She was lean and strong and learned quickly. Her instincts were well developed. She stood about five foot and was considered tall for a Homo Naledi. Her black kinky hair fell over her eyes and shoulders. Thick hair covered her body and provided a measurable amount of warmth, but she knew fur leggings were needed for more protection against the elements. They had been especially helpful on the long journey. Her green eyes were her most striking feature. They drew the attention of the shaman. Green eyes were considered a rare and powerful trait to other hominoids they met on their travels.

She sensed the dramatic change in the weather over the last few days. The wind from the north was getting brisk and cold. As she made her way towards the high ridge her mind wandered back to her childhood. She recalled Drot her father and learning to fish with him. She recalled the first time she killed a deer and sharing the heart meat with him. Drot was always patient. She thought about her sisters and how they worked together. Her mother died when she was young, and she only vaguely remembered her. She did not know exactly why, but her mother lost control of her legs one morning and could not move. Soon after her legs were paralyzed, her heart shutdown and she died. It was quick and sudden. She recalled the body was placed in a shallow grave in a field of purple heather. The ceremony included placing her knife and three arrows in the grave, symbolizing her skills as a huntress. The arrows were symbols for the three sisters, her only offspring. Caek missed her and felt a sadness and longing for her company as she made her way through the dark forest. The neural connections for sadness were beginning to form in the brain.

After climbing all night through the jungle, she arrived at the top of the ridgeline and smelled whisps of the fire. As she snuck closer, she saw the rock circle containing the red glowing embers. Next to the ring rested a single male curled up in a fetal position. He was not from her clan. The man looked as though he was dead, but she could see he was taking shallow breaths. He appeared to be much taller she was, and his leather clothing was notable different. He had no visible weapons other than a knife tied to his waist. As she moved closer, she noticed he had blood smeared over his head, face, and hands. She guessed he was about her age, perhaps a little older. She placed a few sticks on the fire and it crackled to life. She picked up and held a club like stick gripped firmly in her hands, at the ready, in case he awoke and attacked. As morning light grew, Caek became tired. The man had not moved much. There was nothing to eat near him and she thought he may have been starving to death. She eventually fell into a deep sleep as the fire crackled and popped.

A few hours later she woke with a slight jerk. Looking around the man had vanished. The fire was smoldering, and she felt bewildered and frightened as she stood to assess her surroundings scanning the forest and then the horizon. She stoked the fire contemplating her next move. She had no idea where her tribe was or which direction to go. Because of the number of Jakkar, she knew the area was rich in game. If Jakkar were here, the top of the food chain, then all else was in place. She noticed the cave entrance and moved to get a better look. As she stooped into the first chamber she saw bones from various animals, including bears and boars. The hollow descended into darkness and Caek was too hungry and weak to expend the energy to venture inside. As she turned away from the entrance, the man was standing there looking at her. He had a rabbit in one hand and a small crudely fashioned bow and arrow in the other. As she stepped out of the grotto and stood tall, the man spoke pointing to himself: "Noolan."

CHAPTER 6

THE NEXT MORNING KAZAN HEARD THE CRUNCHING OF footsteps approaching and stood to welcome the visitor. He always had many visitors throughout the day. It was Drot and the pregnant woman called Anga. They stepped up over a few rocks into his dwelling. As they looked around, they noticed several objects that appeared ceremonial. Two large tiger skulls with leg-bones slid into the eye sockets were placed on a rock ledge above a well-used fire pit. Feather plumage from eagles were laced together with sinew cord forming an elaborate headdress and cape. Several skins were hanging in various stages of being cured for clothing. A crudely constructed tree limb rack was propped up against one wall and held numerous leather pouches tied in no apparent order containing herbs and homeopathic treatments for a variety of ailments. Several bows and an assortment of beautifully made arrows stood tall in a skin quiver. Numerous stone and bone tools were placed neat and orderly from largest to smallest near the fire. A gazelle stomach was filled with water and hung off to the side of the fire just far enough to keep the water warm. Flint knapper and antler chippers were in a place to themselves.

Kazan greeted his guests with a warm smile and extended open hands. Drot responded. He signaled to sit. The pregnant woman moved close to Kazan and pointed to her belly mimicking baby. Kazan shook his head knowingly and paused. He motioned he wanted to feel the belly, and with a bit a trepidation, she relaxed for the examination. He could sense she was in pain and duress. He could feel the strong muscles of her labor beginning to tighten. She tensed and let the wave of contraction ripple through her body. Then she started a patterned breathing that quickly helped the contraction pass. Kazan new the baby would be born soon. He witnessed childbirth with many of the women in the clan.

He went to one of his vessels and pulled out willow bark and coca leaf and handed some to her. Chewing it released a pain numbing sensation. He then moved the water bag closer to the fire to heat the water. It quickly came to a boil, and he immersed small amounts of willow to steep. The young woman calmly sat next to the fire. Drot motioned with his hands, grabbing them close to his heart and motioning forward in a signal for thank you. Kazan smiled and gestured back, "You are welcome." The linkage of gratitude was developing, and the emotional bond of kindness was evident between the two.

They had an instinctive connection. They could sense each other and understood no harm or aggression was warranted. They quickly realized this was one reason the species would survive. They understood how and when to help each other. Kazan offered Drot tea, and they sat in silence. The girl was shifting as another contraction started to sweep into her body. She got up and walked to the edge of the cave, stepped over a small rock wall, squatted down and with tremendous concentration, force, and focus, she grunted deeply and gave birth to a little boy. Drot went over to cut the umbilical cord; Kazan brought some water and a recently tanned antelope skin for the new child. It didn't cry. There was something wrong. The girl let out a whimper squeezing the child. The baby did not respond. Kazan rushed over and looked closely at the child. It was turning a deep bluish color and was limp in her arms. The baby suffocated on its own mucus lining its throat. Early hominoids had not figured out a way to clear obstructions in the throat and lungs, a procedure done to newborn homo sapiens today with a simple rubber suction device used to clear the nostrils and back of the throat. The baby died within a few minutes, another random victim of evolution.

Once the death was realized, Kazan communicated there was a place for the dead. He described it as a sacred area, a place where scavengers would not be able to get to the bodies. He wrapped the child and included the afterbirth after inspecting it. He noted that it looked and smelled healthy. He also noted blood loss was minimal during the birth. Placing the small lifeless body in the antelope skin, he tied it with a piece of leather strapping and gave the child back to its mother, motioning her to follow. They moved swiftly up the hill and then walked along the ridge a short distance. A small herd of antelope moved gracefully off on a far hillside. On the horizon was a Wooley rhinoceros in silhouette as the sun continued rising. Around the back of a bolder they came to a gate fashioned out of a set of uniform wood sticks and bound together with leather straps. One branch was pushed sideways acting as a lock. He removed it, pulled with minimal force, and proceeded to enter a chamber. Next to the entry, Kazan picked up a torch with animal fat and lit it with a practiced flick of two flint pieces hitting each other. The fat spattered to life.

The three moved down a well-worn path, then up a wall by ladder, and down another corridor until they entered a large chamber. Kazan motioned where to place the baby and they would cover it with rocks to protect it. Anga scrapped out a shallow depression and placed the child down. As she gazed upon the tiny hairy body, her heart felt heavy, and she let out a soft cry. She knew the numbers in her clan were getting small. She had not seen others with the same features since they left their home. She was sad as they placed rocks to cover the child. This was her second child, the first died after three days of life. It froze to death during an unexpected ice storm last winter while on the trail. Kazan started to chant an ancient song of mourning. His voice was gravelly and moved between high and low notes in a harmonic hum with melodic inflections that grew into a mono-tone chant as they placed the last rocks on the small hairless body. Then he went silent. All one could hear was a drip of water deep in the cave and the flicker of the torch, it was burning out. As he turned and started to walk back to the opening, Drot and Anga followed in silence.

They reached daylight near the cave opening and Drot noticed the glorious paintings on the walls. Detailed depictions of various animals and images of people in bright ocher and coal covered the walls and ceiling. He stopped to review one panel. It showed a group of people moving towards a tiger. The images of the people had open hands and no weapons. A recognizable row of mountains rose behind the image of the tiger indicating a great beast lived in the high mountains. Drot then had a flashback to when Caek was separated from the tribe. It was near those mountains. He began to wonder if she may still be alive. He gestured to Kazan indicating he wanted to go in that direction. Kazan responded that snow would be coming soon and a trek into the tree line area would not be easy and gestured why? Weren't he and his people traveling south?

Drot thought about what he was proposing to do. It had been almost a month since Caek went missing. There was no reason the believe she was still alive. But Drot had a sensation, a feeling she was alive.

He felt compelled to believe she was traveling looking for him. Or, he pondered, perhaps she was eaten by the Jakkar. That was the most likely scenario.

He abandoned the thought and looked towards other beautifully drawn panels. One showed several elk, and recognizable mammoths. He had seen the massive beasts on the high plains but never participated in the killing of one. It took a small army to bring one down and many times the huge beasts were run off cliffs and killed by the dozens. There were several geometric shapes he did not understand but recognized the symbols for rivers, serpent looking lines with carefully placed dots indicating points of importance such as crossings. Kazan said in his native tongue, "let's go," and started to limp back towards his shelter.

There was a brisk wind moving across the region as they moved over the ridge line and back down the valley. Once they reached the shaman's dwelling, they shook hands and parted. Kazan had more visitors or patients waiting for him; several pregnant women were pacing anxiously. One young boy looked as though he broke his arm and Coll, his daily companion, arrived with the help of his father. Coll, a seven-year-old boy was born with craniometaphyseal dysplasia, a rare condition characterized by thickening of bones in the skull and abnormalities in the region near the end of long cranial bones known as the metaphysis. The abnormal bone growth continued throughout his short life. Except in the most severe cases, the lifespan of people with craniometaphyseal dysplasia is normal. Cognitively, Coll was fine. He was already able to communicate and count. He could not run as the affliction caused him to be off balance. He would spend much of his time with Kazan helping with the mixing of natural medicinal herbs. He could follow instructions and learn procedures and routines at impressive rates. It was shaping up to be a busy day.

Drot and the young mother returned to their cave. She found her sleeping place, arranged a leather bedroll, and laid down. Sinner asked

Anga about baby, but she knew things had not gone well. She brought her friend some water and, in the silence, they understood each other. Junn, the other pregnant woman, was mending leather clothing by the fire with eyes cast downwards in an understanding sadness of what must have happened. As they sat quietly the two young boys, Cahat and Gluet, moved to the edge of the cave. They could see game in the far-off valley. The antelope looked plentiful, and the clan needed fresh meat. They knew how to hunt and with a quick nod from Drot, they grabbed their bows and left in search of game.

There was a sadness in the face of Junn. She understood the baby had died. And she also knew she would be having her baby next, probably sooner than expected. Death was more common during the early Pleistocene from animal attacks, or falls, and illness. The young were usually the first to succumb to death. The long days walking sometimes twenty-five miles over ice fields or high rocky crags, or deep dense jungle was tough even for hominoids accustomed to sleeping on the ground or high in trees for safety. As members of the tribe aged and their usefulness diminished, death would come quickly. It was a law of nature, and the people of the time knew there was nothing they could do about death except to prolong their usefulness as best they could. Drot knew his days were numbered. The best he could do right now was to find shelter for the last members of the Naledi hominoid branch of evolution. He wanted to protect them from the storms looming on the horizon. Little did any of the tribe know that they were indeed the last of the pure bloodline that lasted more than eight hundred thousand years. The only species that lasted longer was Africanus Robustus who had ceased to be a pure species five hundred thousand years earlier.

Their genetics were incorporated into the next hominoid in evolutionary progression. Robustus oscillated over the planet for almost two million years. Extinction was the wrong term and became a complex question. Extinction implies disappearance of something. A fire can be extinguished, and the flame will be extinct. It will no longer produce light. Through interbreeding, early hominoids homogenized their genetic code into the next rendition of our most useful and successful living mechanics. Certain features of every identified creature in our ancient family tree are genetically imbedded in each one of us. The Homo-Naledi intellectual abilities are found in modern homo sapient DNA. Their unique genetics sparked spiritual awareness and emotions that manifested themselves in the Naledi evolutionary track over the millennia. Although the Naledi were small in stature and the brain casement was smaller than that of future hominoids, their ability to reason, create tools for survival, was unprecedented and unique during this period of evolution.

Certain unexplained anomalies were present that can be considered genetic mutations in most cases. If the mutation proves to provide an advantage in some way, it becomes an adaptation and as more individuals present the genetic trait, the more frequently and embedded it becomes. Green eyes are still common in chimpanzees. This is an oversimplification because a lot happens to our genetics on a molecular level to enhance the chance of mutation. A lot also happens due to environmental factors that cause fluctuations in grow patterns be it trees or tigers or humans. It is one explanation of how our planet evolved and how we evolved to be where we are. It has always been a genetic pool of adaptation based on chance.

As Drot pondered the amber coals in the fire, Junn stood up and motioned towards the path. Kazan was coming down the trail with several others. They did not appear to have weapons, and there was a general feeling of peace. As the group filed into the shelter, they presented numerous gifts and made vocal introductions. There were three women, one younger man, two elders and Kazan. This must have been a welcoming committee, and the gifts included several tanned skins, including rabbit, fox, and antelope. Drot signed a welcome to the visitors and wanted to communicate his thanks. The group gathered and sat near the fire and proceeded to inflect vocal sounds and hand signals attempting to communicate. Kazan was the first to understand Drot's hand signs. He could tell they used a similar counting system with fingers and large gestures referenced mountains and then rivers. Drot was describing to the group where his family had come from.

As he drew some images on the dirt floor, Kazan already understood they recently came from the far north. Primarily because of the formidable fur lined boots and heavy fur capes. Kazan was fascinated with the unique foot gear. The bottoms were made from a tough thick hide. They were not soft and supple like the ones Kazan was used to wearing. If he had to guess, he thought they may have been mammoth, or rhino hide. His thoughts kept him wondering if this group had killed a mammoth over the course of their travels. It seems highly unlikely because it normally took twenty strong young men or more to attack and kill a beast of that size. Another scenario was they came across a carcass of a dead one and scavenged the hide specifically for the footwear. The boots were well stitched and looked like they would last a long time on the trail. Kazan thought Junn must have had a hand in making them. Her sewing skills looked remarkable. She had one needle fashioned from antler and another smaller one made from bone. She stored her sewing supplies of extra lengths of delicately cut leather and sinew cord in a large skin pouch adorned with several unusual elongated colorful seashells.

The guests communicated through gestures and voice inflection. There was an understanding of survival and need. They were smiling, a relatively new sensation and facial expression. They seemed to understand working together was in their best interests. Among the several welcome gifts was a cache of smoked fish, dried peaches, furs, and a dark flint nodule for making arrow and spear points. Drot and his clan of travelers felt welcomed and thought about staying for the winter. He motioned to Kazan and asked if they would be able to winter over. Kazan again indicated that the cave was not used. He said it did go back a good way and as long a fire was kept, larger animals would not come near. Junn presented one of the women with one of her sewing needles as a token welcome gift.

One of the women accepted the gift with a smile and inspected it. The workmanship and strength of the tool was beautiful. It would become a prize possession of the women. During the meeting the young boy asked about the two other young men. He wanted to meet them and plan a hunt. Drot indicated they went after game and pointed in the direction across the valley. With that indication of direction, the boy picked up his bow and as he turned to run off his obsidian knife fell from its well-worn sheath and shattered as it hit a flat rock on the ground. He picked several of the pieces in disgust. At that, Drot vocalized and grabbed the recently presented flint nodule gift. He pulled several tools from his pouch and knapped off a good size flint piece. He began a series of focused rhythmic motions snapping off tiny shards around the edges of the stone. Within five minutes, even with his gimpy arm, he presented the boy with a new extremely sharp and balanced blade. The young boy in turn reached into the pouch around his waist and pulled out a small well-worn, deep green jade stone and gave it to Drot in exchange for the knife blade. The jade was special because he found it on a vision quest as part of his journey to manhood.

They both understood the tradition that one does not freely take a blade as a gift without some small gift in exchange. The legend stated that in doing so, the blade would metaphorically sever the relationships of the giver and receiver unless some trade was made at the time the blade was presented. It was an unspoken custom both clans understood. Drot and Kazan smiled at each other as the tradition was kept. The blade fit perfectly in the woven sheath and the boy, after gesturing, "thank you," asked if he could teach him that skill. Drot smiled and nodded. Then, the boy turned and started walking in the direction of the other two hunters. It was early afternoon, and a cool breeze gripped the air. A short way down the trail he heard crashing in the forest off to his right. He stopped and listened. Something or someone had stirred up the normally quiet area.

As he watched the scene unfold, several gazelles were moving swiftly through the forest and into an open meadow. One appeared injured as it lagged behind the others. The boy sat down and watched the animal slowly weaken and eventually lay down in the tall grass. Shortly after that, the two boys appeared. With quick agility and a bit of planning they tied the hooves of the dead animal together and slipped a long pole through and began to carry it up the valley. While moving down the trail, the one single boy saw a large flat nosed bear tracking the other two boys. The bear had caught the scent of blood from the kill. Animals on the plains were mostly opportunistic eaters not killers. For a bear the size of an adult grizzly, anything would do, dead or alive, and it did not necessarily matter how small or large it was to be considered a meal. The boy watched Cahat and Gluet as they moved quickly down the trail. The bear was following close behind.

With a shrill signal call, the boys carrying the gazelle looked up and saw the bear getting closer. They quickly dropped the load and cut a hind quarter of the dead gazelle off and dragged it towards the bear. The massive bear stopped. Once the boys left, it slowly moved towards the meat and started eating. By the time it finished the offering, the boys completed the field dressing and were moving down the trail back towards camp along with the third young boy Vena, happy with his new acquaintances and the afternoon kill.

CHAPTER 7

THERE WAS A NATURAL ELEMENT OF TRUST DEVELOPING between Noolan and Caek. She had taken the rabbit from him and quickly reached for the knife she kept in her boot. Noolan watched her as she swiftly skinned and gutted the rabbit. She stretched it out on two long stick skewers, stoked the coals, and started the process of cooking it. He noted her small but strong stature, longish arms, green eyes, her braided auburn kinky hair, and her unusually hairy skin. He was still feeling disoriented with an excessive pounding headache. Caek noticed the dried blood on his head and neck. She carefully moved towards him and gently parted his hair to show the deep gash in the back of his head. It was healing but she could tell that the gash cut deep into his head. She motioned to wait and retrieved some clear water from a nearby stream. She attempted to wash the area, but Noolan winced when she touched it. She brought back some moss and placed it carefully over the wound. Then, she returned to tending the rabbit. Noolan reached for the rabbit skin and stretched it out over a nearby rock face. He took hold of the entrails and ate the small heart and offered Caek the liver. She shyly accepted the morsel, understanding it was indeed a special treat. It was a gift she warmly accepted. When the rabbit was cooked, they both indulged in the rich savory protein cooked crisp to perfection.

They sat in silence as night fell. The cave offered good shelter, but they both knew they needed to keep a fire going to ward off creatures wanting shelter as well. They both descended the ridge outside the cave to gather wood for the night. They did this in silence, but with an innate understanding of survival. They clicked into each other's understanding of sharing and survival needs in the difficult environment they were in. As they fed the fire, Noolan motioned towards himself and spoke his name "Noolan." again, hoping for a nod of acknowledgement. Caek quickly picked up the signal and smiled, pointing to herself saying "Caek". He responded by saying her name several times, "Caek, Caek, Caek."

As the evening grew to darkness, Caek moved towards Noolan wanting to share his warmth. He opened his large fur cape and spread it out. Caek moved slowly and situated herself near him. He was receptive and warm. Noolan also felt comfortable as they began to relax for the night. Caek spoke to him in a soft voice, but he did not understand. He looked at her inquisitively, as she repeated herself several times then pointing off into the distance. Noolan did not know how to respond. In his mind, he was still lost. He had experienced the fractured skull and deep gash over a month ago, when the earth tremor that tossed him into the tubular gas vent occurred. His mind wandered and he could not remain focused. He had experienced severe head trauma, a concussion that should have killed him. The continual headaches were driving him mad. It thundered and rained hard that night with lighting flashing violently across the skies.

At dawn, Caek woke first. She moved carefully away from Noolan and placed a few pieces of wood on the fire. She then walked down to the stream to wash. She noted several berries and a few onions poking out of the ground along the way. At the stream she noted trout and small crawdads. She always had a liking for crawdads and started catching the smallish crustations, gathering several and placing them on the bank of the stream in a small surround of rocks to prevent escape. Noolan woke and watched her from a distance. He watched as she started removing her boots, carefully inspecting her feet and toes. She dripped her feet in the cool water and scrubbed them clean of small amounts of dirt and debris and peeled off calloused skin. He noted her boots were well made. The soles were a tough hide from a large mammal, either boar or rhino. Her leggings were made from an elk's belly hide. They were soft and supple but durable and protective. Due to the cycles in evolution the pads on her small feet would soften over the next one hundred thousand years. Her distended toe, or foot thumb, would not be as prominent as it once was. This was an adaption that started to limit the ability to climb trees. She could still climb when she needed to, but not as quickly or as agile as her distant ancestors.

As Caek waded through the water she noticed a strange feeling. The water was getting warm. Slowly she moved up stream and as she turn a corner, among the ferns was a gently bubbling warm spring. Warm water from the earth. She had experienced hot springs many times in her short life. She moved in the direction and noted the bottom of the spring was a sandy gravel, it was easy on the feet. She removed her remaining fur, exposing her taut body. Her breasts were firm and not overly large, and her body was covered in fine hair. Over the next millennia hominoids would lose body hair as an adaptation in developing homo sapiens. However, at this period in the late Pleistocene, the hair was an added layer of insulation and given the color, added to camouflage in certain situations. She placed her clothing carefully on the

shore and immersed herself in the steaming hot water and began wash-
ing herself. Swimming gracefully across the pond she untied her hair,
and shook her hair lose. She dove under and felt an easy feeling of safety
come over her. But she was cautiously curious about the man that she
thought was still sleeping by the fire. He was strong though he had been
injured. She knew his head was cut deep but had no idea how to treat it.
An inherent thought came to her. She could use the moss around the
pond as a compress. It had many medicinal uses, and one was that of a
compress. She went back to her boots on shore and removed her knife,
swam back to the area around the mouth of the spring, and cut a six-
inch square pad of moss for Noolan, and headed back to the cave.

Noolan quickly closed his eyes, feigning to be asleep. He did not re-
spond when she gently pushed his arm to wake him. She shook him
gently first, then a bit more aggressively. Slowly he opened his eyes, and
he smiled when she came into focus. Her hair was wet and hanging
down her face and she was naked. She held out the moss, held it to
her nose, then placed it on her head mimicking the action she wanted
to do. Noolan nodded, understanding this was not an aggressive act,
but rather a caring act. The moss felt good and soothing. Since the un-
expected journey into the volcano that caused his head injury, he had
experienced migraine headaches. The throbbing would come and go,
but the pain was getting worse. He had no way to verbally explain the
feeling to Caek.

Caek applied the compress and in doing so, felt something sharp as
she patted it into place. As she looked at the fractured skull, the area
was matted with blood. The hair was thick, black, and course. When
she parted the tangled mass, she saw a shard of obsidian lodged in the
cut. As she pulled it out, Noolan seized, tensing his arms and legs. It
was piece of volcanic glass was a little over three inches and a half long
and one inch wide hidden by a flap a skin and thick blood covered hair.
Noolan should have been dead after getting the shard stuck in his head.

It was so close to the optical never that he should have at least been blind in one eye. The location of where it lodged did affect his motor skills. He was lethargic and moved with careful motions. Once the shard was removed, she placed the moss back on the wound, gave him some warmed water, then disappeared back into the forest.

Noolan picked up the shard as he rested by the fire. He felt it would make a fine point for a medium sized spear point, or perhaps a skin scraper. When he thought of that he realized he did not have any weapons other than his bow. His knife was missing. It had been missing a long time. He thought about the last time he remembered carrying it. He recalled it was when he was stalking a Jakkar with another person. He could not remember who that other person was. A memory started to come back, but he was having a hard time focusing. It was then he thought he heard the bark of a wolf near-by. He knew the wolf was one of the most aggressive and dangerous predators on the planet. What made the wolf so much more dangerous than most animals was it killed more than needed. It would sometimes kill for sport rather than out of necessity, the only creature to do so. Even to this day, wolf packs will play games with prey, such as elk, killing three or four at one time, leaving massive amounts of meat for others. It is a routine has been going on for millions of years. The extra meat was part of the cycle of life providing not only meat for others but nutrients for soils and fungi. The wolf played an important part of the evolutionary cycle, but the game it played was dangerous to all.

Noolan made a mental note of the direction the howls were coming from, knowing he was safe mainly because of the fire. He needed a good knife, a bow, and tools to make them and then he attempted to stand up. His legs were extremely wobbly and unbalanced. He leaned back on a large rock and tried to focus. When he gained his sight, he looked out over the horizon. "Where was she?" he wondered and who was this female? Where did she come from? What was he going to do now? He reached up and felt the moss compress on his head and noticed the migraine was gone.

Caek was down in the forest gathering some fruits including several pears, and some overly ripe tomatoes; she had some onions and her most prized finds were several potatoes, carrots, and the crawdads. She washed them in the stream, preparing them for Noolan. They would eat well today she reflected and started to wonder about her family and where they could be. She had a feeling they were okay. She also knew her best chances for surviving the winter would be to have a partner. Although the male at the fire was injured, he was better than nothing. If he re-gained his health, even better. She sensed he was lost because he had not gestured to move in any specific direction. It seemed to her; he had come to life at that spot. He looked bewildered, malnourished, dehydrated and in generally poor condition, despite the piece of glass she pulled from his head.

Caek had no idea Noolan had traveled seventeen miles underground, through the intestines of an active volcano. He was on the brink of death when he finally emerged on the far side of his world. In many ways, it was the same, and in many ways it was different. He did not know it at the time, but he could smell the ocean as strong winds came from the west. As his mind began to clear he recalled hearing stories of enormous bodies of salt water that stretched the entire horizon. Fish were plentiful, and many clans gathered to share fish and mussels in ancient locations. The bounty was always plentiful. He started to feel an internal drive to trek to the west, towards the setting sun. He felt the answers to his past world was not lost but just over the next range of mountains. As he contemplated his life, he slowly fell into a deep sleep by the crackling fire.

As his breathing deepened, he began to dream. With the glass shard finally removed, his brain was adjusting and calming down, the swelling was going down. Pressure on his optic nerve had been removed and his vision would revert to twenty-ten in each eye. He reached the REM state of sleep and his mind wandered back to his clan. He recalled seeing Kazan in his cave. He recalled holding the tiger skull and being shown the wall painting and how they were done. He vividly recalled what they meant. The flashbacks were random and disturbing. Kazan had given him special mushrooms as part of his journey. His dreams felt strangely like those hallucinations. His sentience was crystal clear. He felt as though he was traveling through the stars. He started to re-call memories of hunts of the past and walking through open fields and the animals grazing and milling about. He was at peace in this place and was able to communicate with everything. He was in a Shaman trance. It was home. Familiar faces flashed through his mind, his father and brother and his sisters and his dogs! He felt connected and they con-nected with him.

Upon the searing imagery of his dogs, he woke up breathing heavily and bewildered. Caek was there, alarmed by Noolan's rude awakening. He slowly smiled. Caek had been there a while and offered Noolan meat, and then the flame roasted potatoes. The carrots were washed and lay on a skin ready to be eaten. The hind quarter of the rabbit was laid out in slices when opened her pouch and pulled out another smaller pouch. She reached in and pulled a pinch of salt out and sprinkled it on the rabbit. Noolan smiled at this special treat and savored the seasoned mor-sels. He motioned to Caek asking to see her knife. She reached into her boot and produced the elegant well used razor-sharp blade. The handle was made from small pieces of shaved cottonwood that were covered by clean skinned rabbit leather. It was sewn tight on the handle. It was nice work. The blade could be sharpened easily with a small knapping tool, but most of the edge was already as sharp as a surgical scalpel. Caek reached back into her pouch and produced a small knapping tool and handed it to Noolan. He smiled and started to look around the cave area for discarded flint and then he recalled the obsidian shard she removed from his head. It was lying next to his leg near the fire ring. He cleaned off the dust, flecked off the blood, spat on it to clean it and wiped it with a piece of leather. It was perfect.

The center was about an inch thick, and it tapered off in almost equal proportions to either side. The edges were razor thin. With minimal knapping, his knife blade was complete. Caek turned and went about her business of eating and thinking about her next move. Would she stay with him? How were they going to survive the coming winter if they stayed together? When he showed her the blade, she reached for the rabbit hide and motioned she would fashion a handle like hers. She quickly found a piece of wood, carefully shaved it, and put a split in one end. Gracefully, she carved out about an inch of wood from the end. She shaved the remaining area into a grip. She then reached for the blade and slipped it in. The handle needed a bit of adjustment for a snug fit. She cut a length of cleaned rabbit skin and wrapped the handle snuggly and sewed it tightly with a small needle and leather thread she pulled from her pouch. She cinched up the threaded weave tightly and tied it off with a strong non-slip knot. She took a length of sinew and started to wrap the shank of the blade affixing it to the grip with the sinew. She tightened the thin cord with her teeth. She then moved out of the cave and peed on the handle. The acid in the urine would act as a binder and tighten the leather thus securing the blade tightly once it dried. Noolan watched her knowing the practice. It was interesting to him that she knew of such things. She was different in appearance but used many of the same survival skills he knew. They shared a common ancestry and several rituals and routines for survival. The heft of the knife was solid. It was also well balanced. He looked at her with gratitude and vocalized a few sounds she did not understand. She knew he was grateful.

The rabbit had been totally consumed and Caek was cleaning several of the bones. Rabbit rib bones made fine sewing needles and she was happy to replenish her supplies. She packed a few into her pouch along with varying lengths of sinew and leather straps. She went on to scraping the rabbit hide removing all the fur. Once the leather was cleaned, she washed it, and stretched it out over a nearby pile of rocks. When it was damp, she took the skull of the rabbit, cracked it open, and removed the brain matter. There was less than a cup of gray mush brain tissue. She rubbed it deeply into the leather. She learned that this would make the leather supple and soft enough to wear close to her skin. Next to mink, rabbit skin was an exceptionally soft and useful material.

CHAPTER 8

THAT NIGHT KAZAN INTENTIONALLY INGESTED HALLUCI-nogenic mushrooms and slipped into a trance like state. As the chemicals started to infuse his mind, he sat cross-legged in front of his fire. There was no wind. At one point he rose, reached for a tightly tied bundle of sage sitting on a nearby ledge. The bundle was about an inch in diameter and six inches long. One end was already burnt from previous ceremonies. He brought it close to the fire and let it catch. It only took a few seconds. When it was lit, he blew out the flame letting it smoke profusely. Then he brought it up to his nose and inhaled deeply. He walked around the cave letting the waft of white smoke mix with the air. It produced a calming and cleansing effect. He returned to his seat and sipped a little water. He then produced a small leather pouch. From it he pulled out a shaved cedar wood chip. He held it to the flames, and it caught quickly. He then inhaled the sweet-smelling smoke stirring memories of his ancestors.

The mushrooms started to take conscience-altering effect within twenty minutes. Visons started to flash into Kazan's mind. The sky was a brilliant indigo blue with scattered bright white clouds, waters intensely clear, and creatures of all kinds invaded his thinking, some with ferocity and others without. He saw vast bodies of water with heavy white waves crashing on jet black rocks protruding out of the water as it became foamy and bubbly. He saw a beach with bright white sands stretching for miles, and there were hominoids walking with a massive Jakkar. He could not tell who they were, but he did know they were different from him. They walked with an upright posture and were wearing unusual looking clothing, not skins or hides. Their heads were large, shaped differently from his and others he had known. He could see their mouths move as though they were speaking but could not understand what they were saying. He watched as they walked past him. They stared at him intensely and smiled. The tiger stopped and looked back with eyes reflecting sadness. Kazan felt profoundly emotional at that moment, understanding his life was but an instant in the spectrum of time. He understood there was going to be great change in the people and world around him. Evolution of humanity was moving fast as he sensed that extinction was going to happen slowly. The experience was profound. Kazan understood his visions would chart the course of hominoid species ability to infuse creative thought and forward thinking into self-actualization. Kazan saw the face of a man and thought it was Drot rolling a circular shaped gold colored stone attached with wooden poles. The image had similar skin and facial features as Drot, as he was walking towards a hill then disappearing. It was a sign Kazan understood that Drot would be leaving this world soon. Sacred colors of red for immediate times and trials, yellow for the flames of fire, black for the inner soul and white for the ability to think were seared into his mind and then the entire color spectrum filled an exploding indigo blue sky.

Kazan was reaching the crest of the effects of the mushrooms with the psilocybin connecting synapse neuro-links at cosmic speeds. He was vividly aware of himself and his surroundings. He then found himself experiencing an elevated feeling and how he was connected to the earth as its steward. He and the tiger were on the same trajectory of existence and extinction, and he understood they would share the same demise. He started to experience a sensation of floating, and then flying over the forests seeing animals running in panic, and volcanos spewing massive flows of magma setting the forests on unquenchable fire. He saw great rivers loaded with mud and water flowing across the lands. He watched hominoids of all kinds vanishing into oblivion under the mud flows. He witnessed glaciers rapidly melt into watery cascading falls. Unexpectedly his mind flashed back to Huut's dead baby and how blue the boy turned. That imaged intensified, searing into Kazan's mind the infant's death. The tiger stayed next to him and once the image of the baby started to fade, then tiger turned to him and said, "A tiger must do what a tiger must do." Then it turned and walked away disappearing into white smoke.

An easing sensation swept over Kazan as his eyes fluttered opened, straining to focus. The fire had burned down to only glowing golden embers with a teasing pop and shooting spark every now and then. The color images were starting to subside and Kazan was still, breathing deeply pondering the lingering reverberations of the experience and what insights he would gain. There was always a lot to understand. He knew everything had a purpose and the images were a foreshadowing of things to come. He did not fully comprehend what he experienced but understood there was always glimpses of the future embedded in ancient practice of a mind-expanding ritual. He put a few more sticks on the fire and settled down in his warm furs to sleep. As he drifted off, he started to dream. Noolan came into focus and was alive. Kazan felt this was odd. When others he knew died, they were always quickly forgotten. There were no recordings of individual life, and any memories would fade quickly. Kazan was mesmerized by why was Noolan so prominent and visual? He started to wonder how he could record important lessons and pass them down for future generations to learn from. He wondered intensely about the vision, and then gently fell off into a deep slumber.

The psilocybin mushroom was used in ceremonies as far back as Kazan could recall. It was part of the integrated cultures that roamed the world. The hallucinogenic(s) were an integral part of comprehending the past, present, and future of evolving hominoids. The qualities and experiences of a trip were not the same for everyone, but everyone was introduced to the effects as they reached early puberty. Each child was watched carefully for signs of unusual interactions while experiencing the effects. Some exhibited minimal reactions, and others would go into long trances displaying elliptic seizures. Each child was questioned by the shaman as to what they saw and experienced. Depending on the answers, some children were then trained in the art and science of cultural shamanism. Some children were gifted with uncanny powers of observation and communicated experiences in graphic detail, while others with negligible effects were identified as hunters and keepers of fire. Noolan was both. He was a different being; he was a highly skilled hunter and exhibited unique understanding of creative thought and ability. His aptitude to understand the connection to the earth provided by the experience was profound. Noolan found every experience was connected and coded for recall at some time later. Every leaf, cat, emotion, dog, every item in the line of sight, or by ear, touch, taste, smell, was connected to thought and being connected it was an experienced resource for survival. It was then mapped in the brain tissue as the neocortex continued developing and growing. He and Kazan talked many times about what was thought.

They discussed concepts through a series of geometric designs, floral symmetry, seasonal routine, and numerical sequences, and felt all early hominoids were establishing a system accounting for and recalling all experiences. Rituals provided access to creative thought integrated into all parts of the flora and fauna of the early Pleistocene and beyond. This was and always would be the fragmented parts of future ecosystems. Mushrooms and other hallucinogens provide elucidating and expanding effects on the brain. The experiences could be pleasurable, but it sometimes led to death. Kazan understood that as dead bodies were to be left out to rot in nature, they would eventually be absorbed by fungi for further dispersion into the ecosystem. He knew the carbon-based world and the essence of the process of evolution would meet and combine and be absorbed into another. He understood what happened when an egg was fertilized, and creation took place. Evolution would then occur. He could see evolution and understood growth would happen not only on this planet but all others in the vastness of time and space. Noolan was learning this at the time he vanished.

It was raining heavily as Kazan opened his eyes. The rain smelled good. The earth was dry over the last few weeks and the water was welcomed. The forest looked fresh and smelled pure. It was deep green, and he could hear birds of all kinds singing as the rain subsided. He reflected on the visions the night before. He thought about the Jakkar and why he felt so real. He began to realize they shared a common future; one would exterminate the other, and because of that action, the other species would also fail. The challenge was to keep both alive and live in harmony for as long as possible. He reached for a bowl fashioned from a boar's skin, filled it with water and brought it close to the fire. When the skin was full of water, it would not catch fire or burn. The water acted as its own insulation and with a little care, it boiled. He poured the steaming liquid into a clay cup and mixed in a few dried mint leaves and sat back.

Drot appeared on the trail leading up to the cave and Kazan motioned him over. They greeted each other with an arm embrace, were each of the men gripped the others forearm muscle tightly. Then they sat down in silence for a while. Drot wanted to know about the people living in this region. He used hand gestures and a series of voice inflections, then fingers in a pointing fashion. "You, me how many others?" was the question.

Kazan understood and pointed in different directions, "Over in that area on the other face of the canyon sixteen, up the canyon, about twenty-five. Over the ridge, many. Why do you ask?" Drot responded that he was worried about the amount of game they had encountered on their trek south. He told Kazan that as they kept moving south it seemed the game was becoming scarcer. Kazan looked at him inquisitively, thinking what this observation could mean for the future of the area and its people if it was indeed true. He understood if the game was gone, the people would be quick to follow. In the shadows of his memory, as a youth of three years, he recalled traveling to this current region. He was a young child identified by the tribal shaman that he was suited to train. Kazan had keen powers of observation and an uncanny sensitivity about the future.

Due to the size of the brain, specifically the cortex monopathic low frequency wave of thought, Kazan's brain absorbed two-hundred-fold greater thoughts than the hominoids yet to come. As other regions of the brain developed, others died out. The small glands in the brain, the hypothalamus, pituitary gland, and pineal glands were in full developmental mode. The entire endocrine system was increasing, and some regions worked well, and some did not. Kazan's hunting skill left a lot to be desired, but his ability to heal others was remarkable. People of all kinds and distances came to visit the shaman, most leaving with positive results. It was due to homeopathic rituals and herb mixes, and tea extracts, with suggestions of improved hygiene. Kazan had been able to help with numerous ailments, most being injuries while hunting. Lacerations and broken bones were the largest volume of his customers. There was no form of payment, only gifts given to show gratitude. Kazan never went hungry. If he needed anything he knew he could ask, and it would appear. This was especially helpful if he ran out of certain roots, or fungi used in his practice. He would ask one of the young to seek out what he was looking for. Sometimes he needed to go along and train the child to find certain root, plant, or animal. Everything had its own special and unique environment and once he taught someone how to find it, it was always available. Kazan was becoming the most revered shaman in the region. He was training the three boys, Noolan, Hook and Rit. Now that Noolan was gone, it seemed a link to the pattern of passing knowledge forward was missing.

CHAPTER 9

As night began to fall, Noolan noticed several ravens cawing and moving into the trees down the valley. They were on to something. Probably a kill of some kind. He looked over to Caek; she was watching it as well. Then Caek turned to Noolan and nodded yes. Together they started to walk in the direction the crows were moving. Moving through the jungle was easy and quick. Noolan noticed how agile and aware Caek was. He noticed her smell. She had not had her cycle. He knew that women bled on a routine basis. He did not understand why, he could tell by certain smells the woman would be receptive to reproduce. Caek was young and was capable of breeding but showed no interest.

After a few minutes they arrived at a freshly killed boar. A quarter hind was missing. It was a clean kill done by a tiger. The neck was crushed, and the angle of the teeth marks indicated it was a quick fight.

They scanned the area and cautiously moved over to the animal. Noolan flipped it over and with his knife, started to cut through the hide. A boars hide was the toughest in the animal kingdom due to the thickness and toughness of the thick course hair. Once through the skin, Caek held the leg and bent it back in such a way it was easy for the connecting sinew and muscle to be cut. When the hind quarter was free, Caek paused and motioned for Noolan to stop. They listened intently. The level of focused was uncanny, as though their lives depended on it, because it did.

In relative terms, the boar's leg was easy removed with fluid actions learned and repeated countless times before Australopithecus made the scene, three million plus years ago. It was also approximately when the taste for meat was acquired, and the primary vegetarian diet started to change. Obtaining meat was always cause for thought. Many times, the hominoids would get lucky and did not have to make a kill. Early hominoids were opportunists and scavengers along with most other animals.

Caek looked past Noolan and spotted a tiger lying motionless on a branch high in a tree eighty yards away, watching. It was well fed and did not need more. It had enough. There was no concept of mine and yours, but rather an understanding of survival for all. The two took the meat knowing that when they made a kill, they would also take what they needed and leave the rest for other animals including bears, tigers, badgers, mice, snails, ants, maggots, and microbes. A replenishment for them and an offering to the earth.

The couple would eat well that day and save small amounts for another meal. Caek pulled some wild Arrowroot out of the ground on the way back to the shelter. Noolan skinned the quarter, cut slices of meat off and carefully slid them on skewers with the arrowroot tubers. He then sat back watching it cook. Caek settled next to the fire and was looking out over the lands wondering about her clan. She spoke to Noolan in a soft voice, "What are we going to do?" she queried. Noolan looked her blankly, wanting to engage with her and learn more about where she came from and where she headed and where her people were. Not being able to fully understand each other, they sat in silence for a long time.

Once a fair amount of the meat was consumed, Caek motioned to Noolan to follow. She led him down to the water's edge. She removed her skins and stepped into the warm pool. Noolan followed removing his skins and the moss compress. He submerged himself and started washing his head. The pool was geothermally heated and steaming as it left the source. Large ferns and other unique flora lined the smallish reservoir. The water was not flowing fast, but rather a consistent and steady movement and then emptying into a nearby creek. As Noolan moved toward the source, he noted the temperature change. He stopped when it became too warm. Caek perched herself on a log watching as he swam and then floated peacefully. She did not understand what she was feeling but she was enjoying his presence. She knew he was a year or two older than she. They seemed to understand many of the same deeply ingrained traditional routines of survival. Noolan moved closer to Caek and looked her in the eyes. He needed a partner and understood they could survive if they worked together. He touched her face, stroking and outlining her features, the nose, the lips the hair line and sloping brow-ridge. He reached his hand down to her small but firm breasts. Caek tensed up, looking deeply into his eyes. She pushed him back in the water and climbed on top of him. Noolan was in full erection. Caek mounted him and began an up and down motion, rhythmically stroking. Noolan felt the upwelling in his loins and quickly ejaculated into Caek. She also experienced an orgasm. They rested together in the clear warm water, floating in each other's arms for a long time. An emotion was being felt by both, but they were not quite sure what the feeling was.

As they made their way back to the shelter, Noolan gestured to the mountains off to the north. With an aggressive response, Caek shook her head in a negative way implying it was not a good direction to go. She had come from the north and knew the winters were getting longer and tougher to survive. Caek then gestured back to Noolan indicating a southern trek. Noolan looked south. He did not know how to tell her that he had never been far out of his home valley, and he did not know where was. When he emerged from the cave several weeks earlier, he had no idea how long he had been underground. Little did he know he survived two weeks in the tunnels. The injury to his head caused some memory loss and he could not recall what direction his home was. He was lucky Caek found him and was becoming a companion and helper. They picked up firewood on the way back. As the night settled in, cold winds from the north started to blow down the valley. The temperature was dropping quickly.

The next morning, Caek was up early and headed down to the water. She noted several herbs that looked interesting and several fungi popping up in random areas. She knew the use for many, which ones could be eaten and others to avoid. She listened to an orchestra of wild birds, each with a song unto its own, chirping for attention from its mate. She spotted red, blue, and green macaws high above the canopy migrating in a southernly direction. She saw numerous finches darting in and out of the ground cover into the lower limbs of the old growth trees. Pear and apple trees grew in abundance. Nut trees including pecan and walnut grew in random pockets. As she moved around the area, she started to realize this was a good spot. With good water and shelter, this could be home. After a short walk she turned and started back. A forest grouse popped up ten yards ahead. She slowly bent down to get a stick resting at her feet. Once her hand reached the weapon, in a lighting fast reaction, she hurled the stick end over end striking the grouse in the head. The grouse was not killed, but rather stunned. This gave Caek just enough time to grab it by the head and twist its neck. Breakfast was going to be fresh mint infused roasted grouse and fresh pears with salt. She proudly plucked the bird clean as she made her way back to the cavern saving the larger plumage for arrow shafts. When she arrived at the shelter, Noolan was gone.

CHAPTER 10

KAZAN KNEW A JOURNEY TO COLLECT AND TRADE SPECIAL medicinal herbs and fungi was going to be necessary. He was running low on arrowroot, marijuana, poppy oils, rock salt, chili peppers, mushrooms, sage, sweetgrass, willow bark, coca, and flint nodules. He had access to a good supply of obsidian for knives and spear blades. Obsidian was always in demand and a valuable trading commodity. He knew his list of needed items was getting long and was beginning to think about the gathering of shamans from different regions. It occurred in the spring and was the best time to trade for needed items. He also knew this next gathering would be special because of the moving lights in the skies. It was going to be a period of great change. He decided that if he made it through the winter he would travel west, on ancient trails through many forests until he reached the great salty waters. He would turn south and walk along the coastline for several days until he came to the gathering place under the great towering trees of life where the waves pounded energy into the lands. He made the trek two times before over the years. Once when he was young and the next several years after his transitioned to adulthood and becoming a shaman leader. His father died on that trip, attacked by a flat nosed bear. Kazan was almost reluctant to go, but it was time. He sensed the needs of the hominoids in his care, and he understood the necessity of special herbs for healing.

The trick to the success of the trip was to prepare well for the journey over the winter and this meant letting the people know he was not going be around for three or four full cycles of the moon. He would need to pack provisions; he wondered if he should take others with him. He would have invited the three brothers, but Noolan was dead and Kazan was not sure Hook and Rit would be willing to go with him. It would be a dangerous and long trip.

As the winter winds took grip of the region, Kazan noticed Gluet, one of the boys from Drot's tribe, seemed to have a strong instinctual sense. Gluet appeared to have a firm sense of empathy which was a good trait in a leader. He was also a good hunter. Perhaps he would be able to spend some additional time with him and get a better feeling for his abilities. Perhaps over the winter he could teach Gluet some healing methods and see first-hand if he possessed good shamanic power. He needed to pass his wisdom and his abilities on to others. He wanted others to follow in his footsteps and pass on knowledge from the ancestors. It was an imperative obligation to the clans that would come later. He would speak to Drot and the others about Gluet and coaching him alongside of Hook and Rit.

Mid-day Kazan noticed a change in the weather. Winds from the north were picking up. The ravens were on the move heading south, and off in the far distant the familiar V-shaped formation of geese was also moving south. The sight triggered a memory. Kazan did not know how old he was in the number of years he had lived, but he did know he was born in winter. It was the first season of his life. It was a custom that new skins were given during the remembered birth of an individual. His mother would present new skins to him when the first southern migrating geese showed up. He needed new skins now. His were showing wear in the usual places. He stood up and started to select tanned antelope hides when he heard footsteps coming up the trail from the direction of Drot's cave.

It was Junn, the other pregnant woman, showing signs of labor. She pointed to her mouth and a chewing like motion with her lips. "Willow bark please? I am out." Kazan reached for a leather pouch and produced a small amount bark and then some marijuana bud and handed it over. She smiled, putting the herbs into her mouth, and started to chew. As she turned to walk away another contraction hit hard. The baby was coming. Kazan moved her to a flat area near the fire. He then gazed into her eyes and started a chant. Junn locked on to his gaze and focused on the journey of giving life. It was time for the baby to come, she squatted down and the crown of the head was visible. As the contraction continued, her breathing deepened, and then holding her breath, she pushed with all her force. The baby moved a little more down the birth canal and Junn reached down between her legs and carefully grasped the baby's head with a gentle but firm pull. The baby came out. She looked at the baby with curiosity, it was her first.

The new mother cleaned off embryotic membranes from around the face and Kazan cut the umbilical cord. He reached for a newly tanned rabbit skin and handed it to her. The baby had not cried. Junn looked closely at the child shook it, the head bobbed back and forth then a tiny coughed erupted and a wad of mucus flowed from the tiny mouth. Then a tiny cry squeaked from the infant. He was alive. Junn and Kazan both smiled. Once the afterbirth was ejected and buried, Kazan made some mint tea and gave it to her. The baby was nursing and looked comfortable, warm, and stable.

Kazan had not seen her mate and he wondered where he was. He gestured to her, and she replied through a series of hand gestures that he was killed about four months ago. He was attacked by a cave bear and mauled to death. She explained they were seeking shelter and they spotted a cave, but a huge sow was in the cave with her cubs. The men attempted to chase the bear away, but she didn't want to go. The men yelled, fired arrows, threw rocks, and threw long spears but the bear was stubborn and angry. She ran out and chased the men. He caught Jike, her mate, and killed him along with six other men of the clan. The bear ran away full of arrows and spears. Kazan sat in silence and listened as the fire crackled and popped.

After a short time, Junn stood up with her newborn and with a kind glance and smile, she turned to go back to the cave. Drot met her on the way. He had been looking for her. He knew she was going into labor and thought she would have already returned. He knew something must had happened. Then, he saw the bundle in her arms he smiled. It was not uncommon for females to walk a short distance into the woods to give birth. To have a healer and shaman around for a birth was always good. Junn acknowledged him showing off the new child. After a few words, she continued back to the cave and Drot headed towards Kazan's dwelling. He had an idea he wanted to talk about. Communication between the two and others improved significantly over the last month. The primary means to communicate was a clear ability to comprehend each other with an instinctual type of understanding. It was a sense of knowing based on circumstance. One of the common understandings between hominoids was that of long-term survival, rather than a day-to-day basis. It was an ability to communicate that would sustain the evolution of the hominoid for the next two million plus years.

The communication similarities were uncanny in their simplicity. Both early hominoid types developed remarkable skills, tools, and understandings of the surrounding environments. They did not look for patterns in a conscious way. It was an intuitive feel of survival. Everything had a pattern to it and a degree of symmetry. They investigated by trial and error and favorable actions were incorporated by routine; thus, a pattern of successful actions that enhanced hominoid evolution was established. Some of the trials resulted in death. These failures were remembered and logged into the collective memories. Don't eat that little brown mushroom was a known principle during the Pleistocene. It was a precise routine that enabled survival and the ability to thrive. The shaman was the keeper of the learned wisdom, and the routine was to pass the learned wisdom down to the next group. It was not a choice. Kazan knew some others that may have been good learners. But in truth, the learners would find him. It would stem from natural curiosity and intellect and on occasion the ingestion of special hallucinogenic fungi and plants. The net effects of the plants were mind expanding and illuminating, providing glimpses into a dimension of awareness that proved to be more real than not. It was a world of possibilities and creative energy. During one ceremony several years back, he experienced negative feelings. Kazan had felt evil. It was an emotion he was not familiar with; one he was not expecting, and it lingered.

Evil was a developing emotion for the early humanoids. The cortex was still small and the hypothalamus even smaller in terms of today's hominoid, the homo sapiens. The cerebral neural connections during the Pleistocene were in their infancy and still developing. The synaptic connections were coming together despite a long, long, long, period of evolutionary development. Nevertheless, an event that enabled the feeling of selfishness and evil began to take hold in Kazan and anger was the result. Why would an animal need to be selfish? He would wonder.

In the span of five million years the status quo and balance of the planet and ecosystems were never in jeopardy. Billions of species had come into existence and then, randomly became extinct. Kazan felt these irrational emotions would cause more harm to evolutionary trajectory than anything before on an instinctual level. The horrific reality that more floral and faunal extinctions would occur than at any other time in the last one billion years, excluding a meteor impact sixty million years earlier in the Gulf of Mexico's Yucatan region. That impact caused the unprecedented extinction of small and large land-dwelling creatures until the hominoids arrived and started to spread over the world. From the initial random blending of these two clans, the Australopithecus Robustus and Homo Naledi, the world would never be the same. This was the epicenter and genesis of humanoid knowledge and spirituality seen in our own legacy; it is the same one left to us over five hundred thousand years ago.

Over the years Kazan acquired several objects of divination. Several stone animal carvings, exotic seashells, a set of nine-inch incisors from an Amir tiger and a small clay figure of a woman. They aided his efforts to understand and make sense of natural patterns. His hope was to help others. There were mysteries Kazan did not understand, places where the veils between worlds were at their thinnest. He felt compelled to attend the gathering in the spring and trade for goods and knowledge from the other spiritual travelers attending. He would begin to make preparation over the winter and leave when the geese returned, and the nut trees sprouted leaves. This sign meant no more frost for the region, making the trek a bit easier on his aging body. It would take several moon cycles to reach the coastline going west towards the setting sun.

Once at the ocean he would turn south and continue until he reached the gathering place. Kazan knew it was held in a grove where the oldest and tallest trees lived, known as the ancients. He recalled the red-wooded trees were magnificent and reached high into the skies.

It was a stunning landmark that clans from every corner of the world knew about. The trees stood in the ground for eons. The gathering itself was a time to re-kindle alliances, gather news from other regions, and perhaps find a mate. It was a time to trade for rare and unique herbs and medicines. It would be a time for visceral experiences with other shamans. As the short winter days pasted, Kazan grew excited about the journey.

Drot walked up behind Kazan and startled him. His mind wandered off to distant places easily. Drot motioned and spoke of others that may have passed this way. He went on to describe Caek and recanted how long she had been missing, and that she was chosen and chased off by the Jakkar. Kazan stopped and listened intently to the story. It was strange that a Jakkar would chase someone off from their clan and not find any evidence that they were eaten. He remembered nothing was ever found of Noolan. Normally, the Jakkar would leave some remains, unless there was a score to settle. There were stories and legends about past hunters who had bad encounters with the tiger. If a hunter harmed the tiger or of one of the cubs of a tiger, the tiger would hunt the hunter and eat him to the last morsal as a means of revenge. There was a belief that if one ate their foe, they gained its powers and strength. But in all Kazan's life, he never knew anyone to kill a Jakkar. Drot felt this had not happened to Caek. His small band of travelers had no issue with the tiger. It was an unusual occurrence and Kazan never heard of this type of Jakkar action.

With this Kazan told Drot they should think deeply about the meaning of the encounter. He reached for a leather pouch and withdrew a shriveled yellow herb carefully and offered a piece to Drot to chew on. Kazan took one as well. After a few minutes a calming effect engulfed the two men. They sat in a semiconscious state with thoughts racing between them. The net effect of the dried herb stimulated pituitary and thyroid glands and the hypothalamus. These glands were extremely active during this phase of hominoid evolutionary development causing elevated levels of growth hormones. The glands themselves were the size of a smooth walnut, part of the small endocrine gland collection located at the base of the brain below but including the hypothalamus. The yellow herb triggered the released of an array of hormones responsible for the controlled release of endocrine system hormones including testosterone in males and in estrogen in females. The herb acted as a kind of thermostat for the body regulating an important variety of glandular secretions. It controlled a specific hormone secreted by the thyroid gland. In early hominoids, the thyroid glands were about the size of a peanut and still descending into the neck region. It regulated amounts of an awareness-stimulating secretion to the system. With the herb they ingested, Drot and Kazan were able to feel their surroundings and it caused the hypothalamus to go into overdrive influencing the autonomic nervous system and establishing a new elevated level of alertness and thought. Their minds began to think in a different modality and subsequently opened new neural pathways sparking creative thought.

After several hours in a state of mediation, Drot spoke first. He confirmed the desire to stay the winter in the cave but continue traveling south in the spring. Kazan agreed saying the weather would be getting bad, if they started to store the late tubers, including gourds and squashes, they would survive. The small group had already started to collect food stores over the last few days in hopes they would not have to leave. Drot left Kazan in a state of elevated thought, knowing Caek was still alive. The yellow herb opened his mind to understanding complex thoughts. He felt a bond with Kazan and was engulfed with a peaceful easy feeling of trust with his new friend. Kazan was feeling the same way. He was glad they were staying.

CHAPTER 11

NOOLAN WALKED BACK INTO THE CAVE FROM WHICH HE had emerged six weeks earlier. He found a side chamber with paintings on the walls he had not noticed before. There were a few flat faced obsidian stones with images chiseled in them. He lit a torch and began to decipher the cave paintings first. He recognized the large snowcapped mountain images to the north. The artist caught the landscape well. He noticed the bison's images to the south or bottom of the stone canvas. The dark cape was detailed enough, and the shading was right on. He recognized the rivers and then far off to the west side of the painting was a large body of water with no boundaries. Then he saw the trees to the south concluding it was a large forest. The painting also included the image of the Jakkar, and a small representation of a herd of ungulates that looked like elk. This told Noolan meat was plentiful but so were the hazards. The mammoths, also drawn near the top of the cavern ceiling indicating they were to the north. He started to understand he had found an ancient shaman's dwelling. The paintings were magnificent and detailed.

As he surveyed the dwelling, he recognized numerous items that resembled those that Kazan had in his cave. Several pouches were stored on racks hidden behind a stone wall for protection from the elements. Those were the herbs and medicinal items he was familiar with. Several clay pots with lids were lined up against one wall each containing unique colors for painting, ocher red, charcoal chunks for black, and sulfur for yellow. He picked up a soft tanned leather packet, tied closed with a strap and opened it. Inside the packet were exquisitely made knapping tools along with several pieces of obsidian, the material of choice for spear tips and arrow heads occasionally used for ancient hunting ceremonies. Obsidian, when knapped correctly, was as sharp as a surgical scalpel. The items he found had been carefully placed and Noolan felt someone left this place in good order. He wondered if they would ever return. He could tell a lot of time passed since the place was last inhabited. The paints were dry and some of the herbs left out to dry were void of any medicinal value because they were too dry and turned to dust when touched. He began to wonder if the shaman may have died. But he also understood not to take things that he was not given by a shaman. But what if the Shaman was dead? he wondered.

Caek was beginning to wonder if Noolan was coming back. Several hours passed when he popped out of the cave and startled her. "Where were you?" she asked.

With a short series of voice inflections and hand signs he conveyed his find. As they sat by the fire, he explained the items of interest. He knew what most everything was, but also knew there was more inside. Caek listened and then asked him to take her into the chamber. Noolan fashioned two torches, lit them, and handed one to Caek. They traveled in silence, squeezing past a long narrow fissure and stepping into the large room. Caek looked in awe at the figures painted on the chamber walls. Noolan described what he understood were the mountains to the north, and the river in the valley as best he could. There was even a pool with squiggled lines for the stream and the location of the cave for orientation. Caek agreed with Noolan's understandings. As she turned around, she found a long spear with a long tip made from obsidian leaning against the back wall. The spear point was nearly translucent as she held up to the glow of her torch. Next to the spear she picked up an unusual carved wooden tool she did not understand. She handed it to Noolan. It was about arm's length with a long groove carved in the center and a hook stub at one end. He picked up a longish arrow laying on the floor near the clay pots and placed it in the whittled groove. It fit perfectly. The nock of the arrow was carved into a conical stub that fit perfectly into the hooked end. He immediately understood it was a tool for hunting and launching the accompanying three-foot arrows.

As they continued to explore the cave, they found another passageway to a chamber hidden behind a large moveable oval obsidian panel. They ducked under a low ledge and entered the concealed chamber. As Noolan held his torch up the room became alive with more extraordinary paintings and markings on the walls and ceiling. Caek was able to stand up easily in the room, but Noolan had to keep crouched over or risk hitting his head on protruding rocks sticking out of the ceiling. Every edge of the mysterious chamber was taken up by elaborate paintings of objects, animals, or landscapes. A ring of carefully placed rocks was in the center of the chamber and remains of burnt wood in the ring of rocks. Noolan noticed that a slight breeze was flowing towards the entrance, realizing that smoke would exit the cavity. This was undoubtably a ceremonial chamber. Noolan recognized this as the belly of the mother. From his early training, he knew that hominoid cultures referred to the earth as the mother; it is only through entering her womb, through a ceremonial chamber such as this that the shaman could learn her secrets. This was a lost cavity that had not been used in several generations.

There was a crude shelf chiseled into the basalt on the edge of a wall near the entrance to the chamber, upon which were clay containers of additional dried ceremonial paints and powerful hallucinogenic compounds. Noolan instantly had a flashback to Kazan's face. It was a ghost like vision from his past, though he did not recall who Kazan was or where he was from. He recalled the power of hallucinogenic plants and fungi and seeing Kazan's image but could not make a clear connection. The injury to his brain kept him from remembering specific things and connecting information about his past. It was a form of injury induced amnesia. He knew something was there but could not recall the specific details. He could only recall what the items were for, but not how or why he knew these things. He explained to Caek that he understood what the items were used for. As he did this, his vision blurred but then cleared up. This would happen repeatedly at unexpected times.

She understood more than he realized. She also had the ability to communicate with perceptive thoughts; without realizing it, they had been doing so for a while. Her clan also had a shaman, and she was aware of the power of plants and herbs, but the Naledi great shaman died on the trail several seasons ago due to old age, and Drot had taken his place. Caek and her sisters were learning from him, but their training was not complete. She asked lots of questions Noolan could not answer. She went on to explain that her father, Drot, was able to understand the way of the shaman and how to make medicines. Noolan, did not fully understand what she was telling him.

Their torches were beginning to burn out and with a knowing glance they turned and walked to the entrance of the passage and then through the narrow corridor. It was a tight fit, and they had to crawl to get to the outer chamber. Noolan picked up the well carved stick and the quiver of long arrows. As he grabbed the quiver, the bottom gave way and the contents scattered on the ground and several of the well knapped tips broke. He picked up the array of arrows and knew he would have to repair the gaping hole in the quiver and knap new arrow tips if the weapon was going to be useful. He was excited to tryout the new device. Once outside, a strong cool wind hit them in the face. It was moist and they both could smell snow in the air. The far horizon was billowing with large gray clouds full of moisture. That was then they realized they were going to have to stay for the winter.

Caek signaled to Noolan to follow. She walked to a large tree and started to climb it with ease. Her slightly longer arms and marginally distended large toe made climbing second nature. Within a few easy reaches of her arms, she was safely sitting on a branch laden with pears, eating. Noolan watched knowing what was going to happen next. He positioned himself under her perch and she pick several ripe pears, and gently tossed them down. Noolan caught them with ease. Caek picked another one and started to eat it on her way down. She caught a whiff of scent on the winds that stimulated an immediate alarm through her mind and body. She looked and scanned the forest and out to other trees and she spotted a male Jakkar perched eighty yards away laying prone on a large thick tree trunk, gazing dead at her.

The Jakkar were ambush hunters. The practice of stealth coupled with the element of surprise was its calling card. This skill allowed the solitary hunter to kill quickly and silently. The Jakkar perfected this practice over the last five million years. They were capable of navigating through vast complex climates, landscapes, and over great distances swiftly. Attacks were relatively common, but all indications were that this beast was not interested in Caek or Noolan. It made no attempt whatsoever to conceal itself. Caek watched the beautiful creature as she slowly made her way down the tree recalling how the mother tiger caused her to become separated from her clan in the past. She also remembered that the three Jakkar cubs and their mother had left her alone after she had rescued the cub several weeks earlier. A spark of curiosity made her feel there was a bond developing with the beast. She felt a gravitational pull towards the animal and started to change her direction; instead of moving away from the tiger, she moved towards it.

Noolan watched her in disbelief, grunting with worried intonations asking, "What are you doing?" Caek kept moving and found a branch to sit on ten yards away. She sat there silently looking at the animal. He was magnificent. His fur was rich and deep and thick. His eyes were bright yellow, with a red flame dancing in the center, seeing every movement all at once. His ears rotated and perked up to the smallest, slightest noise undetectable to Caek. It heard every minute sound in the forested area. He was the dominant predator, rarely the prey. She could see his whiskers, as long and thick as sweetgrass strands at the base and tapering to a thin curved threads at the end reaching more than twenty inches in length. His wet nose flexed with miniscule muscle movements as hundreds of scents filtered past on the gentle breeze. He did not pay much attention to Caek. She sat for a long while, gently speaking to the beast with tongue clicks and guttural locutions, asking the Jakkar to be her guardian and totem and to keep her safe. She could hear the heavy breaths, and then a deep peaceful and rhythmically rumbling emanating from deep within him. The tiger was at peace.

After a while she climbed back down the tree and joined Noolan. She looked back for the tiger, but he had vanished without a sound. They walked back the shelter in silence, each thinking about the beast and what the sign must have meant. They began to go about the chores that needed to be done in preparation of the coming cold. Noolan understood that if he could kill an elk, the fifteen hundred pounds would be more than enough meat for the two of them for months. The incoming cold would allow them to keep the meat in an earthen hole like a wine cellar, maintaining a stable cool temperature. It would also protect the cache from other hungry animals. The large antlers would be broken and carved to make tools including flint knapping instruments and implements for cooking. The bladder would be used as a canteen and the ribs once cleaned and dried, for supports in a pack frame. The hide would be made into numerous articles of clothing, including head coverings, and leggings for protection and warmth, boot soles, and external coverings like ponchos. One of the massive creatures was enough for the winter.

Caek was in the lead as they made their way back to the shelter. She spotted a rabbit in the direction they were traveling. She stopped and stooped to pick up a hand sized stone. In a practiced smooth motion, she brought her arm back, focused on the rabbit watching it's every twitch. She knew she would have to lead the rabbit once it took off, because it would be alarmed at her fast arm action. She understood where it was going to go. With an inflection of her voice, like a lynx growl, the rabbit jumped. Caek launched the stone with lighting fast actions and precision. It met the rabbit's head, stunning the furry animal long enough for Caek to retrieve him and snapped its neck to ensure it death. She smiled at Noolan thinking this was a going to be a good dinner. Noolan warmly smiled back.

The rabbit was cooked and as they were eating, Noolan started to explain a strategy to hunt the elk. The animal is difficult hunt. He recalled the large obsidian spear tip Caek retrieved from the shaman cave and asked for it. He picked up a strong eight-foot-long pole he found in the forest, carved a notch at the wider end, and fitted the spear point in. Caek produced a supple leather strap and handed it over to be used to securely lash the spear tip to the long pole. They would hunt the giant elk together. Caek picked up several of the long arrows and asked for the unusually carved launcher Noolan carried from the cave. She stood outside the entrance of the cave and with great effort, she placed an arrow into the cut groove in the flat piece of wood and placed the notch-end of an arrow on the hook. She aimed at a tree a short distance away, and with a smooth throwing action, flung the arrow towards the tree. The tool seemed to fit her arms. It flew past the tree with tremendous speed and force. The projectile landed well past the target and stuck in the forest floor. They both looked at each other amazed at the distance it had gone. The capability of the new hunting tool was fascinating. Caek secured another arrow and with a little more concentration hit the tree, striking the arrow deep into the bark. She launched another with the same result. Noolan began to think Caek could drive an elk towards him and perhaps wound the animal with an arrow or two at a good distance. The plan was coming together, and they decided they would start the hunt the next day.

Noolan was up early the next morning and gently nudged Caek awake. There was a cool low mist lingering in the valley. They ate a meager meal consisting mainly of fruit and started out for the open area far below one side of the shelter. After about twenty minutes of hiking, they came to an opening near a quick flowing crystal-clear stream. The water channeled into a ravine with gentle banks that transitioned to steep walls. Noolan watched elk grazing in the area several days before. As the mist began to lift, several elk were spotted grazing near the creek.

Caek look at Noolan and signaled she would wait for him to get into position and then start stalking to get closer. Noolan circled around and climbed to the high bank just above the flowing waters. When he reached a strategic vantage point, he soundlessly watched Caek maneuver into position. When she was about forty yards away, she loaded an arrow on the launcher. Noolan crouched down and then motionless he watched events unfold. Moving towards the stream, knowing what direction the elk would run to escape once hit with an arrow, Caek began to advance towards the prey. Noolan readied his spear, watching Caek prepare to fling the arrow. She led the animal understanding when it would run, the arrow would have to be ahead of its target. The timing was critical. With a natural aim she swung her arm forward releasing the arrow with strained force. It stuck in the elk's neck cutting an artery and lodging in its esophagus. It started spewing deep red blood. The animal jumped in alarm and started a panicked run down the ravine directly towards Noolan. The other elk scattered in all directions in an alarmed frenzy. He launched the spear with deadly accuracy, hitting the huge beast in the side just behind the front leg causing it to stumble and then fall to the ground.

In an act of swiftness, Noolan jumped off the cliff and on to the flailing, animal unsheathing his knife, cutting the animal's neck deeply just below the jaw to hasten death. He then jumped off to avoid injury from the animals thrashing dying kicks. As he jumped off, one of the hooves struck Noolan in the chest cutting him. The force of the blow threw him back and took is breath way. He lay in the tall grass gasping for air. Blood seeped out of the wound. Caek ran to his aid. She applied pressure to the cut to stop the bleeding as he lay in a semi-conscious state gasping for air. He slowly recovered his breath as the bleeding began to subside. The cut as not as bad as they thought and within a few minutes the bleeding stopped. As the two recovered from the incident they took account of the massive dead elk. They looked at each other in a knowing way understanding what work now needed to be done. Noolan gained his senses and stood smiled feeling a sense of elation at their success. Caek smiled and knew they made a good team. They both paused at the lifeless ungulate, feeling gratitude for the gift of the meat.

As they were butchering the animal, the Jakkar came into the clearing and lay down a short distance from the kill. Caek stopped and took several large chunks of meat offering it to the massive cat. The tiger accepted the fresh meat eating it quickly. Caek returned to the kill and carved off more for him. But when she turned to present it to the Jakkar, it was gone. He had enough, reinforcing the underlying tenet of survival for all and only eating what was needed.

Once they completed the field processing of the carcass, they began packing the meat, entrails, bones, and antlers back to the shelter. They made jerky with the bulk of the meat, eating what they could of the fresh meat. The heart was sliced and eaten raw, being the purest of muscle, they believed it would bring strength and healing. They cooked the liver and feasted on the iron rich organic delicacy. Every part of the animal was used. Caek set upon tanning the thick hide, cleaning every fleck of meat and fat off the cape. She decided to leave the hair on, for warmth.

The days were getting shorter and the winds from the north brought bitter cold to the region. Snow was falling and the stillness in the forest was peaceful. One evening as they were sitting by the fire, Noolan said he was being pulled by some unknown force to return to the shaman's ceremonial chamber. He felt the need to search for a path to walk and entering the mother earth through the cave he had come out of. He had a vison it was the path to the womb. He felt, with a special mix of powerful medicines, he would see what his destiny would be. He could not remember his past clearly and he was troubled by that. He told Caek the next full moon would be the right time to enter the chamber and begin the search. She understood the drive and experienced similar thoughts over the last few days. She then expressed a desire to engage in a search with him. It would have been common in Noolan's tribe for women to be part of ceremonies. In many instances, they were the focus of ceremonies symbolizing rites of passage, rebirth, survival, and the birthing of lineage.

CHAPTER 12

A BITTER COLD AND WINTER SNOWS CAME EARLY TO THE region. Although they did not know it, Kazan and Noolan were separated by only twenty-seven miles. Both were experiencing the changes, but it was much more severe than in any past seasons they had known. The snow piled up in drifts and made hunting all but impossible. Footpaths were stomped smooth to make it easier to move from one cave shelter to the other. As the days grew shorter, the clans spent more time sleeping. They fashioned protective doors from wood and stretched skins, preventing the cold winds from entering. It was warm and comfortable inside the dwellings. It was the natural cycle of the seasons, but something felt different this time. The shortest day of the year was known as a pivot to the next season and the clan celebrated by coming together under a rock overhang.

Kazan announced his desire to go to the gathering in the spring with several members of the surrounding community during the winter solstice ceremony. Of those in attendance several declared the desire to go including Drot, Sinner, Huut, Cahat, Hook and Rit. Kazan told them he had not been to the gathering in many seasons but knew how to get there. He told them it was a special event and stories of moving lights in the skies would bring good fortune and open visions to the future. He also told the hominoids the trip was long and would be dangerous. They had to hunt as they went, and forage for foods. No one backed out at the warning. The group was healthy in most respects. He and Drot would be the oldest members and Cahat, would be the youngest at nine years. Hook and Rit, Aberns sons were fifteen. Huut, Sinner, the identical girls were both thirteen. Although Junn came to the meeting it was decided that she and her young child would not make the trek as it would be too dangerous. She understood the wisdom in the decision.

As preparations began, meats were dried over open fires and other supplies such as berries and nuts were gathered and packed into tanned skin backpacks. The area was known for several deposits of excellent snowflake obsidian used for knives and elongated elegant spearheads. The snowflakes speckled in the volcanic glass was unique to the area and highly prized. Kazan also collected numerous small basalt rocks and tenuously shaped them into figures of horses, bison, bears, and tigers. He decided he would spend some of the dark winter hours carving the totem creatures to trade for medicinal herbs.

Kazan kept going over the route in his mind. He had a good sense of direction and how to travel, only taking what was necessary for the trip. He knew he would walk toward the setting sun. He recalled it took at least two cycles of the moon going that direction to reach the great salt waters. Once there, he would turn left and walked until he came to the great forest trees. The gathering was held here, among the old father trees with the great salt waters and healing warm springs. There would be game and fish and fruits and vegetables.

He began to remember the others he met numerous years back. Many would have traveled many more moon cycles than his small band. There would be several different kinds of genius homo, but nobody would be considered an outsider. He hoped Geon would be there, he was the short light skinned man with the chocolate beans and coca leaves for pain that would have traveled for a year from far south. Maybe the most beautiful female he had ever seen would be there. She was there the last time he went. He remembered her tight kinky hair and how it smelled. They had coupled. She was powerful and capable of vast thought projections and Kazan found her engaging. But he knew he was getting old. If she was at the gathering, she would surely have a mate. But if she didn't, would she leave with him? He wondered about the possibilities and the journey. The return trek always seemed more challenging because they would be laden with trade goods and supplies. This might be the last time he would make the trip to the gathering. A trip like this always took a toll on the body. It was important to prepare well for the journey.

Out of the seven in the group of chosen travelers, he knew it was possible that one or more would not live through the entire expedition. Either by an injury, or sickness, or animal attack, some would probably die. Each of the travelers could protect themselves with knives and spears and being able to outrun one or more of the others. There was always the threat of being attacked by other hominoids. Being able to move silently and quickly through the forests and on the trails was vitally important. Kazan would be the slowest and as such, the most likely to be brought down by a bear, wolf, hyena, or other predator as he typically fell behind the others due to his short leg malady. But the true threat to the small band were the ones they would not see. Viruses and infections were the silent killers. Kazan knew small cuts and uncleaned sores could develop into infections causing illnesses and slowing the group down. He would pack his mosses and cleaning items with the intention of protecting his fellow travelers as best he could. In turn, they would provide meats and foods for him. It was a good symbiotic relationship.

As part of the shaman gift to the clan he served, Kazan provided special forms of divinations. In preparation of the journey, a vision ceremony to gage obstacles and challenges would be performed. A few weeks before the journey, as winter snows began to melt, he invited the travelers to join him in a ritual. It was evening when they entered the sacred chamber of his cave, the shaman took some herbs and mushrooms from small clay and wooden containers and began grinding them into a fine powder with smooth rocks. Once they were well crushed, he added water, blending a strong black tea. A robust fire was burning, and their shadows moved ominously on the walls adding to the painted drama etched in choreographed sequences on the walls. The flames of the fire caused the painted images to move, bringing life in the reflections and the mixing shadows. The group sat cross legged around the fire as Kazan provided each a small amount of an elixir. He started a rhythmic chant in a smooth baritone voice. He then started a slow rhythm with a small ceremonial drum, a round section of hollow tree limb with antelope skin stretched and tied across the top. Their heartbeats becoming syncopated with the steady beat of the drum. One by one the participants joined in the hypnotic vocalization, some swaying in circular motions and others back and forth absorbing the intoxicating chemical elixirs potent affect. After twenty minutes the concoction was taking full effect. They saw flashes of tall mountains in a vivid array of colors, animals with large asymmetrical bodies, and a series of erratic abstract geometric shapes moving in chaotic patterns. Kazan turned to Cahat, the youngest of the group, asking him what he saw and what he was feeling. When Cahat opened his eyes said he saw people of all kinds and strange noises coming from their mouths. He described feathers on their bodies and brilliant eyes of green turning to stone. He saw great bodies of water, flashing red and green and undulating shades of purple. Each of the partakers went through an array of thoughts streaming towards each other, trading a bond of understanding. There was a comfortable rhythmic synergy and soon they were all chanting in unison, and as the evening progressed, they sang ancient rhythmic songs in a low deep harmony as the drumming kept them tied to the earth.

Kazan then brought out a larger tightly stretched antelope skin drum and slowly and softly started the syncopated beat to match his heartbeat. He could feel the steady pulse in his chest, and he could see the beating moving his skin on his wrist. The deep sounding beats resonated off the cave walls and travelers found themselves slowing their own heart beats to match that of the slow pulsating drumbeats. He was lowering the energy in the room into a contemplative state of relaxation. The feeling was a strong tangible pull into a peaceful calming state. Kazan passed around water and each of the participants took long refreshing gulps. The fire died down to red and then golden yellow embers, pulsing against the darkness of the cave. Several hours later as the elixirs effects started to subside, the travelers began to silently exit the chamber. Each stood and faced the four directions of life, relating to the four seasons and bowed down. They paid a simple homage of respect to Kazan, turned, and left the small gathering. Kazan knew that each had an immersion into their own future for the coming journey. Each would have a message to share at the right time. The aftereffects of the solution would linger for days and during this time their minds would be sparked with insights of creative thought, intensifying the sensation of all their senses. Smells would sharpen, sight would be laser-focused and hearing so sensitized that a mouse could be heard squeaking one hundred yards away. They would identify personal challenges to overcome on the trail to the distant place of gathering. Drot left that evening with a bewildered look on his face. Kazan took that as a bad sign.

CHAPTER 13

Caek and Noolan entered the shaman cave as darkness shrouded their world. The night was crystal clear, and the temperature dropped to well below freezing. The stars shown brilliantly like billions of pinholes in a black felt canvas. Caek often wondered what was out in the black abyss of the night skies. Noolan brought good amounts of firewood and started a fire in the center of the room. As the flames grew, Caek took noticed of the array of magnificent paintings spread across the walls. They came to life as did other paintings in other caves. As Noolan watched the stone canvas begin to move with animated action, he immediately had a flashback to an experience with Kazan, where the vibrant animals came to life and then as the light from the flame shifted, they became still. Kazan told an intricate story of what the animals were doing, and how the hominoid would be to blame for the extinction of many forms of life. The flashback faded quickly, but he kept the images and vision of Kazan alive in his mind.

After a few moments he opened his eyes and returned to mixing the dark red concoction he and Caek would ingest. He started to chant an ancient melody; Caek was strangely familiar with the melody. It was not coincidental. The tune was something she'd heard before. The practice of inducing visions had developed over the last two hundred thousand years; the original hominoid inventers tried many techniques and practices to concentrate the powerful energies. There was a pattern to induce the full effect of the rituals. The effects for individuals varied, but the net result was the opening of the mind to creative understandings and foreshadowing of coming events. There was an understood process to visions and opening the doorway to the spirit world. The drumming, vocal music, swaying, and hallucinogenic concoction were rituals used to enhance the results of the drug. Caek knew the tunes and the basic patterns of the ceremonies. She started to hum in harmonic repetition with Noolan and swayed back and forth rhythmically.

Noolan passed her the dark red tea. She took a large swallow, half of what the container held. She passed it back and Noolan drank the rest. Within twenty minutes both were experiencing the mind-altering effects of the hallucinogenic mixture. Caek stared into the fire seeing her past life with her sisters and Drot her father. She felt waves of pleasure shoot through her body. Her long arms spastically twitched with erratic movements. She started to wail in guttural tones, emanating from deep in her diaphragm to the point of causing her to convulse in a vomiting action. Noolan was going through similar gyrations. The drug was incredibly strong and coursed through their bodies quickly reaching every cell. Caek looked deep into her partners eyes seeing strange things made of bright flashy metals, shining and flashing silver, brassy, and gray frequencies of light then the infrared rainbow of intoxicating waves started. Noolan was silent and stared into the fire, focusing on coals and amber colored embers. He saw images of Caek walking with a tiger. They were protecting each other and as they walked Noolan had a vision of a disfigured tiger's front paw causing a slight limp. He realized the Jakkar was limping just as Kazan did.

After about two hours the intensity of the medicine was starting to wane. The effects would linger for several more days resulting in a calm warm feeling that would consume their minds. As the night drew on, they eventually moved closer together stepping into a trance like state, seeing visions, and experiencing vividly lucid color filled dreams. Their visions continued long into the early morning.

Awakened by the unmistakable rumbling of falling rocks, Noolan felt the cave starting to shake, and the room became filled with a fine dust. Spotting day light towards the entrance, Noolan grabbed Caek and ran through it. As they darted though the entrance, groggy from the aftereffects of the drug, they saw the rippling undulations on the earth's surface causing the forest trees to surge up and down as though it was an ocean. Hundreds of thousands of birds filled the skies and the resulting squawk of alarm was deafening. It was still ice-cold and light snows blanketed the area, but something different was happening. The skies were gray with a thin layer of homogenous high clouds. Gaping gas vents randomly opened across the landscape and started spewing hot vapor clouds into the sky.

The quaking stopped after several minutes, and they took a quick inventory of the area and walked back in the direction of their shelter. When they arrived, several boulders shifted and the egress to the interior of the main chamber was blocked. After moving several boulders away, Caek as small as she was, shimmy through the opening. She lit a torch and noted that several large chunks of the ceiling had fallen and filled much of the chamber making it difficult to maneuver around. She located several useful items, such as skins and hides, the arrow launcher, some of the food stores and Noolan's knapping kit. It was neatly wrapped in a leather pouch and stored on a small shelf near the entrance. As she handed the items through a narrow portal to Noolan, an aftershock started, and a loud rumble ensued. Noolan lost his balance and fell backwards tumbling down the scree covered slope hillside hitting his head and becoming disoriented. Caek was still inside the room as it was shaking. In an instant she found herself in total darkness. She felt and heard more of the ceiling collapsing around her. Hugh chunks were slamming on the floor missing her narrowly. She made herself as small as she could crouching against a wall, riding out the tremor as debris filled the room stirring up suffocating dust all around her. Then an unrelenting heat welled up from deep in the chamber. A smell of noxious gas started to waft into the chamber.

Caek coughed violently gasping for air. She heard Noolan faintly yelling. When she tried to respond she broke out into an intensive cough, spitting out strangling dust uncontrollably. She gasped and yelled waiting for a response, but nothing came. In the total darkness of the small pocket, she was scared. She could barely move around, and she wondered how she was going to get out as panic began to set in. The only solution was to try and dig in what she thought was the right direction. In total darkness, handful by handful she started to remove rubble. She started to feel weak and lethargic, moving slower and slower. A few seconds later she heard Noolan yell, and she excitedly howled back. He heard her and continued to remove rocks in the direction of her voice. Rock by rock they worked from either side until they finally met. Caek squeezed through a narrow portal welcoming daylight gasping for fresh air. Noolan felt relief and an overwhelming sense of happiness that she was alive. He held her tightly for a long time as her breathing and coughing began to relax.

Both the shaman cave and the shelter they lived in were destroyed. The quake changed the landscape in dramatic ways. Hundreds of trees were down making it extremely difficult to traverse through the forest.

They tried to get to the warm water spring, climbing up and over hundreds of downed trees. When they arrived in the general vicinity, the water was no longer flowing. The shifting earth altered the flow, and the creek was drying up. When they realized this, they knew it a sign was they needed to leave. They needed to find a new shelter and water source. They walked back to the remnants of the old shelter, picked up what skins and tools they could find and started to trek away from the destroyed volcanic vent. A foul sulfur type gas from the vent engulfed the area. They remained in a dazed and confused state for a long time as they made their way off the steep mountain slope into the freezing cold. The north winds started to blow with strong gusts.

The first night without shelter was the most challenging. Noolan had been able to salvage a skin large enough to cover the two in a crude but effective lean-to. The temperature was well below freezing. Their clothing provided much of the insulation for keeping warm, but they also had a large amount of hair covering their entire bodies, mother nature's way of retaining body heat. They each wore a tanned skin with fur left on for warmth. This was used as an over covering or top layer as they huddled under the makeshift tent. Their second layer of clothing consisted of a soft elk hide in a poncho-style covering with a drawstring-type leather thong to cinch tight. Men typically fashioned soft leather undershorts as a base layer next to their bodies. On that same thong type garment, two small pouches were secured. The pouches sported Noolan's flint and magnesium nodule for starting fires, and the sheath for his knife. The cover for his blade was made from tightly woven plant fibers, decorated with a single half of a small bi-valve seashell, a gift from Kazan. Noolan also carried a fur covered larger pouch which contained small wooden carved amulet figures of significance for ceremonies. He was having a hard time remembering all the details, but he knew they were important. He fashioned a backpack-type bag to carry water and nuts and carried the elegant long spear.

The clothing Caek wore was much different. One of the main differences was the type of skins. They were not from the immediate area. Her clan had traveled from the far north and the garments had fur lining the outsides and insides for warmth. The stitching was a unique cross-hatched pattern not seen by Noolan. Caek also wore a thong that would hold absorbent moss during her menstrual cycle she recently started. Her hair was pulled back in a tight dreadlock bundle tied with a simple leather string and her leggings stretched up to her mid-thigh. She also sported an outside strap to cinch her exterior that pulled the coverings tight. On that strap she carried several items including her knife and fire making tools. She wore a small leather pouch on a single leather lace around her neck. It held her scared objects. When they were ready to move, Caek deployed a tumpline strap across her forehead. This strap was tied to the load on her back. The muscles in her neck helped support the weight of the pack and made walking long distances more manageable. For such a small-framed woman, she was able to carry impressively large loads.

They did not know exactly where they were going but decided to head in a westerly direction. They would keep looking for uninhabited shelters. They had not seen any other humans, but both knew they would more than likely run into some clans. The only question was if they were friendly or not and if they lived in shelters they could share until winter passed. If a large snowstorm came through, they both realized they would more than likely succumb to the elements. Going through the forested area was hard, but as they gradually made their way west, the cold and snow became less and less of an obstacle.

CHAPTER 14

KAZAN STOOD UP AND LOOKED OUT OVER THE SNOW-COV-
ered forest. Something was wrong, his mind was sensing an
overwhelming burst of energy. The birds were squawking cha-
otically and flying in erratic patterns. Then the earth shook. Back and
forth at first, with a vibrating sensation. Then a loud rumbling and the
up and down undulating motion started. The epicenter of the quake
was a long-distance away, but the shaking was intense. As he ran out of
his stone shelter, several pieces of the ceiling crashed down around him.
He stood outside watching the trees sway violently, branches snapping
and falling with loud thumps and huge trees snapped at the trunks.
Massive rocks were rolling down behind him and over him ripping
down the mountain at horrendous speeds. He dodged a large bolder
and fell to the ground hard. Then as quickly as it started, the shaking
stopped. Kazan stood up and did a self-check and realizing he was not

injured other than a few scrapes from hitting the ground hard. There were no sounds, it was eerily quiet for a few minutes.

He started to inspect his refuge as the dust settled and he realized the collapsed material from the ceiling was not as bad as he thought. As he started to move some of the fallen rocks and debris out of the living area, Drot showed up running, asked if he was okay.

"I'm good, just a mess to clean up. Was anyone in your cave hurt?" he asked.

Drot shook his head and said "No. But a new chamber opened further back. The fissure is big enough for me to get through and then it opens to an even bigger room, but the air was not good."

Kazan thought about the new chamber as he kept moving debris out of his way. Then he told Drot he wanted to investigate the opening. The two headed for the cave and along the way met several others from different shelters. The reports stated no one was injured too bad, but some of the shelters may have to be abandoned. Kazan was glad the shaking stopped so quickly. He experienced quakes in the past with much more intensity than this one.

As he neared Drot's cave, Kazan noted how much it had change in the little time it was inhabited by Drot's group. The new occupants were tanning skins, and a fire was burning in the fire ring. Foods were being dried, and something was cooking. Junn's new baby was already sitting up on his own. His teeth were starting to come in and he looked healthy as he chewed on a small stick. Huut was sewing skins for clothing, Junn was sitting by the fire heating water for a tea. After a short greeting, Kazan asked about the two boys. Junn said they left earlier in the morning on a hunt. As they reached the open fissure in the back of the cave, Kazan picked up a torch, lit it, and squeezed through the opening. After a few seconds, he emerged into a vast cavity. He was able to walk across it and the ceiling was high above him but sloped quickly into a small conical passageway. He was feeling it was new way into the belly of Mother Earth. Mother Earth had given them another portal to her secrets, but it would need to be explored further.

As the two men looked around Kazan noticed another small opening going deeper into the mountain. He pushed his torch into the crevasse but could not tell how far back it went, and he was not ready to go further in without some additional torches and rope in case they had to climb. Kazan felt that the chambers could be used for ceremonies, though that would have to be decided later. The air was foul, and he needed to exit. As Kazan emerge from the room with Drot closely behind, he started to talk about the upcoming journey. The trek to the Gathering was coming up. He was waiting to see the flying "V" the geese used to chart their course while high in the sky. When that occurred, he would know it was time to go.

Kazan recalled attending two other gatherings in the springtime. Hominoids of all kinds would be present. Many were related in some way being grandfathers or grandmothers, fathers, mothers, aunts, uncles, and the newest generation of adolescent children. Many were elders and respected for their knowledge of the known world. Kazan chose not to go to gatherings, mainly because his short leg gave him pain as he walked long distances with loads. He told Drot this might be his last unless he could find another way to make the trip. His short leg was starting to cause him greater pain. He went on to tell Drot he had seen a man riding on the back of an animal in a dream. That kind of help would be a good thing. Drot agreed saying that was an interesting idea. Kazan said his goodbyes and limped off towards his shelter gathering firewood along the way.

The quake brought out many of the people in the valley. Several had minor injuries such as scrapes and bruises. One young boy experienced a broken arm due to a cascade of rocks hitting him. Kazan set the bone and the young boy was off with his peers later that afternoon. Despite the aftershocks, life returned to normal quickly, but Kazan knew change was in the air. He could feel it as a light snow started to fall across the valley.

Three days later, he saw the familiar "V" shape of geese moving north. The weather would be warming, and he was ready to start the journey west. He gathered up the travelers and told them he would be ready to leave in the next few days. He then said he would be gathering all the residents of the area giving them updates and telling them of his planned return. He brought out a drum made from boar hide stretched and tied tight across a short hollow wooden log. He summoned Gluet and asked him to beat the gathering drum teaching him the steady pattern. The deep baritone pounding sounds reverberated and echoed off the valley walls send the message for several miles. By evening, sixty-eight mixed hominoid species living within hearing distance arrived at Kazan's shelter. Most were able to gather inside, out of the snowy surroundings. A fire was burning, and low voices were murmuring through the crowd. Most knew about the planned trip. Kazan wanted to be sure people understood the details and that he would try and return by the end of summer. He also stated he wanted someone or a family to live in his shelter while he was gone. Teeock, one of the older neighboring men, who was recently injured on a hunt volunteered. His woman died two years earlier and he was living with his daughter's family. Teeock felt it would be a good change for him. It seemed there was always conflict with her man.

There was an unwritten rule during the Pleistocene time, if a shelter was not occupied it was available. This rule was always enforced because good, protected living areas were hard to come by. The point he made was that he planned to return but would be leaving behind many sacred objects. His most prized objects including medicinal herbs, tanned hides, antler and bone artwork, small sculptures, weapons, ceremonial drums, and most importantly, a picture story etched on stone tablets he was working on. It was all packed into a small alcove carved in the basalt wall. Several years earlier he chiseled an oval obsidian panel to cover and secure the items for long term safety. When he placed it over the alcove and slathered a mud and ash mixture to the outside edges, the small chamber became airtight. He felt good about having someone to cave sit so that an animal, such as a tiger or bear would not take refuge in his space.

The meeting was brief, most people knew of the plan. That night a short ceremony was held. His cave was cleansed with sage and braided sweetgrass in an ancient traditional way. The travelers were also washed in the smoke of sweetgrass, told to inhale deeply as the shaman presented the offering. The use of sweetgrass was a way of cleansing the spirit of a person, a home, and places of sacred significance. It was a blessing. Kazan understood the use of sages and sweetgrass from his teachers. He knew the plants were from the open plains of vast continental areas. As hominoids were evolving so was the availability of sweetgrass and sage. In his visions he could see fields of such grasses and shrubs burn regularly, especially after long periods of drought. They were one of the longest-lived grasses on the planet, sustaining herbivories for eons. The aroma of the smoke developed a peaceful connection in evolving hominoid mind. It was a synaptic relationship of wellbeing. The herbs and practice, with no clear beginning, was found in ancient dwellings and the rituals continued to evolve. Kazan developed the practice eventually waving smoke in circles around people that were coming and going. It was his way to offer a cleansing of community. If a person had bad memories, he would use it as a way of purging the mind, body, and soul.

Many hominoids claimed to be able to feel the essences of others when he used the special herbs in ceremonies. The origins of loss, grief, and love surfaced during the brief rituals. Essence came into focus, and a powerful feeling of devotion seeped into their minds. The feelings would linger for days. The burning herbs were much more than a soothing smell. They were a connection to their past humanity, weaving back hundreds of thousands of years forming a bond with the earth. It was always a welcomed practice, attracting good energy and spirits and allowing the mind to understand influences from the past. It had the connection and provided telling signs of the future that only the shaman could understand. Kazan Understood.

CHAPTER 15

Noolan and Caek walked for three days, camping in snow so deep it sometimes reached their waistline. Caek was light enough to be able to walk softly on the surface most of the time, only sinking occasionally. They constructed a snow cave the fourth evening and were warm as they slept under skins next to each other. The rhythm of the journey was beginning to set in. As the days began, they would eat what they had and there was always an abundance of foods. Walnuts, pine nuts, small game such as rabbit, beaver, rats, and birds they would knock down with the accurate throw of a rock or well-balanced stick and in some instances, a well-shot arrow. Root vegetables were plentiful, and they knew where to look in the snow-covered landscape. The two complemented each other in the foraging task. Caek knew some things that Noolan didn't and vice versa. It was remarkable how quickly they could start a fire and find foods.

On the afternoon of the tenth day of travel the snow all but disappeared. They came to a vast river. The current was swift, and they knew they could not cross it by wading or swimming. Moving down the bank they came across a well-worn path. It was not uncommon to find such a path, but the more worn it was, the greater the chances of encountering a bear, tiger, boar, wolf, hyena, or hominoid that would be unfriendly. It was a chance they were taking by being without a formidable shelter at night. As they moved down the path, Caek motioned to Noolan saying she felt as though she was being watched. Noolan agreed as they kept moving cautiously, Caek walking backwards, with a spear in hand. Noolan was leading, mindful for who or what was stalking them and maybe in the bushes alongside the trail.

As the evening approached, they agreed to find a location to rest. Caek motioned to stop. She looked high into the canopy. She quickly placed her load on the ground and climbed an eighty-five-foot tree with stout enough limbs to support their weight. She broke a few branches and wove them together to make a sleeping platform. She then climbed back down, grabbed her load, and climbed back up with Noolan following behind closely. This was when he realized he was truly frightened of heights. It was an unexpected reaction, but he was able to climb to the platform with a bit of encouragement from Caek. He felt secure next to her, high in the boughs of the tree canopy. They both knew something was tracking them but whatever it was, it was less likely to attack them in the tree. Caek was able to easily move up and down the tree, making the trip to get water for both. She managed to grab a few nearby pinecones full of nuts. She sensed something was watching them. They sat in the perch watching. As night fell, she managed to drift into a peaceful sleep in Noolan's arms, but he felt uneasy and did not sleep as the tree swayed with the wind.

The next morning, they resumed walking on the banks of the river looking for a place to cross. They could see trees on the far side but did not see the riverbank coming closer. Noolan took note of a large log floating by and had an idea of catching it and using it to float across. He waded into the river and was able to pull it close to the shore. He tried to explain to Caek what he was going to do. He motioned her to follow. The log was long and wide with several thick branches protruding out various places. He broke of several and then fashioned a crude stone axe to shave the hull. He and Cake peeled off the bark from one side making a somewhat smooth surface to stand on. Once that was done, Noolan went in search of two long poles. As Caek was tying her load to the log when she turned to see someone she did not recognize for an instant before she was hit over the head. Her world went dark.

Noolan returned with the guide poles looking for her, but she was nowhere in sight. He thought she may have gone to get food or some other materials. He looked at the unfinished knot that was in place to secure the load. The line was cut, and the load was missing. Then he looked down on the ground and saw some blood and several hominoid tracks. Immediately his hackles went up and he grabbed a spear looking for whomever attacked Caek. He stopped and listened. He put his nose into the air trying to catch a scent. Looking at the tracks he knew which way they went. As he stared closely, he could tell it was two humanoid types with broad flat feet. He did not understand why they would attack travelers. He was used to always welcoming others but knew attacks did happen. He knew something bad had happened; he could sense it. As he walked through the dense forest, he noted the sounds of the birds. Some signaling the alarm as intruders entered their territory. Some of the birds, such as ground grouse, would not take flight until he was right on top of them, startling him. After a short time, he heard unusual voices, then he heard Caek start to yell and scream and then silence. He ran in the direction of the sounds. He came into an opening and stood still. There to his right was an immense Amira Tiger, Caek was next to him, and the two Neanderthals were backing down the trail with spears in hand. The tiger started walking towards the two attackers. They turned and started running. The tiger followed giving chase.

Caek was unclothed and a bit dazed but happy to see Noolan. Her hair was matted with blood, and she was scratched up after being dragged on the ground. Then they heard shrieks of pain and deep unmistakable attack growls, then some shrieks and yells and then everything went silent including the screaming ravens. They quickly gathered Caek's knife, fire pouch, leg coverings, and moved in the opposite direction the tiger had gone. They did not know if the Jakkar helped Caek or was it just luck that the tiger chose to go after the others. If the tiger did help Caek, this would be the second time it happened. She tried to explain this to Noolan as they made their way back to the makeshift standup paddle boat. She was feeling a type of intentional bond with the tiger. She recalled being separated from her clan and Noolan had a hard time believing such a thing could happen but was grateful this tiger chose to spare her.

They moved swiftly to the log and again tied their possessions to a short limb near one side of the craft. Carefully Noolan knelt in the center of the bow as Caek pushed the log out into the current. She then pulled herself up onto the log, balancing carefully before standing up. The current felt gentle but as they started to move down the river they were pulled into the main current, drifting further away from the shore. Noolan kept digging his long pole into the river bottom attempting to slow the craft or at least turn it. Caek used her pole as a weak rudder, providing an element of steering. Together, they struggled to keep the raft under control. It quickly became apparent the log was too large and heavy with water to control against the increasing current. Noolan dropped to his knees and grabbed the bark attempting to balance the makeshift boat. Caek also dropped to her knees, grabbing a short-broken branch.

After an hour of drifting and bobbing, Noolan heard rushing water. He carefully stood up but could not see the river in front of him. The rush of the water sounded like distant rumbling thunder and Noolan realized the log was going over a huge waterfall. He yelled to Caek trying to explain what was coming to no avail. Caek could not understand him. The roar of the water was deafening and then she realized what was coming. She gripped the branch with all her might as the log violently and erratically bounced while gaining speed. Noolan grabbed the bark holding on with all his strength as the log went over falls. Then the bark he gripped gave way and as he was free falling in the cascading torrent of the rushing waters, he lost sight of Caek.

CHAPTER 16

"It can be said a tiger is an inspirational beast. The tiger does create awe due to its size and strength. What is truly awe-inspiring is how cunning and resourceful the beast is."
Anonymous

KAZAN AND HIS BAND OF TRAVELERS STARTED OUT EARLY IN the morning. As they moved towards the setting sun, the snow was starting to become spotty in some places, mostly in the dark shadows of rock formations. The temperatures were rising, and trees were beginning to show early spring foliage. He knew he would be able to travel about fifteen miles per day if the weather was good and his leg held up. The travelers seemed well prepared. Cahat asked to lead the group down the mountain footpath. Each of the travelers had some sort of weapon to be used for hunting and self-defense. The group was loaded with skins for warmth, food supplies, and goods to trade. They would spend several hours a day hunting; they hunted as they walked in the general direction of the setting sun.

They made their way down the trail Drot spoke quietly about his past. He explained his partner died two summers ago. She was bitten by a snake they never encountered before. She died quickly. Huut and Sinner's future mates died while trying to kill a mammoth. A total of six men from the tribe of travelers had perished during that hunt. Two others were terribly wounded and ended up staying behind with another tribe several months ago. The number in their band was dwindling. He was not sure where they were going, but he was willing to go to the Gathering to seek other areas to live. He was getting tired of traveling and wanted to settle down, he just didn't know where.

As the days started to wear on, a sense of uncertainty descended on the group. They maintained a constant vigilance of hazards and the potential of animal attacks. The path they were on was well-defined. It had been used for eons by both hominoids and animals. It followed a stream which connected with a large river. The group fished and hunted small game along the way. They harvested nuts of all kinds and several root vegetables and fungi. They would set up camp in the late afternoon with a large fire in the center, sleeping close to the flames for warmth and protection. Kazan knew they would have to travel through a high mountain pass with a large amount of snow. He explained the coming hazardous areas to the group as best he could recall. They decided to camp and stock up on provisions before getting above tree line and into the snow.

Two days later they found themselves at the base of a range of formidable mountains. They all stood in awe, admiring the thick forest and the snowy hummocks beyond. Hook, Rit, and Cahat took off to hunt. They had seen boar signs in the area and with a little luck they could bring one down quickly. Kazan reminded them to leave some meat for the Jakkar. There would be plenty to ensure they had food enough to make the climb through the pass. Kazan and Drot built a fire ring, gathered tinder, and proceeded to start a fire. Sinner and Huut gathered larger pieces of wood for the night. It was peaceful in the forest as they setup camp.

As the travelers gathered near the fire that evening, Drot and Kazan spent a lot of time gazing at the stars. They queried each other as to what the stars meant. Drot knew certain stars would shine brighter than others and on occasion some move quickly through the sky. He called out the brightest one in the north, and the three bright ones all in a straight line, and the red star that moved slowly across the night sky. The air was pure, and the sky was crystal clear. Billions of stars filled the black carpet of night. Drot also talked about the changes he had seen in the hominoids where he had come from. His family, although many had died, still had roots in foothill of an area in the south of high snowy mountains, but the winters were bitter and getting longer. Only the those who could not travel due to physical ailments stayed behind and surely succumbed to the harsh winters. Drot spoke of the open plains they walked across that appeared to continue in all directions. It was where the mammoth and bison walked. He started to speak, "The snow started staying year-round, and game became scarce."

The Bering Land bridge was open, and hominoids moved easily across the barren landscape staying close to the water. Some used boats to move along the shores. There were many seals and fish, but they kept moving further away from dry land as the ice sheets started expanding. The mammoths, and other large animals, were beginning to move too. Many of the travelers stopped in cave areas when some could not continue due to injury or illness. Many others died of various ailments. Drot understood mating rituals were different and burial ceremonies differed a bit, but, in general, they were like all the hominoids they encountered. Other travelers travelled the way they did, and others were going back to their homes in the far north and beyond. Most of the hominoids encountered were in good spirits and wanted to flourish and live peacefully just as Drot's clan did. They understood their environment and living in a balanced way. Drot had seen visions and feared their time as a species was going to end unless they could find hospitable places to live and breed. He knew they possessed strong genetics. For some unknown reason, he knew he was a traveler with a special purpose.

Drot spoke of a great vision he experienced once. In the vision, he saw a great abyss of white clouds. They had been moving towards the setting sun for many seasons and he felt it was time to stop. He stood on a boundless cliff surrounded by the great trees. His three daughters Caek, Sinner, and Hutt were with him in the vision. They were the hope of the species. They were to bare many children of the Naledi hominoid line and would ultimately be important for the evolutionary journey and genetic linage of hominoids. Through the strong genetics of the identical triplets, the continuation of his genetic line would survive. He knew the line would never become extinct. As Kazan described where the Gathering was, Drot recalled his vision. He felt if he could make it to the Gathering, he might finally stop wandering. It was then Kazan realized Sinner, Huut and Caek must have been powerful sisters. The third, Caek, broke Drot's hopes with her disappearance.

Drot continued, "Caek was different from her sisters. Her senses were strong, and she could do things and create new processes. Her mind was sharp. Her skills in knapping points were brilliant and she was fast. She knew medicinal plants and her deep green eyes were the sharpest of any. Her hunting skills with a bow, throwing sticks, and rocks were perfect. She understood fire. At one point she placed a heavy yellow rock she collected in fire. It melted into a bright golden-colored blob. Then she figured out it was bendable, and she made me this."

Drot reached into his small amulet pouch around his neck and pulled out a small golden wheel with a hole in the center. He showed Kazan the simple object and then tied it on his wrist with a simple leather strap. "She knew secrets and practices from past ancient generations. She was following in the footsteps of her mother and grandmother becoming a strong medicine woman. All three sisters were enabled with strong gifts." Drot knew that finding the right mates, who also possessed powers, would provide for the continuation of their strong genetic coding, enabling the sustainability of the line for generations.

Kazan responded that he understood the power she must have held. She was clearly a medicine woman with strong bindings to rituals even if she was not formally mentored. He knew people like her existed and reminded him of Noolan. He said he was sorry she was gone. He asked if Drot's other two daughters had the powers. Drot said Sinner was given some power of medicine and Huut was given the power to be a skilled huntress. Both had strengths and weaknesses. He hoped they would find males with strong medicines and shaman skills. Caek was given both gifts and he witnessed that as she grew into a woman.

Triplets in the Pleistocene era were rare. Rarer still was the fact that all three survived into adulthood. Even rarer was the fact that they survived so many years on the trail with Drot and the clan. Kazan wondered what they must have been looking for and it came to him that Hook, Rit and Noolan, triplets themselves, could have been the link joining the two species together and making for a strong and knowledgeable offspring. He understood as new species, their combined genetics would expand and provide for stronger species among hominoids growing in mind and physical ability. In time and given the chance, they might expand their genetics over great distances. This would be a territorial gene pool gain, in the intellectual arena was well.

Drot and Kazan both understood the value in travel and expanding their minds through attentiveness of self and surroundings. The opportunities to engage with other hominoids and their cultural practices provided insights to different tools, foods, and detailed sustainable practices. Travel also offered opportunities to develop new hunting strategies and partner with other groups. New techniques also allowed ways to defend themselves and their families against attacks. The controlled use of fire was an early indication of communal interactions and the opportunity to tell stories of the past. Both Drot and Kazan knew fire was a recently controllable tool. They had both had taken advantage of communal gatherings to teach and tell stories of past events and practices. They understood their ancestors were not mindless apes wandering through the forests without a purpose. They had developed purpose and skills, and emotions including those neural connections that would keep them alive and thriving. There was a harmony to the world and Kazan and Drot understood this and wanted to pass this knowledge on.

As the evening grew into a dark and cloudless night the two men kept talking by the fire. The fact that the girls were a set of triplets was consuming Kazan's mind. Huut and Sinner were sitting nearby and Kazan asked if they could hear Caek and her thoughts. They both said yes. Huut and Sinner could hear each other's thought as well. They could feel each other's pain and elations. Caek being gone was an unusual feeling because they had never been separated for any length of time. Huut went on to say she still felt Caek in her thoughts but did not know quite how to interpret the messages since she had not been around. Sinner also talked about feeling Caek's present even though she believed she had been eaten by a Jakkar. They both felt she may still be alive in some way, perhaps through the essence of the Jakkar.

Drot told Kazan if any of the three girls could survive on their own and alone, it would be Caek. Kazan thought about this for a long while and then asked Huut and Sinner if they had any visions of Caek since her disappearance. Huut responded the only time she saw anything it seemed Caek was in danger and Sinner nodded in agreement. There was a fearful sensation she occasionally received from her sister, as though she was silently yelling for help. Kazan asked how long the visions lasted and Huut said it was usually a short time. She went on to say she dreamed of Caek with Sinner often. They had a bond of knowing with each other. The feeling was strong.

Kazan thought Caek may still be alive. He did not say anything to Drot, Huut or Sinner. He wasn't completely sure, but given the history of the girls and what he knew could happen, the girl was alive somewhere in the region. He wondered if he should talk to the girls and find out more details about what was in the area where they saw Caek. Were there any discernable landmarks he might be able to recognize? Perhaps they would look for identifiable landmarks as they traveled.

Late that night, as the moon began to rise, the members of the party started to drift off to sleep. The next few days would be tough, climbing up and through the mountain passes. The snow looked deep, and that night the temperature steadily dropped.

CHAPTER 17

CAEK LET GO OF THE LOG AS IT WENT OVER THE FALLS. THEY were free falling and became shrouded in the cascading water, losing sight of each other. Hitting the water hard they both sank deep into the rush of water, nearly hitting the bottom of the splash pool. They struggled fiercely and eventually bobbed up to the surface, coughing and flailing, attempting to swim. The top outer skins they wore were buoyant but becoming soaked and heavy, adding to their struggles. Their leggings and footwear were made of the same type of skins and became waterlogged. However, the hairs of the hide were hollow and acted as a type of life preserver, helping them in the struggle to stay afloat. They were both taken by a swift current away from the thundering waterfalls, pulling away from the vortices, finally coming to rest on the large gravel bar downstream. They were exhausted and uncertain of their condition. Noolan was the first to stagger to his feet. His first action was to survey the area and look for Caek or any of their belongings. Caek was a short distance away, coughing as she got up. She also started to scan the area. When she gazed back up the falls, she could not understand how they survived the huge fall.

They both knew they needed to find their belongings, and they started to move back towards the falls searching. Once they were in sight of the enormous splash-pool, they stopped and looked in several whirlpool eddies circling the front of and around the fall area. Jammed against the bank was the log but the hide bags full of the belongings were gone. They had nothing but what was on them. Thankfully they each had their knives and pouches with fire making tools. Caek started look for shelter and stopped when she spied a dark cleft to the right side of the waterfall. It looked as though it was a cave a good distance up the cliff. To get there they needed to climb over numerous debris piles consisting of huge ancient old growth trees, most of which were covered in dense green moss. The trees were huge, making the hike slow and tedious. As they moved towards the cliff, two large eagles became aware and interested in the two intruders. The birds started to dive bomb the couple trying to knock them off balance and halt their progress towards the cave. Noolan found a hefty two-foot-long stick. When one of the birds swooped, he wound up and launched it hitting the attacker in the head. It shrieked in surprise and fell to the ground just ahead of Caek. She picked it up, rung its neck and smiled at Noolan saying, "Dinner!"

Once they entered the cave, there was evidence other humans used the shelter. The front portion of the cave was being used as a bird nesting site. It was evident no humanoids lived there recently. There was a fire ring and knapping chips littered the floor. Noolan quickly lit a fire and began warming himself while Caek plucked and cleaned the bird. She then used a stick to support the bird over the flame. They were both exhausted and warmed themselves while glancing about the shelter. Caek noticed the knapping flakes were mostly obsidian and held flecks of white. She showed several pieces to Noolan who also found them unique. A jarring vague memory stirred in him he could not quite place. The snowflake patterns felt familiar. He put a few larger pieces into his pouch planning to work them into arrow points later. They thought the cave may go back a long way, but they were not ready to investigate. Once the bird was cooked, they ate it quickly huddled together and fell asleep.

Noolan awoke with a jolt of not knowing where he was. His head was hurting. The crashing thunder of the waterfall was loud and the roar was pounding and causing him pain. Caek was curled up in the fetal position sleeping. He looked out the mouth of the small cave searching for the packs through the spraying mist. He thought he saw something snagged on a large tree resting on the shore far below them. He shook Caek awake and told her it was time to go telling her about what he thought he saw. They climbed down the cliff face and searched the debris wood piles for the pack of supplies. They never found it. Once they gave up the search, they moved into the dense forest and soon came across a well-worn trail that ran parallel to river. The number of tracks in the mud showed that it was heavily used by many animals. Noolan were sure humanoids used the trail as well, but no hominoid footprints were visible.

Noolan set up a crude lean-to out of tree branches early in the afternoon. Caek went back to the river to find a spot to catch fish. There were rugged black basalt crags cutting at her footwear. After scrambling over and around the formations, she found a shallow pool and saw the shadows of fish passively swimming around. She went to the far end and piled rocks to seal off the escape to the river. She then fashioned a spear out of a long straight pole and stood motionless surveying the pool, waiting. After a few minutes she thrust the spear and came up with a large trout. She knew it was enough to provide sustenance for both.

As she made her way back to the camp, she could smell the fire Noolan made. Caek cleaned the fish quickly and secured the two large fillets on two sticks she skillfully sharpened. It cooked quickly and they ate it in silence. Noolan wanted more once he finished.

After the meal they discussed what they should do next. Noolan said they needed to continue until they found a suitable area to live. Caek agreed but was cautious because of the many hazards. She did not want to try and cross the river again. Noolan said it would not be his first option and traveling west along the river would be a good option. They would try and stay ahead of the weather. In the morning they decided to keep using the pathway as long as it trended in a southwestern direction, and it did. The trail crossed many small rivers and tributaries, but none as large as the main river. As they walked down river, keeping to the path, they were able to ford many water filled tributaries. The path became more worn, and after a long distance they spotted humanoid tracks in the mud. Looking at each other, they knew they would need to be careful and be aware of the possibility of encountering others.

Caek started to notice the array of birds flying about, some she had never encountered. There was one that caught her eye, with bright red tail feathers and a blue cape over its head. The beak was large and hook shaped. It flew with others of its own kind and made a horrendous racket when they all squawked in unison.

It was later in the day Noolan caught a whiff of smoke. He noted the wind direction and asked Caek if she smelled it as well. She did. It was not just smoke, but the odor of meat cooking. It was unmistakable. They did not want to get into a fight with anyone, but they were hungry, and they thought that perhaps whoever was cooking the meat would be willing to share. They quietly and cautiously made their way down the trail. They spotted the camp through the dense vegetation and from a short distance they saw two men and two women engaged in camp chores. They looked to be travelers and pitched a tent like structure made of skins a short way up the trail. Noolan walked into the camp. The four people stood up in a startled manner. One man reached for a club. Noolan put his weapons on the ground then his hands up in a surrendering "Hey! I'm unarmed!" position. Caek also put her arms up as she slipped in beside Noolan.

She looked at the two women, and then the two men. She recognized the facial features as that of the Naledi, the same line of humanoid she was from, but they held skeletal traits from the Australopithecus Africanus, with shorter arms, longer legs, and a larger eyebrow ridge across the forehead. She made a gesture with her hands a gesture and one of the women gestured back. It was an ancient sign of friendship. At that point, the man with the spear relaxed his defensive posture and motioned to them join the fire. Noolan was cautious as he felt like an outsider. Caek took the lead and introduced herself in a high-pitched vocalization Noolan had never heard before. It was a different language with completely different dialects of sounds and intonations. With several clicks of the tongue and twists of the lip, some specific teeth type clicks and over emphasized eye movements, the four engaged in a conversation. It was a rapid-fire song-like discussion. The female hominoid said they were travelers but lost from their hominoid families. Caek asked where they were from, then asked where they were going. At that time, one of the men offered some boar meat that was well cooked. There was more than enough to go around. It was a nice sized; they had a full hind quarter on the spit, carving off slabs as it cooked. Noolan began to relax but was still curious about what was being discussed. They both received offerings of meat, accepting it with nods and smiles of gratitude. Noolan was able to understand some things about the others from innate consciousness and observation.

Caek told them she was separated from her clan a long time ago by a Jakkar. She explained some of the encounters she experienced, such as being kidnapped, and how she came to be with Noolan. One of the women said she was a healer, a shaman. She said they were traveling to a gathering many days away. Caek said she was not sure where they were going, other than looking for Noolan's clan. He could not remember certain things and one was where he was from. They had been wandering for a long while looking for a place to stop. Caek explained the conversation to Noolan. She explained one woman was called Ovla, the other woman was called Hetra, the two men Kuni and Vena.

Ovla's stories started to sound more and more familiar to Caek. The Naledi tribe had deep roots in lands far north and far south. Ovla drew a crude map on the ground indicating the direction of travel for generations and the underpinning to spreading out and multiplying. Ovla asked how many children Caek had, but she had none. She thought she was still too young because she had just recently started to bleed. The other woman, Hetra, and the men listened with great interest although Noolan was somewhat lost in the chatter. His head was still giving him problems. He kept experiencing migraine headaches. Sometimes he would just space out and stare off. It looked as though he would go into a trance. As the evening grew dark, one of the men rolled out some skins and laid down. The women joined in preparing their sleeping spots. The other men put some wood on the fire and motioned to Noolan, who indicated that he and Caek did not have skins for sleeping as they lost them over the waterfall. Vena rolled out another sleeping skin. Noolan and Caek moved over and laid down near the fire to sleep.

As the flames died down to golden embers, she could feel Noolan breathing deeply. Caek started to dream. Her mind flashed to the Jakkar and the complex interactions she had with them. Then she saw a dead tiger on the end of a spear and then she saw someone that might have been Noolan at a great distance, limping as though he was injured. Then she had a flashing image of being lost on a great body of water. The skies in the dream were an indigo blue and lightning arched in erratic frightening patterns across the horizon. She twisted and turned, waking Noolan with her sudden flailing movements. Over the course of the next few hours Caek began to relax and fell into a deep sleep but kept mumbling sounds Noolan could not understand. He did not sleep the entire night.

The next morning as the sun was beginning to rise, Caek was up early watching the fire. Noolan could tell she was in deep thought. Everyone except Caek ate a morning breakfast of leftover boar with some carrots, nuts, and greens that were easily gathered. Several dried fruits were offered to her by Ovla, but Caek politely refused. She remained silent and distant from the others. The group of four headed down river, the same direction as Caek and Noolan. With the efficiency of a well-organized team, they packed their belongings and departed down the well-worn path.

CHAPTER 18

BY NOON THE SNOW WAS WAIST DEEP AND THE TRAIL WAS progressively steeper. Drot lead the group as they reached tree line. Kazan lagged a little behind the group. He was slow and methodical in his advance and made good headway, despite his shorter leg. About mid-day, as the sun drifted higher into the clear sky, Drot eyes became blurry. He looked back over his shoulder at the rest of the travelers. He could tell they were having problems seeing because of the brightness. He pulled a thin piece of bark with two quarter inch slits across his eyes and tied it to his face around his fur lined hoodie with a thin leather strap. He explained to Kazan and the others that it helped with the blurry vision in the bright snow. This simple and effective matter of protection helped when navigating through the deep snow especially when the reflection was bright. The others immediately peeled fresh bark of nearby pine trees and copied Drots eye protection device. As the day grew into evening, the party realized they would not make it out of the pass. Drot started to dig a snow cave into a deep bank with his hands. Huut, Sinner and the rest of the travelers understood what was needed. During the last winter as they traveled south, they were trapped in a blizzard for eleven days. It was evident that Drot and his crew of Naledi learned to survived in many environments. The entrance to the snow cave was small and as the interior carving continued, each person dug their own small sleeping platform moving snow out efficiently and effectively.

The temperature plummeted to well below zero overnight, but the travelers stayed warm and comfortable in their new shelter. As the sun crested the eastern horizon, Kazan was already preparing to get moving. They shared foods and helped each other prepare to move quickly. Once outside, the crew took turns relieving themselves, the deep yellow streams burned an oblong hole through the deep snow staining it brightly. The freezing air outside the snow cave quickly crystalized the breath on the scruffy and wily beards of the men. Within a few minutes, eyelids became crusted with ice. Every now and then a member would rake a hand across their faces clearing chunks of ice away. The travelers slowly started up the path as Drot began to push through the thigh-hi snow. along. Kazan was the last one out.

After two hours struggling up the pass nearing the top, the group heard a deep heavy rumbling. Drot looked up and yelled to the other to run, an avalanche was shooting down the mountain. The group started to plow through the mid-thigh deep snow. Drot shot forward seeing a black outcrop of basalt boulders ahead. He ran as fast as he could plowing away a path for the other to follow. The roar of the coming snow was deafening. He threw himself behind the nearest boulder and the others followed suit, diving behind and on top of Drot. Within a few seconds they were engulfed in snow.

Drot was trying to yell because the others were crushing him. He was being suffocated at the bottom of the pile. Huut started screaming; Kazan felt the crush of the snow as did the others. The weight was overwhelming. Hook was the first to realize the snow stopped coming, but he panicked because he could not breathe. Rit and Cahat were lying near him and pushed up with all their might and were able to move the snow on top of them. They frantically dug upwards finding the edge of the bolder. They eventually broke through. In a daze, Rit pulled whoever was under him to the open air. It was Cahat. He immediately started moving snow away as fast as he could, still semi buried to his waist. Sinner was next and Huut was under her. They were both dazed but gasped for breath. They immediately started to dig for the others, and quickly found Kazan. He was struggling for air and started coughing It was the first full breath of air in several minutes. The rest kept digging for Drot. Sinner yelled and yelled for silence: she yelled for everyone to be quiet. They all listened for any sound of life. Hearing nothing Kazan said he must be near where he was, so they continued digging. After several minutes, Drots fur lined outer shell was uncovered. The group dug frantically and finally extracted him, but it was too late. He was no longer breathing.

As they pulled his body from the snow, Sinner and Huut began to weep. He was also the leader of the Naledi and their most reliable defender. He was the wise one of the band of wanderers. The travelers held a high respect for him. He lived as an honorable and loyal hominoid. Sinner wanted to think he died for them, bringing them to safety without considering his own. Drot was like that. She knew it would be more difficult without him. They all understood this. All his wisdom would be lost. Rit and Cahat also began to grieve the loss with soft whimpers. The two had known Drot since they were young. He was their teacher of many things including, hunting skills, special tricks to lure and track game. He taught them how to make certain flint knapping tools for shaping well-balanced spear points and efficient sharp scrapers. Drot could make the most elegant scraping and carving tools. He was a master at many things. Drot was also tough. He had battle scars to prove his courage, and in some cases, the stupidity of his youth. His disfigured arm never slowed him down. Kazan understood the loss would be significant to the travelers. Drot was carrying some valuable pieces for Kazan including trade items such as obsidian and stone carved figurines. Kazan would also miss him as a friend. They were about the same age, and he enjoyed the comradery they were developing.

It was still bitter cold, and the band of travelers knew they had to keep moving or they would freeze to death. Sinner started chanting a repetitive whaling-type vocalization. Huut joined in and then Cahat, Rit, and Kazan. It was a song of respect and love for the dead. This was a funeral song, a tune reflecting the concept of grace, forgiveness, love, and courage, new emotions for the Pleistocene hominoid brain. As they gathered around the smallish man, Sinner removed his pack and strapped it to her chest. Rit gathered the flint knapping kit still strapped to his side and his knife. Cahat picked up the spear. Another item Sinner removed from Drot was his small pouch. Most hominoids carried one. It was like a wallet and held items of significance to the individual. Drot's contained a small one-inch wheel shaped nugget of gold he was given by Caek. Drot knew it was important and remembered Caek demonstrating the concept to reduce work. She would hold the heavy disc shaped item between her fingers and then on her roll thigh. Drot was going to build a large one out of wood when he found a place to call home. It was one of those projects he never got around to. He carried the trinket knowing it was unique. Sinner gave the disc to Kazan. The bag also contained several finely made tiny obsidian bird arrow points along with a wrapped bundle of sage and sweetgrass. They were for ceremonies to ensure good hunting and refreshing the spirit. He also carried a small intricate carved image of a tiger. It was to be a gift to Caek. He and Caek had a special bond and Drot never stopped believing she was still alive.

Kazan reached into his personal pouch and pulled out an ocher stone. He then removed Drot's fur lined hat and marked his forehead in ocher with a circle with a dot in the center. It was faint against his dark skin. The circle was the symbol for going home. Once the circle was closed, as Kazan had drawn it, it signified the life was complete and another would eventually begin. The small dot represented the first drop of water in the pond of life. The outer circle was seen as the ripple from the drop or mark in the center. It was a wish for a pleasant journey home, wherever it might be in the cosmos. They dug his shallow grave in the snow near the base of the basalt rock and placed his bow and quiver of arrows next to him in a respectful and dignified way and covered him. When the ceremony was complete Kazan turned and lead the party down the mountain. His short leg was starting so show signs of frostbite and his limp was becoming more pronounced.

As the group moved swiftly down the trail, short stubby juniper trees eventually started to appear. They were reaching tree line and would soon begin entering the forest. The trail was more visible, and patches of forest ground started to emerge. Birds began to sing and chirp as the trees began to get taller. That evening they found a small crude hollow near a riverbank that appeared to have been used as a temporary shelter. It was vacant except for an ambling porcupine that was quickly chased away. A rock fire ring was near the entry, surrounded by several sitting stones. The group started to prepare for the night. Sinner was relived to put both her and Drot's packs down. Cahat, Rit, and Hook set their loads down and wandered off to gather wood. Kazan started to gather nearby kindling and quickly started a small fire. The boys arrived and placed larger pieces of fuel on the flames. Within a few minutes, they were all gathered, warming themselves in silence. Sinner started humming a melancholy tune as they stared into the flames. Each of them began recalling the life of Drot. They were truly going to miss him. He was a good-natured man.

At some point during the evening, Huut pulled out some dried meat and started to eat. The group slowly started to realize they had gone the entire day without food. Cahat remembered seeing some plants while gathering wood and went into the forest to gather some Salal, a dense green foliage with a sweet yet faintly tart taste. Sinner opened up Drot's pack and pulled out his food reserves to share with the group. While she was exploring the contents, she came across a small leather pouch. As she unrolled it, she discovered it was his cannabis. She recalled Drot would smoke cannabis and sometimes ate it. He said it helped with the pains in his bones. He also said it helped women with cramps and their monthly bleeding cycles. The herb was also used for recreation. It gave him a euphoric feeling and allowed him to see and experience humor, a new sensation and feeling in the developing brain. He said it was always enjoyable and one would always return to their normal state of mind. Drot was an interesting man, she thought. Sinner presented the cannabis to Kazan, thinking he might get better use out of it than any of the younger travelers. She told him it was for his bones, but Kazan knew it had many uses.

Other contents of the pack included his sleeping skins, several well-worked soft leather pieces and most important to the group, strong cord. Sinner valued strong cord. She used it for securing loads and hanging meats. Well-made fine cord was used for snares. Drot always seemed to have good cord when it was needed. Then, she recalled, one of the things Drot always used to do was roll and twist and braid cord. While sitting around the fire, his hands were always working. She gave some of the cord to Hook and Rit and held onto the fine strands for setting snares. That night, as the forest grew dark, and the fire started to dwindle, they heard the roar of Jakkar not too far off. Kazan added wood to the fire.

As the morning sun quietly opened the forest doors, Huut was able to survey the surroundings, keeping a watchful eye open for Jakkar. She walked down the trail a short distance to relieve herself and as she was doing so, she spotted a series of cliffs and then caves in their direction of travel. She thought that the Jakkar they heard must have been living in one of the caves. Then she caught sight of another humanoid. It was a fleeting glance for just a fraction of a second. But the rustling of the leaves confirmed it was not her imagination. It looked like it might have been a young one. She slowly backed out of the area towards the camp, cautiously watching. All her senses were on high alert.

When she returned to camp, she reported what she saw to the group. She told them it looked more like a distant developing cousin to the Naledi, but she wasn't sure. If it was the species she was thinking of, she knew they were extremely aggressive hominoids and usually stayed in groups and caves for safety. They were also cannibals. The travelers encountered a few others on their journeys and Drot was the only one who fully understood how to communicate with them. He was teaching Huut the sounds and gestures of their developing language. Kazan said he knew of the type of hominoid, but he had never seen one or had the occasion to meet one. He believed they were a species that was adsorbed into the hominoid gene pool. He also knew they could be peaceful, but only on their own terms. They typically had no desire to fight and had the ability to stay in the shadows of the forests undetected. They were adept at climbing trees, and they could run at a good clip if they were chased. They hobbled and wobbled from foot-to-foot because the development of the knee and hip joint was still progressing. They had a lot more body hair and did not find it necessary to cover their bodies in another animal's skin. They were masters at concealment and moved about the forests quietly, surviving primarily on a raw meat diet. To see one was considered rare occurrence. They moved with the stealth of the Jakkar.

The Jakkar, of course, was an ambush hunter and its technique, the coupling of slyness, concealment, and surprise gave the predator the ability to kill large fast-moving and dangerous prey for eons. The Jakkar almost never revealed itself unless it was attacking. Later that day, Rit, Cahat, and Hook saw the Jakkar and it made no effort to conceal itself. The band of hunter travelers watched as the massive beast moved ahead of them casually walking down the trail, occasionally looking back over his rump at the men and women trailing it. It was as though the tiger was leading the group to a specific location. The group stood ready to defend themselves should the Jakkar attack, but it didn't. It kept walking down the trail, staying within eyesight. Kazan watched nervously, as did the others. As the trail started to climb, they watched the Jakkar gracefully leap from one rock outcrop to the next. They watched as the muscle groups in the legs flexed and relaxed and then rippled in unison with each movement the beast made. The tiger was not in an attack posture or seemingly all that interested in a humanoid snack. All the while, they cautiously moved up the trail matching the pace of the beast and made sure they could see him.

CHAPTER 19

As Noolan moved down the trail with the small group he made attempts to learn more about the hominoids by observation. Caek seemed to fit right in and experienced no issues communicating. How she communicated was fascinating, with multiple hand gestures and vocalizations in high pitched frequencies. The clicks lips were loud and clear as two rocks being hit together. Caek would interpret and relay important information to Noolan as they walked on the now sandy path. The ocean now paralleled the trail, and the waves could be heard crashing on the shore like thunder. On occasion, the group would catch glimpses of the vast ocean and the foamy white waves crashing in the surf. As one point, Caek turned to Noolan and explained the two men had been successful fishing in the surf and at the mouths of some of the small streams that flowed over the beaches and into the deep blue waters. The group also harvested clams and caught crabs. The group prepared them much the same way Noolan remembered, baking them in a small pit.

About noon, the unit of travelers stopped and put their loads down. With several motions and short sounds, they started to hike across the dunes in the direction of the ocean. There was a strong wind coming from the waters and off in the distance large billowing clouds were building. As Caek walked over the stringy beach grasses, she noticed several small delicate brown mushrooms tucked tightly among them. She had not seen this type of fungi and was intrigued by the small caramel colored cap and the thick white stem. When she squeezed the stem, it bruised a deep purple. She knew what it meant. The mushroom was special, but she did not realize how unique it was. She knew it could offer a spiritual reflection. It was the creative consciousness of thought she understood was powerful enough to create processes. It was the genius of self-reflection, deep thought, and a profound spiritual harmony with the environment.

Caek collected several of the unique mushrooms not understanding the full coming consequences. During the evening she ingested many and began to experience profound effects. The surrounding sounds were amplified and Noolan knew something was not right. He suspected she was experiencing visions. She was experiencing insights and connection to her environment in a metaphysical state. The others watched her fall into a trance, occasionally mumbling incoherently. Noolan became worried and watched her as she began swaying in a rhythmic pattern and then asking to lay down. Her body twitched with small spastic motions. She would smile and laugh and then her forehead would wrinkle with concern and deep thought. Her mind was being transformed with the massive psilocybin ingestion.

Caek was seeing things she could not understand. Drot walking beside her down a wide path into a grove of Redwood trees. She could see everything around her in minute detail, seeing the fibrous connections to the earth through the fungal threads, the mycelium, the root system, tree trunks and full-spread coniferous canopy. The bark on the tree moved as millions of ants climbed up and down its surface. Then an enormous flash of fire seared her visions, she was sitting near a lake with green calm waters. Other hominoids she did not know were in a boat-like object moving away from shore. As the event went on throughout the night, she found herself walking with the Jakkar. She looked down at her feet and found they had turned into the paws of the Jakkar, pads and claws covered in bright orange and black strip of fur. She wiggled her toes and she saw claws stretch out in front of her. But one claw was overextended in a crippled and crooked way. It was the same foot of the tiger cub she rescued long ago. She then noticed how quiet and dark the forest was and began to shiver violently. All went soundless and starkly motionless. She then found herself floating among the stars in the quietness of outer space and a calm and peaceful feeling descended over her. She found herself aware of the world in a surreal way, witnessing connections to all things, the plants, animals, and all hominoids. As the effects of the drug started to subside, she grew tired and lethargic. Noolan wrapped her in a soft fur-lined skin, and she fell asleep, breathing deeply and rhythmically. He lay beside her, holding her, eventually falling asleep.

As the sun started to rise Noolan was awakened by a faraway loud booming sound. Caek was not next to him. She was gone. Frantically, he jumped up looking everywhere nearby. The others of the group were slowly rising and Noolan used what gestures he knew to indicate Caek was gone, asking if they had seen her. With blank stares they looked bewildered and did not quite understand other than the fact Caek was not in the area. Noolan started to search the immediate area, looking for tracks and other indications where she may had gone. The others soon understood and began searching the area, eventually climbing over the sand dunes towards the ocean. By late afternoon, the booming thunder intensified as they made way towards the water looking for Caek. As they looked out over the waters, they witnessed expansive lightning bolts striking the water's surface and then heard the enormous explosions off-shore that shook the ground they stood on. They did not understand but could see vast dark clouds billowing with tumultuous erratic and chaotic undulations. Over the next two hours, the waves grew larger and began hitting the shore with powerful blows of energy, eroding the sands, and sending millions of cubic yards of materials back into the frothy waters. Rain started fall as the wind whipped the droplets into small stinging needles hurting with each hit. They could barely hear each other's screams as they motioned and yelled to retreat from the dunes for protection.

Once under the canopy of the pine forest, trees were bending with each blast of hurricane force winds. Branches were breaking and falling all around them. Ovla motioned to the high caves. As the darkness of night started to grow the group gathered what possessions they could and started to run for the high volcanic crags scrambling over fallen branches and trees. As they climbed up the side of the basalt outcrop face, Noolan kept looking back for Caek, but she was nowhere in sight. The winds were whipping the group brutally and the rains were drench-ing. They made slow progress up the face of the steep rocky cliff face and eventually found the entrance to a cave sheltered by a large over-hang and reaching a good distance back. Once inside, the group sat in silence as the storm raged and ravaged the beach. The flashes of lighting illuminated the cave for milliseconds and the resulting thunder rever-berated against the walls of the cave making it impossible to hear voices. Huge sixty-foot waves pounded the dunes where they had been looking for Caek and digging clams. The entire beach area was now under wa-ter. The storm continued to build in intensity, pounding the cliff rock face heavily making it difficult to hear anything. The thick clouds bil-lowed continually on the horizon and visibility was limited.

One of the young men, Kuni, cut his leg severely from mid-thigh over the knee and down his shin bone while scrambling up the rock face. He was bleeding profusely and was in excruciating pain as they huddled in the shelter. Ovla inspected the wound and could see his exposed kneecap and shredded ligaments and bone. She applied a soft skin compress and tied it tightly with a leather thong to stop the hemorrhaging and keep the kneecap in place. As the darkness of night grew, Noolan kept a watch at the opening of the cave looking for any sign of Caek.

The storm raged for the next three days trapping the band of travelers. From the safety of the cave, they watched the entire shoreline change. Runoff waters washed mountains of sand away, huge thousand-year-old trees were downed, washing away into the ocean to become driftwood for eons. The path they were on was now under the ocean waters. The base of the rock outcrop, where the cave was located, was now the shoreline. They would have to find a new way to return to the forest. Scrambling down was not an option at this point.

Noolan began to lose hope of finding Caek alive. It had been three days since she was last seen. Being able to survive the storm out in the open would have been impossible. Extreme hunger was setting in.

On the morning of the fourth day, the sun broke through the cloudy skies. The exhausted and hungry travelers decided they would have to scale the rock face upwards to reach the forest if it was still there. Their food reserves dwindled to nothing, and they all knew that finding food was a priority. Once they packed their belongings into backpacks and prepared for the climb, they realized Kuni was in no condition to climb or walk. His injury was infected, starting to smell of gangrene and he had a high fever. When Ovla untied the leather strap holding the moss and deer skin compress, greenish-yellow puss oozed out. Kuni immediately knew his time was up. He tried to stand as the other travelers, knowing they could not stay, began to sing the ancient song of life. It was a repeating rhythm of low, melancholy sounding voice inflections. Noolan understood and he started to load his pack. Kuni had two choices. He could starve himself or when he felt the strength, throw himself off the cliff into the ocean below. Hetra was his mate, and she fully understood what was next. As brutal as the conditions were, it was a matter of survival and for Kuni it was not looking good. Any sense of attachment to one another was negated due to the conditions. Hetra was entering the prime of her child-bearing years and her goal was to have as many offspring as possible before she died. She would have to look for another mate if she made it out of this situation. She knew Noolan was looking like a possible choice. In the mind of Hetra, the mating ritual would be short and there was no courtship. She did not know if Noolan would stay with them. She would not want a hominoid that was not of strong genetics. She knew it was a relationship borne out of necessity and interdependence, not a feeling of love or happiness or compassion. It was the evolution of the species. It was procreation and although they did not realize it, they understood it was the way it was. It was a simple act and love was not an emotion she or the others recognized. She knew she had to mate, and it was her time.

As the group began the treacherous climb out of the cave, Vena turned and bid farewell to his lifelong friend. He was the last one out of the cave, but before he left, Kuni gave him several arrow points and a small carved image of a mammoth. With that Vena reached around the side of the cave wall and started to climb up the sheer wall, following the others.

They both began singing the ancient song of life until they could no longer hear each other. Noolan was in the lead, followed by Ovla and Hetra, then Vena. The climbers were agile and lean. Their well-sinewed bodies rippled as they reached for hold spots on the cliff and pulled themselves up, straining to find the next hand grasp. Slowly they made their way up the cliff, moving laterally and then up, and then laterally again, straining to cling to the sheer cliff face. The wind was still blowing, but the rains had stopped. As they climbed, Noolan looked back over his shoulder, where the beach used to be. It was nothing but ocean as far as he could see. After several hours of climbing, he found the far side of the cliff face and the terrain, although steep, did not require his hand to hold on. As he stood up, he yelled back to the others with the voice inflection that he was okay. Ovla was next to reach the edge. She smiled and then yelled something Noolan did not understand back to the others. Soon enough, Hetra came and then Vena. Each were relieved to be off the cliff.

They began to descend the far side of the mountain into a heavily forested area, having to go over downed trees, branches, and pools of water. A short time later, Noolan motioned to stop. He spotted fresh track of a wild boar. With a stick he drew out a plan to hunt the boar on the ground. He grabbed a long pole and quickly sharpened it. Then he opened his pack, pulled out a large flake of chert and knapped a point for the spear tying it to the shaft. Vena acknowledged the workmanship and a bond started to develop between the two. Ovla and Hetra understood the plan, as well. They would be part of the team drive to herd the animal into a kill trap.

Noolan moved out to one side of the forest over several downed trees and Vena to the other. Slowly they moved on either side of a small draw. The fresh tracks were between them. Ovla spotted the boar first and let out a series of clicks and squeals. Noolan readied the spear and Vena raised his. It was a young boar and sensed something and grunted loudly spinning around to face the two women coming up on his backside. Hetra squealed mimicking a female boar call, Ovla joined in making wounded pig calls. This confused the animal and he charged towards Hetra at full speed. The tusks on the pig were eight inches long razor sharp and could easily penetrate flesh. The pig weighed about two hundred pounds and packed tremendous muscular power. As it started to charge, Noolan launched the spear hitting the beast in the side just behind the front quarter. Vena quickly threw the spear hitting the pig in the neck. The pig twisted in convulsions screaming and squealing. Ovla grabbed her knife and as the pig started to die, she jumped on it and rapidly cut through the course hair and slit the throat to silence the screams and bring death more quickly.

The team moved swiftly and pulled the pig into a small clearing. The first order of business was to remove the skin. This was done effectively with the crude but more than efficient flint and obsidian cutting tools. The entrails were removed, inspected for damage, and separated. The animal was cut into quarters. One quarter shank was quickly removed and placed a distance away on a log. This was for the Jakkar. They all understood the Jakkar was there. He always was. Noolan started a fire as Ovla gathered wood. She then prepared a spit and skewered a hind quarter of the beast with the help of Hetra and soon the waft of cooking meat filled the air. Vena easily found some eatable tubers scattered in the area and the feast began. After gorging themselves, they constructed a lean-to shelter and rested. Noolan's thoughts wandered back to Caek.

CHAPTER 20

CAEK WAS WAKENED EARLY IN THE MORNING BY A CENTI-pede crawling on her face. She swiftly brushed it off. Her mind was still reeling from the powerful dose of psilocybin the night before. She was startled by the sound of a Jakkar far off in the distance. Moving gracefully and swiftly she slipped away from Noolan's relaxed arm while he deeply slept and started walking in the direction of the distant roar. Again, she heard it, and her pulse began to quicken, and heart beat hard. Adrenaline started to course through her veins and body. Within a few seconds she found herself running with all her might towards the Jakkar. The winds were picking up significantly as she scrambled over fallen trees and dense vegetation. Thick vines draped over some of the obstacles helped her to climb over larger obstructions. The tiger roared again, giving its location away and Caek turned to refine her direction of travel towards the cat. Then she heard what she thought was another Jakkar far off to the north. She stopped and listened, canting her head and ear in the direction of the slightest sounds. Then another roar not too far off to the east. She kept moving deeper and deeper into the forest following the alluring roars. Each roar drew her further away from Noolan. She kept going, losing herself in the tantalizing, gripping call of the Jakkar. In the back of her mind, she knew better. But the thundering roar was an invitation captivating her body, mind, and soul. She became absorbed in the chase, losing all sense of where she was and how far she had run. She lost all thoughts of the small band of travelers she left behind.

Eventually, by late afternoon she made her way to a large clearing. The field was green with dandelions, Johnson grasses, and sweetgrass. Looking high up in the canopy skirting the field, trees were swaying violently with the whipping winds. Trees were beginning to snap and fall to the ground near her. Then out of the corner of her eye at the edge of the forest she spotted three massive Jakkar, watching her.

She realized she had had a vision of this place but with only one Jakkar, not three. She was still gripped in the after-effects of the mushroom infusion and was just beginning to think of her surroundings. She felt she needed to find shelter. With this thought, the three Jakkar stood up, slowly turned, and walked single file deeper into the jungle, farther away from the coastline. The last one stopped and looked back over its rump to see if Caek was following along. She was drawn to them and started to walk behind them.

The Jakkar led her on a semi-well-developed trail. It was apparent to Caek that the trail allowed for game animals to move swiftly through the dense jungle. The Jakkar was using the path to lead Caek somewhere. By dark the rains began and Caek was growing tired. She had not eaten anything the entire day. The effects of the psilocybin were subsiding, and a pleasurable afterglow was setting in, but she was hungry. As darkness shrouded the forest, Caek grew tired and felt ready to stop and sleep but the winds were becoming more and more harsh whipping tree limbs wildly. When the lighting started and the resulting thundering booms exploded, Caek felt consumed with exhaustion and fear. As a bolt of lightning struck a nearby tree, she was able to make out a small fissure in a mound of rocks leading down into the ground. It was a narrow squeeze, but she was able to wiggle her way in and found herself in a dark but dry chamber. She reached for her fire-starting tools, felt around on the ground for sticks, and proceeded to start a small fire. Once the light illuminated the cavity, she realized had been a dwelling for hominoids, that was abandon. As the flame of the fire grew, she was able to make out a fire circle and then paintings on the walls. She fed the fire and examined the painting and found Jakkar was the main theme in several panels. She watched in awe as the Jakkar came to life as the flames of the fire danced across the walls creating moving shadows across the rockfaces. The images seemed to move and created a flow of beautiful motion. After a long time, as the fire began to fade, Caek laid down and quickly drifted off into a deep asleep.

She awoke the next morning to a loud clap of thunder; the three Jakkar were in the cave with her; they had somehow slipped in while she was sleeping. Caek realized there must have been another entrance to the space. The cats were much too large to have entered the chamber as she did. She arose and shimmied out into the open, but the storm was still violently raging. She found some fruits on the ground nearby and collected enough to give her nourishment for the day. She then collected wood for a fire and slipped back into the fissure. She ate what she could and put herself into a trance-like state focusing her thoughts on the meaning of the signs she received. The three Jakkar watched her calmly.

It was then she started to experience a vision of Noolan, Drot, and an enormous hide of a Jakkar. As the images came into focus, they were standing in a forest of incredibly huge trees. The bed of the forest was thick and soft, piled deep with pine needles and mushrooms. There was silence as she felt time and space moving together. She witnessed men and women working, living, fighting, loving, and worshiping together. She wondered what worship would look like hundreds of thousand years into the future. She knew humankind, whatever it managed to evolve into, would need some form of worship. She envisioned it coming in many different forms. Deities would exist, multiply languages would exist, things would be worshiped. But the most important connection—that of the earth's bounty and balance—would be forgotten. She felt her future essence linking the humanoid to all things would grow weaker and more complex with time. She understood and felt the connection to time and space as she dreamed. She felt connected to the Jakkar and understood her connection. It was her power and, in a sense, her idol of worship. She was at peace.

Caek floated in and out of the self-induced trance. As she did, she started to hum an ancient melodic tune. She slowly swayed to either side, rhythmically moving. After a long while, she stopped and opened her eyes. She stared at the golden embers as the fire slowly burned down. She could feel the presence of her ancestors who used the caves and trees as their homes. She felt the essence of their lives and the many offspring they would bare. She felt drawn to motherhood. She understood she needed offspring to complete her mission on the planet. She knew why she was alive and what her purpose was. She needed to find Noolan. He was strong and he knew of the healing arts. She knew they would take care of each other and their offspring. Her trance lasted three days. When she awoke, she was lying with the Jakkar, nestled in the middle of all three, warm and secure. She arose from the comfort of the cats and headed to the small opening. As she emerged, the sun was beginning to shine through thick fast-moving clouds. The rain was stopping, and the winds were beginning to subside. She watched the three Jakkar emerge from an opening and slowly vanish into the forest.

Caek did not have a good idea of which way to go, and she was hungry. Once she obtained her bearings, she determined which way the sun was moving and walked in that direction. She started to walk and climb over downed branches and trees. A Jakkar sprang out in front of her, stepping directly into her path, surprising her. She froze and the Jakkar growled with a deep low raspy tone, moving closer and then a curious thing happened. One of the other Jakkar appeared and dropped fresh meat at her feet. Looking at it, she realized it was the hind quarter of a young wild boar, neatly cut and removed from the animal with great skill and care. Caek did not quite understand how it happened, but she picked it up. Meanwhile the Jakkar had silently vanished. She efficiently built a fire, stabbed the chunk of meat on a stick and began roasting it. She savored the taste and consumed a large portion. The meat replenished her muscles, mind, and spirit. She soon felt strong and able to resume her search.

She rested infrequently, only enough to catch her breath and eat. She had packed several large slices of the meat before continuing her trek towards the ocean, leaving the rest for the Jakkar and other animals in the forest. As she made her way towards the coast, the area became a mangled mess. Many trees and branches were down making travel difficult. Caek realized the waters had moved inland and the encampment she had left was gone. Sadly, she the chances of finding Noolan were fading. But where would she go from here, she started to wonder. Was she supposed to live with the Jakkar?

As she moved inland, away from the beach devastation, she found that traveling became easier. Later in the evening, she found a worn path heading south and she became keenly aware that others would be using the trail. She needed to be cautious and move silently and unnoticed until she could observe other hominoids she might encounter and evaluate them for friendliness. She was alone in a strange place and the chances of her survival were not extremely favorable.

As she walked silently down the path, a thought occurred to her, and she wondered where the Jakkar was. She felt they were watching her. Why had he given her meat? Where did the meat come from? Was she his mate now because he cared for her survival? Would she ever escape the watchful eyes of the Jakkar? What did this mean? What kind of power enabled a Jakkar to befriend a hominoid or a humanoid to befriend a Jakkar? How could this be possible? Her mind was wandering when she heard the distinct sound of hominoid voices. It brought her back to reality and she immediately went into a high alert knowing how careful she needed to be. She took off to one side of the trail springing quickly into the bushes and concealing herself. She was completely silent and could barely hear muffled sounds. She slowly moved in the direction of the voices, trying to discern who they could be and if they were friendly. She quickly discovered they were moving away from her but traveling the same direction she was. Caek made her way back to the path and started to follow the travelers. She could tell there were four in the group by the tracks. As she got closer, she smelled something familiar on the wind. It was Noolan. She moved swiftly and cautiously down the trail and finally caught up to the travelers. When she spied Noolan, she yelled. He immediately stopped and turned in disbelief. She ran to him excited to see him again. He was in shock, it was Caek, and she was alive! He was elated and erupted in excitement to see her. The others stood and watched in disbelief, excited to be reunited with her. They all embraced her and displayed a kind of unusual affection, an emotion that was new but enjoyable to the species. It was love.

CHAPTER 21

BY THE TWENTY-SECOND DAY OF TRAVEL, KAZAN AND HIS group had developed a defined routine. He was normally the first one to awaken before the sun crested the horizon and would prepare an herbal tea. After stoking the fire and pushing the hot coals into a small pile, he would place a hot rock into a skin cup and heat water. He would then dispense a small amount of dried plant flakes and herbs he collected into the hot water. It was a calming ritual he enjoyed. Soon Cahat and Sinner would awaken. They too found a warm beverage in the cold morning enjoyable. They would sit in silence, except for the crackling of the fire and the echo of birds waking in the dense forest. Smoke from the fire infused their lungs, each particulate of the inhaled charred alder or pine wood becoming imbedded into their being. It was a peaceful smell and triggered memories of family and rituals. They all understood that smoke would always be a token for entry to remembrances and connections with ancient times.

As they stoked the fire, Hook, Huut, and Rit roused. The early morning sun was shining bright in the cloudless eastern sky. The group broke camp quickly and efficiently and started towards the west, foraging as they went.

Later that morning, Kazan caught a faint whiff of the ocean. He could not hear it, though he was excited to sniff the salt air. Soon they would make a turn to the south. He remembered there was a precarious rope bridge to cross. Eons ago, early hominoids figured a way to get vine made ropes across the ravine and tie them off on the other side, thus creating a manageable way to cross the river. When and if the group made it safely across it would be only four days away from the meeting location. Although they recently experienced the great loss of Drot, the grouped was in good spirits. The changes in weather brought some relief.

Kazan told the travelers to expect some unusual things at the gathering. Some of the hominoids traveled a full year to get to the jamboree. There would be different foods, and tools, and ideas. Master tool makers would be teaching others and would trade blades and scrappers. Sometimes one of the craftsmen would have long elegant spear points. There would also be games of skill and strength for the younger crowd and the elders would gather and talk of ancient times and medicinal herbs. Kazan then remembered the golden disk in his amulet. He wanted to share an idea he had been thinking about with the elders when they arrived at the gathering.

They came to the bridge the about noon. Kazan was surprised to see how worn it was, but still appeared functional. The roar of the river below was deafening with tumultuous rapids gargling and frothing wildly. Occasionally the group could hear a bolder rumbling down the rapids bumping along frenetically. Kazan explained the trouble he had crossing when he was young. The bridge was a series of three ropes strung across the ravine. The idea was to hold onto the two ropes at the top and walk carefully along on the bottom rope. Because of the distended large toe on developing hominoids, grabbing the rope was easily done as was balancing. Kazan went first and the others followed cautiously.

A short while after crossing, Sinner and Huut spoke saying they negotiated many large rivers on their journey and could help in the construction of a raft. They had knowledge building options with logs and use long poles to navigate the crossings.

As they walked through the forest, Kazan started to get a sensation of being watched. He alerted the group to keep an eye open for threats, both from animals and other potentially unfriendly hominoids. Rit and Huut felt the tingling sensation of being watched also. Soon, they were all on high alert, carefully watching as they quietly walk down the trail. Something or someone was tracking them. They talked in hushed voices among themselves, wondering what to do. They agreed that if whatever or whomever was going to attack, it would have done so. They quickened their pace as fast as Kazan could manage. He was having difficulty with the walk-run everyone else was achieving and his lame foot started to ache and throb. He had always been slow but would always eventually catchup. He started to lag further behind and was soon out of sight of the others. Rit noticed first and stopped so he could catch up, then Cahat stopped. Both the young men took up a protective posture as Kazan hobbled towards them. As the young men came into sight he turned around and froze. Rit spotted the Jakkar and instinctively raised his spear in self-defense.

The Jakkar's eyes were locked on Rit's eyes. They both intensely stared at each other. By this time Cahat saw the Jakkar and ran towards Kazan to provide what protection he could. The rest of the band was a good way up the trail and did not know what was happening. Rit could see what looked like glowing red embers in the center of the Jakkar's eyes. Rit launched his spear with swiftness and hit the Jakkar in its side just behind the front leg as the Jakkar moved to try to avoid the attack. Although the spear penetrated the fur, it only went in six inches. Not even close to enough to kill a Jakkar. But it was enough to anger the tiger, all nine hundred pounds of killing machine. Kazan had his knife out and Cahat was preparing to throw his spear. The Jakkar started towards Rit and stopped in preparation to leap in an attack killing lunge. Instead of throwing the spear, Cahat charged forward and with all his might, just as the Jakkar was leaping into the air towards Rit, he plunged the spear deep into the chest of the beast. The creature released a death-defying roar of agony and tumbled to the ground forcing the spear deeper into its chest. With its last instinct to kill, the tiger reached out and clawed Rit deeply wounding his leg with three deep bloody gashes.

The three stood looking at each other out of breath, the adrenaline rushing through their bodies. A few seconds later Hook, Huut, and Sinner showed up. They stood in silence, Rit laying on the ground applying pressure to the wound. After a few more minutes, Huut asked what they wanted to do with it. Kazan spoke up saying he was not sure why this Jakkar was given to them but felt compelled to use everything the tiger could offer. It was the first time he ever knew of a Jakkar being killed by hominoids. From his perspective it would be a curse to not use everything and that which was waste would be buried in ceremony.

He went on to say that by eating and sharing the tiger, they would share its wisdom and strength. The first thing they did was to remove the internal organs by cutting the skin away from the neck to the groin, opening the chest cavity. The heart, liver, lungs, stomach, esophagus, and intestines would be removed and evaluated for use. Kazan would keep the eyes, tongue, and brain to eat during later ceremonies. He felt the eyes of the tiger would bring him greater vision to see the future. Each of the other items would be prepared by cutting them into thin slices and dried. They worked efficiently with scrapers and obsidian blade knives. The cape was magnificent, it's length was enormous from the nose to the tip of the tail. In its fresh state, it weighed more than three hundred pounds. They surgically removed all meat and slowly worked it with flint scrapers. Over the next three days, Kazan would travel to the ocean and retrieve salt water and instinctively used it to salt the meat. Kazan knew the group would not be able to carry all that had been provided. The wisdom of the ancient people told them to always leave something behind for the Jakkar. Not in this case. Kazan knew institutively nothing of the Jakkar would be left behind, except the blood that soaked into the ground.

As a group, they decided to leave loads packed ready to be transported to the gathering site. They would tell the other hominoids what had happened and request help in hopes they would share in the gifts of the Jakkar. As they left the site, Kazan looked back and paused. He thought about what he had heard as a child, "Being killed by a Jakkar was not much of a contest but being able to kill one is different. The tiger must want to die. The tiger will do what the tiger must do."

By this time, Rit's wound was beginning to heal. It had small signs of infection, and it was tender. He was limping and occasionally winched in pain because the claws penetrated deep into his thigh muscles. It slowed the progress of the group. He asked Kazan for one of the claws and strung it on a light cord, and then put it around his neck. Cahat did the same as a small trophy of the kill. On the afternoon of the seventh day, they arrived at the gathering.

Kazan was surprised at the number of humanoids attending. Camps were littered all over the place. He wondered where all the people had come from. The group found an open area near the edge of a twenty-foot cliff. At the bottom of the cliff was a small stream. Kazan instructed the group to pitch camp and he would go find some help to retrieve the remaining parts of the Jakkar. As he walked, he looked for camps with strong and able men. A short distance away, he came up to a group sitting around a fire. He gave the universal sign of peace, two open hands pointed downwards, and stood in silence waiting for a response. The group stood up in unison and all of them responded in the same way, presenting two open hands, and then smiling. Kazan started to speak but there was an obvious communications barrier. They appeared to be of Denisovan- Eastern Neanderthal origins, a newer looking species. They looked strong and capable. One of the older men of the group stepped forward, and with some additional hand gestures, said his name was Huki. Kazan emulated the gestures and said, "Kazan."

There was always a short drawing stick within reach and Kazan picked it up and drew a crude Jakkar in the soft dirt. He then drew a spear in its chest and showed the group the claw on the string around his neck. The claw still had a red stain of blood on it and some of the cuticle was still stuck to the keratin claw. Huki could sense what he was saying but did not believe it. He had never heard of anyone killing a Jakkar. He kept shaking his head in disbelief. Through a series of drawings and gestures, Kazan got his point across and Huki selected six young hominoid men to prepare to help. Later that evening they met at Kazan's campfire. Cahat and Rit told the story of the kill with animated acting and loud clicking and guttural sounds. The group was in awe as they shared some of the meat ceremoniously.

As Cahat and Rit danced about the fire, Kazan thought deeply about their trip. He thought about his friend Drot and the small golden wheeled object he inherited. He pulled it from his leather pouch looking curiously at it. Then he put a small stick through the hole. He grabbed both ends of the stick pinching it between his fingers and rolled the wheel on his thigh. Sinner was watching him curiously. Kazan had an idea, but he had to think it through. He noticed Sinner's interest and asked what she was thinking. She pensively grabbed two more small sticks, tied them to the one going through the center, and then rolled it around in the dirt using the two handles. Kazan then placed a few other sticks across the handles and put a rock on the platform. Using the handles, they looked at each other with an excited sparking glance that said, "This could work!"

The others sitting around the fire stopped and focused on Kazan and Sinner and their invention. It was the first wheelbarrow in the history of humanity. It would reduce work, but it would have to be built to scale. The wheel would be fashioned out of wood, rather than stone because of the weight. With potential supplies scattered all around them, they had a prototype by nightfall. Kazan was remembering Drot and wondering if he knew what the small wheel meant, and he smiled to himself. It was getting late, and the group was starting to dwindle. Huki motioned to Kazan and gestured they would be ready to travel in the morning to help retrieve the Jakkar. The crowd of visitors soon started to head out to their respective camp areas to sleep.

Before the sun was up, Kazan, Sinner, Cahat and Huut were well down the trail. Rit was staying behind; his wound was still healing, and he needed to rest. A groggy band of seven volunteers straggled behind inquisitively pushing a crude wheelbarrow-like device. The trip was uneventful except for the occasional modification to the unwieldly thing. They would stop and retie the wheel in place and adjust the test loads. But the idea was sticking. After four days of trial and error, they had a functioning wheelbarrow and took turns riding on the contraption and being pushed down the trail.

Sinner was sneaky and she liked to laugh, enjoying the relatively new emotion. She would take a long, narrowly small stick and tickle Kazan or Huut and whoever was in front of her behind their ears. Everyone enjoyed a good laugh as Kazan never caught on and would swat the stick as though it was a fly. Kazan must have though he smelled bad having so many flies to swat. At the next stream crossing, he jumped in to wash off. The swim felt good on his tired bones. He then rolled in the dirt to freshen his scent. Sinner began refined humor and playing jokes as the band of travelers made their way down the trail. The travelers looked at her confused when they did not understand the intention of what she was doing. With a snort and the curled lips, she would open her mouth and let out throaty gurgling sound. The others followed suit, not sure of what it meant, but feeling good with the gestures and sounds. Soon, a whimsical gurgling band of travelers echoed through the forest.

CHAPTER 22

CAEK WAS ELATED TO FIND NOOLAN AS WELL. SHE QUICKLY acknowledged Ovla, Hetra, and Vena and asked what had happened to Kuni. Vena explained that Kuni had been injured and was not able to continue and that he was left behind. Caek understood and felt empathy for Vena realizing she now had no mate. Noolan quickly realized there was something different about Caek. She was much thinner than before, and she did not talk as much. She had a faraway look in her eyes and her hair was not in the tight braid she typically kept. Noolan explained the others were walking to the south to a gathering of hominoids and explained it would be a good way to hear from other travelers and what they were experiencing. He also explained it might be a chance to find her original clan and meet up with her father, Drot. Caek was a bit indifferent. It was as though she did not remember some things and Noolan felt confused and awkward when trying to relate to Caek. Caek went on to describe what she had been through after she had eaten the mushrooms. When she got to the part about sleeping with the Jakkar, she stopped. Her heart was beating fast. She looked around spying each leaf of vegetation, feeling the aura of the Jakkar. She stopped and closed her eyes and with her mind searching for the Jakkar realizing they were gone.

Caek then started to feel isolated, and a cold shiver embraced her body. She began to shake violently for several minutes. When she regained her composure, all were watching her with curiosity and fear. She thought about the Jakkar and why they mysteriously cared for her. For two weeks, she lived with them. It was sinking in with Noolan and the others that what Caek had been through was extraordinary. There was no explanation for what happened, and no one ever heard of this type of encounter before. As the group gathered their belongings, Caek passionately embraced Noolan, being grateful for the unexpected reunion. It was the feeling of caring for another.

After a short period of time, they moved down the trail in silence. Ovla lagged a bit back and started to speak with Caek in a hushed voice so the others would not hear. She asked Caek what the mushrooms had done to her and if she was okay. Caek said she was feeling good but could not explain the effects completely. The experience made her feel connected to the trees and sky and clouds and part of the tumultuous storm that had come through. The experience made her connect with the Jakkar in some ways. She described a vision of a web of fibrous materials growing everywhere and on everything. Ovla found this comment fascinating and asked if she had a supply of them because she wanted to try some. Caek did not but she knew where to find more. She told her they would find more when they stopped for the night. But she cautioned Ovla, too many might prove to be dangerous.

After several hours hiking down the trail, the group came to a large flowing river. Caek and Noolan told the others about the experience with the log and how they almost died getting swept over a waterfall. They decided to go inland and seek a safer crossing other than where the river emptied into the ocean. Within a mile they came across a colossal log jam. Trees of all sizes were being stopped by sand bars that had shifted in the recent hurricane. and the logs were being caught up in shallow sand bars of the river. It created a natural blockage. There were huge redwood and sequoia trees with branches reaching out like hungry hands of a child. It looked as though the natural dam stretched across the entire width of the river. After some discussions they decided to attempt a crossing, Noolan went first as he carefully walked on the stuck trunks of the aged trees, jumping, and leaping to make progress. As he reached the top of the jam, he was able to scan the surface of the river as it stretched out for miles in every direction. The current was swift as if flowed through an opening in the logjam and could have easily carry someone away if they missed a step. Caek came up behind him and slipped, catching herself before getting completely soaked. She quickly recovered her balance. Vena, Ovla, and Hetra followed a good distance behind looking for hand grabs and good foot holds. As Noolan kept moving, he could feel some weakness along the tangled mess of jammed logs and trees. Some of the older and rotting wood debris would creak and snap off, breaking as he reached and climbed along. He became more cautious and moved slowly and pensively as he inched along.

A little past the middle of the logjam, he spotted something bobbing in the water. It looked like a dead animal stuck in the jam. As he got closer, he thought it could possibly be a bundle of skins caught up in the debris. He climbed down to a small protruding log, reached down, and grabbed the bundle. He strained to retrieve it. It appeared to be a backpack, presumably from someone that did not make it across. It apparently floated down the river to the present location and became snagged in the downed trees. He could not tell how long the bundle had been in the water, but it was still tied tightly with a leather strap.

He pulled the bundle of skins up; it was completely soaked and felt extraordinarily heavy. As he inspected it, he quickly realized it was his bundle, the one he lost as he and Caek went over the waterfalls several weeks before. Still packing his current bundle of goods, he pulled in his old bundle up, climbed to a larger more secure perch and looked at it closely. Caek immediately understood why Noolan was smiling. He had some things inside he thought he would never see again. It contained a few intricate antler art carvings he was hoping to give to Caek when they were finished. Vena curiously witnessed the retrieval and wondered where the fur lined pack came from.

Noolan started moving across the jam again towards the far shore. Just as he was getting close and could see the shore area, the log jam started to rock back and forth with the river under-current. Within a few seconds he heard loud cracking and snapping. The tree he was on was a huge old growth cedar tree, and it started giving way. Caek quickly jumped to the large tree and move towards him grabbing his arms and huddling next to him. He sat down to maintain his balance. Caek did the same. Within a few more seconds, the log started to creak, and more of the large branches were snapping and cracking. Unexpectedly, it started moving away from the rest of the jammed trees and logs and turned into the now-surging river, pointing downstream. Vena, Ovla, and Hetra watched as their new friends started moving quickly towards the ocean in a developing torrent of water. The entire logjam burst and within a few minutes Noolan and Caek were floating in a strong current too far away to hear any yelling. Ovla, Hetra, and Vena started to panic and began the arduous scramble back, making it to shallow waters near the shore when everything gave way and they fell into the river. They struggled in the current and were able to find footing enough to wade back to the shore. Then several other spots in the wooden dam began to creak and branches snapped. The entire logjam started breaking apart began floating down river piece by piece.

Caek and Noolan held fast to the massive tree as it started to move swiftly into deeper waters. The tidal action met violently with the torrent of river surge and began tossing the logs and debris in erratic patterns pushing further into open ocean with the outgoing tide. The tree was much too massive to try and paddle it back to shore. It kept bobbing along and the shoreline kept getting further and further away. When Noolan stood up, he could no longer see the log jam or the mouth of the river. A widespread river filled with logs, branches, and sticks churned around them. Once they reached the open ocean, longshore currents kept pulling the tree and other debris south at a steady pace.

Several hours later Caek was standing on the tree holding tightly to a thick branch scanning the horizon. She was startled by an enormous spray of salt water from behind her. A Baleen whale surfaced next to the tree and rolled slightly eyeing the trapped passengers. Caek and Noolan marveled at the huge mammal having never seen a whale. It slowly drifted off, rolled to one side, and dove out of sight. A short time later, the whale breached the waters causing the log to bounce violently and then massive beast disappeared into the ocean depths.

Several more hours passed and the two were becoming concerned about their future. Noolan was getting more and more thirsty and drank sparingly from a water reservoir made from a wild boar's stomach he had carried. It held about two liters. He instinctively knew not to drink the salt water. Caek tasted the saltwater but was averse to the overwhelming solution and spit out the harshly flavored liquid violently. Noolan proffered Caek the bladder and she also sipped small amounts of water. They occasionally made out a far shoreline, a thin line of cliffs on the horizon formed a discernable black line. They both realized it was too far to try and swim.

As the evening approached, Noolan told Caek to tie herself to one of the branches. He did the same thing, feeling it would be for the best, in case they slipped off during the night or the tree drifted into rough waters. Noolan opened his pack up and found three packages of dried meat and handed one to Caek. She ate sparingly. They could hear the waves pounding far off on the shore and the constant winds. A few scattered clouds dance around the moon as the sky turned almost blood red with the setting sun. Noolan wondered how they would make it out of this.

Caek was quiet as she rocked back and forth along with the churning waves. She started to reflect on her life and her family and two sisters. She could feel them and knew they were still alive. She ached to see them. In the back of her thoughts, she felt she would see them again. Deep in her thoughts, as hunger and thirst rippled through her body, the connection with her sisters became vibrant and strong. As the darkness grew around them, the stars started poking holes in the black velvet background by the millions. She thought about what must have come before her and the rest of humanity far into the future. She wondered how long the stars could exist and where they go during day light. As she watched the clear star-filled skies, a meteor shot across her field of vision. She watched its bright green tail arc majestically across the heavens, wondering about its origins. She questioned what stories were being told by the stars and the earth. Where were they headed on their arc in the skies?

The temperature started to drop as it got darker. In the darkest hours of the night, the moon started to set on the crest of the western horizon. The last minuscule tip shining a captivatingly bright beacon caught her eyes. Moving ever so slowly, the slight brightness of a thin sliver of moonlight disappeared, and the two drifted into a light sleep rocking with the ocean rhythms lapping at the sides of their crude seagoing vessel.

Early the next morning, Noolan half-slumbered, drifted along in his thoughts. It was becoming light, and he kept his arm braced tightly around a branch, balancing himself while the tree bounced and bobbed with the waves. The hours dragged on. Around mid-day Noolan stood up again, looking for the shoreline or a mountain to indicate which way the log was moving. He recalled the last night; the shore was far off to the left of the log. He could not hear any crashing waves or see any sign of the shore. They were adrift, lost in the ocean with no idea how far they drifted or needed to travel to get to land. Both were starting to experience dehydration and stopped drinking water with the thought of saving it for later. They knew that trying to drink the saltwater was not going to do them any good.

The sun was starting to make its brutally slow climb into the skies, and as it did, the temperature began to rise. It was not long before their skin began turning red through their thick-haired arms, legs, back, chests, and face. A patterned cracking of their lips and cheeks continued as they floated aimlessly in the abyss. They drank water from the skin canteen sparingly and by the third day the water was gone. The meager rations of meat from Noolan's pack were also eaten. Their skin continued cracking and blistering in the searing sun. The burning was intensified by the reflection of sunlight off the clear blue saltwater. Skin lesions grew into open cracking sores lined with burning saltwater spray. The occasional curious dolphin swam by eyeing the stranded couple, startling them back into a dazed understanding of their surroundings.

On the fifth day Noolan spotted a smaller log floating near them. With his length of leather cord, he kept around his chest, he lassoed a large protruding branch and strained to pulled it alongside the tree. Out of desperation, he explained to Caek that maneuvering a smaller log may give them the opportunity to paddle in the direction of where he thought land was. There was no way they were going to be able to maneuver the large tree they were on. Caek agreed and quickly climbed aboard the log. Noolan strained to steady the small, waterlogged log. She was able to strap one pack to the bow, another in the center, and the last on the aft of the log. Caek climbed on the front half and steadied the skiff while Noolan sat on the back with his legs dragging in the water. He cast off the large tree and started paddling with a branch be managed to break off. Caek joined in paddling with her hands but quickly picked up a floating branch. Soon they were making way in the direction of where they hoped the shore was. After several hours, Caek was exhausted and Noolan was completely drained and spent. Noolan stopped to rest and then Caek stopped. They both drank saltwater in desperation knowing it would not help. They had nothing else. As they lay back to rest, something bumped the log from behind.

Noolan glanced back and a large black fin was protruding from the water coming up from behind. Again, it nudged the log, not in an aggressive way but more out of curiosity. Noolan stood up, getting his legs out of the water. Caek did the same and when she did, Noolan fell into the water, splashing and struggling to climb back on. As he struggled, Caek slipped but stayed straddled on the log. Noolan crawled back onto the log just as the shark grazed his leg with its jaw open. Breathing heavily, completely spent, they stood to get a better view of the intruder and Noolan readied his spear. As he stood and turned, he saw the coastline. Excitedly, he relayed to Caek that it was not too far off. She resumed paddling as Noolan watched the shark, spear poised to strike. Within a few minutes it swam off and Noolan joined Caek, frantically paddling.

They soon heard the slight roar of breaking of waves growing louder and smelled the spray of the spray of saltwater that lingered in the air. Noolan told Caek to untie the pack up front and hold on to the line. If she fell off the log, he told her to grab the pack and use it as a floatation device and ride it on to the shore. Noolan did the same for the two other packs, lacing the leader lines together. The log started to roll and pitch as the waves started to break closer to them. Sure enough, as the log became caught in the ten-foot surf, Caek and Noolan fell off getting swamped in the curl of the waves. Caek vanished under the water for a few seconds and came up coughing, pulling herself up on the pack. Noolan lost sight of her as he was engulfed in another breaking wave. He was quickly tossed from the log and strained to pull himself up to the two packs. He was again tossed back into the froth of a crashing wave swallowing mouthfuls of salt water as he tried to regain his balance. This time his foot felt the sandy bottom. Pulling the attached cords as hard as he could, he grabbed onto the packs tightly and rode them onto the beach, pushing with his feet. Caek was on the beach a short distance away, walking towards him dragging the pack behind her.

They trudged onto the beach, thankful to be on land. Severely dehydrated, and on the verge of starvation, they collapsed amid the driftwood and sand. Noolan surveyed the area. It appeared to be a cove surrounded by extremely high cliffs on all sides. There was a small water fall spilling to the floor of the cove a short distance away. Caek noticed it right away as well. They started running toward the falls and leapt into the shallow plunge pool at its base. Immersed in fresh water, they frantically drank, feeling life coursing back into their flesh. Their exposed skin was burnt, and the cool water was painful against the open blistered flesh. Both had cracked and toasted sunburnt lips and it was difficult to drink. Their throats were swollen and parched, making the act of swallowing painful. As their elation started to subside, Caek felt weak from starvation. She carefully investigated the vegetation around the waterfall and found a small patch of edible redwood sorrel. There were several varieties of fungi growing around the falls, primarily chanterelle mushrooms bigger than her two hands spread out. She grabbed several and handed one to Noolan. He devoured the offerings. Fish were trapped the pool darting away from the intruders. As the sun set over the horizon, Noolan caught two trout and built a raging fire of driftwood. He gutted and skewered the two fish on sticks and before long they were savoring the crisp but juicy flakes of protein. The blisters and lesions all over their bodies made it difficult to get comfortable, but as they huddled together exhaustion took over and drifted off to sleep.

The fire was coals and ash by daybreak. Noolan was up surveying their surroundings. The cliffs rose dramatically, and it appeared that the ends of the cove they were in was encircled columnar basalt towers reaching far out to sea. He could see waves crashing against the rocks far out to the horizon. Still exhausted and in pain, they decided to stay for a few days until they regained strength. The fresh water and fish, along with the abundance of fungi and other edible vegetation was nourishing and comforting. For the next few days, they considered their options. Going back out to sea was too dangerous. It seemed the only way out of the cove was going to be climbing the surrounding steep cliffs. By mid-morning of the sixth day, they repacked their important belongings into two tight backpacks. They left items behind, taking only what they felt they could carry comfortably as they eyed the climb. Slowly and cautiously, Noolan began to scale the wave beaten basalt walls with Caek tethered close by. Handholds were difficult to find, but gradually they made progress.

By late afternoon they neared the mid-point of the climb, Noolan reached a shelf with a huge mound of bird droppings. As he pulled himself up, he met two brown pelican chicks eye to eye. The birds looked closely at him, not showing any fear. The birds moved back from the face of the cliff edge, cackling a raucous alarm. Standing up he looked further into the shelf. The area was littered with bird droppings, bone fragments, and nesting building materials, including sticks and feathers as well as carcasses of long dead fish. The cave appeared to go deep into the wall. Caek soon joined him and rested while the birds cackled angerly at the intruders.

Noolan piled up some of the bird nesting materials and made a torch, easily lit it, and peered deep into the cavern. Someone had been there before, but not recently. There was a well-used fire ring and wood piled against the side of the cave. Several knapped flakes littered the floor. He looked at the walls and found they were adorned with magnificent images of large birds in flight, and fish. There were also hominoid stick figures, both in groups and single images holding spears, standing on crude looking canoe-type boats. Caek looked asked if he understood what the images symbolized. It appeared that whoever made the paintings must have wanted to convey what was going on at the time. He said they must have been hunters or fishers. Caek asked how old the drawings might had been. Noolan could not answer. He lived in the present and could not grasp time well. The thought sparked a memory of Kazan talking to him about the concept of time. Noolan struggled with the notion of before and after, only living in the now, but he hoped to understand it someday.

That evening, a bright light appeared in the northern sky. Caek and Noolan stopped what they were doing because everything went eerily silent. The birds froze, still as statues. A slight roar started to develop in the background and the two stood up expressing confusion. They watched the bright light grow and the roar get louder. The object crossed the sky near the cave. As it got closer, the ocean started to agitate violently, and the cave started to shake. As they stood at the opening, the heat caused Caek to wince and cower towards the wall of the cave. She covered her eyes, while Noolan stood fast absorbing the radiation given off by the meteor. Little did they know, the heat they felt was radiation, causing small mutations deep in their cells and genetic coding, changing the hominoid trajectory forever.

As soon as the object disappeared over the horizon, an injured connection in Noolan's brain was re-established and he began to recall images of Kazan, his father Abern, and his brothers Rit and Hook. He started to remember his past with vibrant clarity. He remembered being on Jewit peak and falling into a Jakkar den, most likely the one he was looking for, and then traveling for miles in the tunnels under the volcano. His mind reeled with vibrant memories. He began to recall who he was.

Caek watched him as he sat down in a daze trying to understand what happened. He started to mumble to himself, puzzled at some of the things he could not place. He became confused and started to talk in mysterious phrases about encounters while hunting with two others. Noolan was remembering his brothers Hook and Rit and focused on an intuitive connection the triplets had. In a flash of his mind, he saw them among tall redwood trees, among a group of strangers. He knew they were alive. They were carrying a massively beautiful Jakkar skin and a spontaneous connection between the brothers was made. He tried to remember where his home was but could not recall landmarks that made any sense.

He snapped out of his trance-like state and looked at Caek. He said he clearly remembered his two brothers. He told her he was one of three triplets. Caek was astonished to hear this and she looked him in the eyes and said, she was also one in a set of triplets. They stared deep into each other's bright green eyes in stunned silence for a few minutes. What strange power could be responsible for the sudden return of Noolan memory and their meeting? Caek was sure something affected his mind. In a confused state, she searched for some reason for why they had been brought together, and where their path would lead. She knew they were there for a purpose. Though she did not clearly understand what that purpose was, she had an idea.

CHAPTER 23

KAZAN AND THE BAND OF TRAVELERS REACHED THE RE-
mains of the Jakkar by late afternoon of the fourth day. All
the packaged goods were as they had left them. They made
camp, and a hushed murmur rattled about the group, some asking if
they would be at odds with the Jakkar since one was killed. They talked
and speculated that a curse or bad fortune would follow them since a
known trait of the Jakkar was vengeance. Kazan responded that he did
not really know. He went on to say that the Jakkar attack was unique.
It was as though the beast threw himself on Cahat's spear as an offer-
ing of some kind. The group did not plan to kill the beast. They were
not hunting. He said it was in the defense of their lives and the Jakkar
knew it. There was plenty of food for the Jakkar and travelers. There
always had been, throughout the eons of time. Why it focused on this
ragged band of explorers was a mystery. Kazan may have appeared to be

an easy meal, because he lagged as the oldest of the group. He could not run with his gimpy leg and arthritic joints. The Jakkar could have easily killed him and dragged him off without much effort many times. The group became nervous as darkness fell across the forest. There was always more Jakkar in the forest and mountains.

As they shuffled around to find sleeping areas for the night, several men built the fire up to keep predators away. The forest became eerily quiet that night, other than the crackling of the fire and soft snoring. As the night wore on, the members of the group took shifts to keep the fire going. As the fire popped, sending golden embers skyward, the group got needed rest. Those who stayed vigilant during their shift reported feeling as though something was watching the group from a distance. Nothing stirred until the early morning light crested the eastern horizon when each of the travelers quietly awoke.

The sky was ablaze with orange and red clouds as the group awakened and started to pack up the remains of the Jakkar. They tied the hide and head to wheelbarrow type contraption with leather straps holding them in place. The others loaded the pieces and parts into their packs. By noon they were ready to begin the trek back to the gathering place. As they started back, the wheelbarrow became less controllable because of the weight of the pelt and head. Kazan suggested they try pulling the load instead of pushing. He explained that, if necessary, they could help manage the load with one person pulling and two pushing. The idea was easily implemented and seemed to work well. They made good time and by nightfall they came to the bank of a small stream. The group was in good spirits as they set up a camp for the night. Several of the group went to the stream to drink, wash, and then fished with thinly woven hemp line and hooks carved out of bone. For bait, they caught several crickets hiding in the underbrush. This was an easy and practiced routine, a skill mastered long ago. The group feasted on fresh fish, root vegetables, assorted fruits and mushrooms easily collected in and around the camp.

By the time darkness covered the lands, most were bedded down and sleeping peacefully. By drawing straws of different lengths, they decided who would stay awake and keep the fire going. The shortest straw was always the one required to be up in the middle of the night. Kazan always stayed up late sitting around the fire. He told stories of other gatherings and spoke about coming to this area two other times during his life. The first with his parents and grandparents when he was young. His grandparents did not make it back to their home that trip. They both died in separate bear attacks. The last time he attended was more than fifteen seasons ago. Kazan started to recall several of the hominoids he met from other trips. He knew many strong medicines from faraway places and were traded. He spoke excitedly about the random events and celebrations that were held. He knew his group would be revered because of the gift of the Jakkar. No one had ever brought such a powerful gift to share.

The routine for the travelers would be repeated for the next three days. By the end of the fourth day, they arrived back at the gathering amid great redwood trees. The news spread quickly and that night there would be a great celebration.

As evening approached, a lone drummer initiated the call for hominoids to gather in a large meadow. Soon another drummer from a different clan came and joined in and then another. The deep rhythmic sound resonated for miles amid the huge redwood trees with plush deep green ferns growing at their base. A great fire was started. All forms of hominoids, some tall with large barrel-chested bodies like the homo habilis, some short with thin bodies and long arms like the homo africanus, some in-between with disproportionate bodies like the homo robustus, and several others of mixed linage gathered. Although they shared several traits the most visible was that they all walked upright.

Along one side of the meadow was a long hollow with numerous pools carved into a thickly vegetated hillside. Sacred hot water spewed from the earth and formed hot pools that drained from one to the other. Some were soaking in the pools. The moon was beginning to set over the ocean and Kazan found himself drawn to the sulfur aroma of the steaming pools. He walked to the sacred hot waters knowing his aching bones needed their healing. It was one of the most pleasurable experiences he recalled from his past visits. While he was soaking, along with others, he heard talk about places they were from. Some of the Homo habilis talked about huge sand deserts that could consume entire tribes in storms of sand. This was where food was always scarce and water even scarcer. Most avoided the sands, but traveling around the great desert would add a year to one's journey. Kazan had heard rumors of such places and imagined them in his dreams.

As the drumming grew louder into the evening many of the hominoids danced around the massive fire. Their arms flailing about as they hopped foot-to-foot, smiling. The rhythms of the drums stirred powerful and haunting emotions. A palpable primitive sensation grew in the crowd. A bond was starting to grow. After long periods of dancing, some of the hominoids sat down to tell stories of hunts, others told stories about the lands they traveled. Through a series of hand motions, facial expressions, and voice intonations, they managed to make each other smile and then laugh. It was magical to see the attempts and creative effort the gathering caused. The hominoids shared foods and drinks and the shamans gathered. They spoke in hushed voices about powerful hallucinogenic plants, fungi, and animal secretions. Kazan understood many of the compounds, but only a few caught his attention. As the evening grew dark, he looked into the night skies and noticed a light that seemed to get brighter. When he pointed at the phenomena, they all stood and watched. They watched the arching light curiosity. Then the forest went mysteriously and completely silent. The light kept getting brighter and closer. They could see what looked like a green fire streaming off the back as it arced across the skies lighting up the forest and bringing daylight to the darkness. The heat generated caused some of the tops of trees to catch fire. Some of the hominoids shielded their eyes as a wave of intense heat radiation engulfed the region. Kazan felt the heat permeate his body and sensed that something deep inside had changed.

The object traveled at a fast pace and quickly disappeared over the forest. The massive fireball looked like it bounced off the horizon and shot back into the skies. A deafening roar started to engulf the forest as birds squawked erratically and flew out of hiding places throughout the forest canopy. When the uproar began to subside, a slight mummer began among the gathering. Several commented they felt dizzy and disoriented. Kazan knew something unusual had just happened. He watched the people at the gathering. They began to sit down and talk quietly amongst themselves. At that moment, Kazan knew and understood that all hominoids were the species that would rule the world. They were no longer just hominoids, they were people. People with consciousness and purpose.

Ohana was a new term Kazan learned from Huki, his new friend. A term meaning family. Kazan started to think about the words and sounds he was hearing. How could they record their lives and rituals for future generation? He pondered this in silence. Why would we want to record our lives? When he thought deeply about it, he wondered how it could be done, and with that thought, he scripted a straight line in the dirt, put a hook on one end, and made a sound. It was a simple opening of his mouth and he said, "AAH." He then told everyone that whenever they see this mark, it would sound like "AAH". And then he told them that every time they hear the sound, it could always be scripted like the mark in the dirt.

The hominoids soaking in the pool were curious. "What about other sounds? Could symbols for those be created?" one asked. Kazan said yes and went on to say it could be done but someone would have to write the collections of symbols and teach others how to use them. He went silent and wondered about the idea as the drumming continued late into the evening.

As he returned to camp that night the thought kept running through his mind. The rest of his crew were busy scavenging for firewood and setting snares a short distance away. The meat from the tiger was shared by all and much was distributed. Groups setup shelters and made note of places to dump waste and relieve themselves. Water was a short hike away and several camps were within ear shot.

Kazan found the tiger skin, dragged it to the fire and started to clean it with his knife. The blade cut the scraps of meat, skin, and fat off efficiently and smoothly. Over the course of the next four days, he would work the hide, scraping and cleaning. He knew he could not chew one so large to soften it. The common practice was to chew on smaller pelts to make them soft. To make the Jakkar hide supple his teeth would be ground down to nothing but nubs. He decided to keep it moist and work each section as best he could by hand. Cahat, Sinner, Huut, Rit and Vena joined in. At one point Sinner asked about the head. Kazan told them to skin it as best they could, keeping the hair on. Kazan already had saved the eyes. He was planning to consume them is a short ceremony to help himself see with more clarity. He told Sinner he wanted the gray mass in the head. He would use it to keep the hide moist. Once she gave it to him, he carefully mushed it up and worked it into the hide. They stretched it out between two redwood trees, and with flat stones, the group continued to massage the brain mass into the hide, working it deeply into the skin. Kazan had decided to keep the hide and record this journey as a history of the people. He would transport the hide back to his home valley and find a place to store and preserve it.

Over the next number of days, the group engaged in new activities and established new relationships. There were numerous games of strength and games of chance. Vena lost his prize obsidian knife on a bet over which way a rock would roll off a smooth log, left or right. The wheelbarrow was a topic of many discussions and a curiosity for many. A wheel would simply help reduce the amount of work needed to do certain tasks and make transport easier. Kazan was way ahead with the concept and in his mind, he saw many applications for the device. In the evenings, around the campfire, he would work with the Jakkar hide for a while and then draw designs and lines and animals in the soft dirt and ash on the forest floor. Others also engaged in camp floor artwork and by late night the woodland floor would be decorated with wonderfully glorious designs and patterns, only to fade and get trampled by the next evening.

One evening, while the group was gathering, Kazan had an idea he decided to share. He started with the simple mark for the sound "Aah" and began building a structure to communicate sounds, but in writing. He explained to Rit and Cahat what he was doing and asked them if they understood. They indicated they sort of knew but needed time to think about it. It was confusing. Kazan asked Sinner and Huut if they understood. They looked at each other and said yes. It was easy to follow. They understood the concept and started to ask about other symbols for sounds.

As the evening discussions progressed Kazan, made mental notes. As word spread, spontaneous gatherings started to occur in and around the evening fires. Kazan soon found himself espousing opinions on various topics. He was often questioned by others and responded as honestly as he could. Others had concepts about the stars and certain food types, and trails that lead to wonderous places. The entire concept of having evening and then morning discussions was being developed, pursued, and enjoyed. His alphabet grew to nineteen distinct marks in various orientations, indicated concepts of action, time, and emotion. A common language was being written down for the first time in the history of people's existence.

This place was unique. It had become a refuge of thought and healing in a physical and spiritual sense. On several occasions, hallucinogenic fungi, plants, and animal parts were offered. On occasion Kazan would indulge in the offerings. Afterwards, he needed to find quiet places and reflect about the environment and the discussions. Kazan felt extraordinary; it was an opportunity to imagine and create new perspectives. But in the back of his mind, he knew it would be time to begin the journey home sooner than he wanted. He made a promise to his clan that he would return. He realized there were important tasks to accomplish. He explained this to the people at the gathering, telling them that he would be leaving. He asked them to think deeply about what happened and what was said. He had become even more aware of the world and environment and wanted to find ways to make it better. Above all, he felt he needed be kind to others.

On the morning of departure, Kazan, Cahat, Sinner, Huut, and Rit bid farewell to their friends and started the long treacherous journey back to their valley. Kazan was on a mission to somehow record a story and invent a way to preserve it.

CHAPTER 24

A STORM WAS BREWING FAR OUT ON THE HORIZON AS CAEK watched from the lip of the cliffside cave they took shelter in. Noolan was asleep and the young pelicans were no longer interested in the intruders. They were getting hungry, and the mother pelican was tolerating the visitors frequently bringing ocean perch and regurgitating the chum for the nestlings. Caek wondered how far the cave went and pondered how other visitors came and went. It looked like the place had been used frequently and recently and from the looks of the ash and coal remains. There was wood piled up in a corner and evidence of knapping because flakes littered the ground. She did not see a worn path. She had questions bouncing around in her mind. Could others have come from the ocean, stopped in the cove, and climbed to the escarpment, and lived in the cave? They could have she thought. They could have stayed a short while, and then left by the sea in some sort of log float. As far as she could tell there no other way out. Lightning flashed like burning alcohol and arced across the sky, illuminating far off billowing clouds. She could see a huge storm brewing.

She quickly woke Noolan and told him they should keep moving. As he stirred, one of the juvenile pelican chicks nipped at his arm, cutting it slightly. Noolan thought that if the birds were any bigger, they would have made a nice meal. He agreed with Caek, and they started to pack their packs. As the storm began to make landfall, neither of them could predict if they would get be able to get out before the waves reached the cave. They looked at each other and agreed it was time to go. They strapped on their respective heavily loaded packs, still somewhat damp from the ocean adventure. Noolan went first, looking for foot hold and hand holds. The face of the basalt columns was scarred with protruding clumps of lava frozen in twisted positions. Small open vesicles made good holds. The winds started to pick up and the rains quickly became torrents of pricking needles on their exposed skin. Sheets of drenching rain pelted the climbers. Noolan yelled several times to Caek, but she could barely hear him. Noolan threw a cord to her, and she quickly tied a bowline knot around her waist. Noolan then proceeded to tie the cord off as he moved up the cliff. The face became slippery and Noolan caught himself several times.

The progress along the cliff face was slow and steady as the storm intensified. Waves thundered onto shore and swamped the entire mile-long beach, reaching the base of cliffs below. As they slowly moved up, Noolan found various birds nesting among the crags. They seemed much more concerned with sheltering from the storm than protecting territory, their heads tucked deep under their wing. Every stretch and grab for secure holds were riddled with uncertainty. The winds howled at hurricane force and the rains pounded relentlessly. Every footing was hard to gain. It was either up the face or to the side; going down into the pounding waves was not an option. Eventually, after several hours of scaling the cliff, the face started to curve up and around. Noolan felt his grip begin to relax and the ground started to level off. As Caek rounded the corner she untied herself and joined Noolan. Feeling relieved they huddled closely together.

After a short rest, Noolan walked ahead quietly looking for a trail. They were in a grove of huge redwoods. The tops of the trees were swaying rhythmically with the winds, slowly arcing back and forth, and creaking loudly. They found shelter in a hollowed-out trunk of a long dead tree. Caek built a small fire as night began to fall. The trees were pushed by the winds generated by the storm, and branches fell randomly across the forest floor. Some were large and could have injured one of them. The trees creaked in long rhythmic swaying motions, keeping time with the pulse of the winds.

The next morning the storm was beginning to wane. Caek and Noolan had no idea where they were. They were not able to estimate how far they were from Vena, Ovla, and Hetra. They had no idea if they were able to cross the river or made it back to the other side of the river. They drifted on the ocean for five days. The time in the cove was around ten days and the cave another two. The hope of connecting with the other three travelers was not likely. They were alone again with no real idea where they were heading. There was evidence of lots of small game and some large ungulates roaming the forest. They were both exhausted and in need of food and a good rest. Moving deeper into the forest, the raging storm began to subside. They both knew they needed to hunt.

In the early afternoon, they stopped walking and set up a shelter with branches and a skin covering near another large hollowed out log. A stream flowed vigorously a short walk away. Much to their surprise, a short hike out of camp, they came across the fresh tracks of young deer. Within a few minutes of following the tracks, the quarry was spotted and Caek hurled a spear, connecting with the target. The deer went down quickly. It was easy to drag the prize back to the camp, where they cleaned and gutted it. After skewering the meat on a stick, they began grilling a hind quarter. As it cooked, they sliced several strips of meat off and ate well. Caek found some wild dandelions and a few pinecones laden with nuts near a nest. A curious chipmunk darted through the camp, chipping alarms at the theft of his stored goods. As the evening fell, muted sounds penetrated the forest. Crickets chippered sweetly and owls hooted deeply sending secret messages to and from the walls of the forest. A bullfrog hidden in the underbrush grunted, challenging a female to grunt back and show herself. As darkness began to settle in, they heard the roar of a Jakkar far off in the distance. Noolan's first reflex was to ready his spear, and he felt for his knife sheathed and strapped to his leg. Caek, more curious than afraid, sat by the fire and listened to what the roar was telling her. The Jakkar was watching her, and she felt safe.

Sleep came in short bursts that night. Both were in a heightened state and every sharp sound woke them from light sleep. Still exhausted at daybreak, they cooked more meat, and packed a little away for later. Caek looked at Noolan and told him to be sure to leave some for the Jakkar. Noolan had another flashback to Kazan, telling him to leave some for the Jakkar before he went in search of a Jakkar so long ago. The brain injury he experienced was slowly healing and his memory was improving. Flashes of Huut and Rit, his brothers, kept coming back to him. He knew the two were important to his life. He saw his father Abern, but the image was amorphous and cloudy. Then it vanished. Abern had died. He kept having flashes of Kazan but could not understand exactly who he was. As they moved through the forest, Caek started to smell fire. Noolan also smelled it. There was an unmistakable aroma of cooking meat. With their noses in the winds, they cautiously moved towards the smell hoping it was their lost companions. Over a small hill they spotted a camp.

They moved cautiously into the surrounding area and began seeing several camps with people engaged in chores. Some were tanning hides, others were cooking, others demonstrating the use of a variety of hunting tools, and some bent down by the fires knapping new arrow and spear points. As they walked towards the encampment, people stopped and took notice of the newcomers. They smiled, making the Noolan and Caek feel better about where they were. Without any questioning, they found an open area and put their packs down. Noolan leaned his spear against a tree. As they began to relax, Huki came over to greet them. In common fashion, he approached with his hand open, pointed down in a non-aggressive posture. Noolan and Caek make the same gesture. "Welcome" was the understood greeting. Caek immediately responded with several Naledi tung clicks and hand gestures asking where if he knew where they were. With a gentle response Huki said it was a place of gathering, because of the healing waters. This place was discovered eons ago and had a special energy to it. Then he told her about the hot springs to heal their bodies and bones. He told them it was a spiritual place and if they intended to visit, they could not bring any weapons. It was a spiritual setting for ceremonies and celebrations. It was a peaceful place to find healing.

Noolan was able to understand some of what was being talked about. He then asked about others. This question puzzled Huki, and he said many people traveled to this place. Huki went on to talk about the great gathering that just ended and many of the people were already returning to their homes far away or to new regions. Huki said some travelers left many days ago. Those travelers presented the gifts of the Jakkar, including meat and special organs for powers. This was something unbelievable to Caek and Noolan. No one had ever killed a Jakkar. When Huki looked closely at Noolan, he thought Noolan was one of those travelers that recently left. His name was Rit. With this comment Noolan had another flashback. He knew the name Rit. It was the name of one of his identical brothers. Huki said there was a re-markable resemblance to the others and remarked about the same deep green eyes. Then, Huki asked if he knew a shaman healer named Kazan.

Noolan looked at him and with an excited expression. He knew the name. He explained to Huki that he had been lost from his clan and so had Caek. He went on to explain that he had been in training to be-come a healer. He was lost in an accident in a cave and his mind had not allowed him to remember what happened. It was only recently he was able to begin to reassemble who he was and where he was from. Huki told him that the travelers left days ago and were going north and then to the east along a great river. The way Huki described the jour-ney, Noolan knew the river. It was where the log jam was the sent them adrift in the ocean.

Huki look hard at Caek and asked if she had been to the gathering before. The style of the skins she wore reminded him of clothing of the girls that accompanied Kazan. The design was unique, and the some of the pelts were from a different region. The patterning was extraordi-nary unique and Huki knew they were worn only by a few people. He looked hard at Caek; she had deep green eyes. He realized the girls with Kazan were identical to her, including the green eyes. It was remarkable. He shook his head and looked again. He asked if she had family and she told him she had two sisters. She went on to say she was separated from her clan a long time ago by the Jakkar. Huki said their names were Sinner and Huut and then realized they were triplets. Two sets of trip-let's genetics from two entirely different lines. It was extraordinary. If they mated, the offspring would become the first in the heidelbergensis genetic line ever, the immediate precursor to the neanderthalensis spe-cies. That would be the critical link for the eventual evolution of the homo sapiens.

Huki wondered what the likelihood of two set of identical triplets, both missing one sibling, and those two siblings randomly meeting, and the other two siblings meeting and surviving to this point. He knew there was strong medicine at work. He looked at the pair; she was smaller, obviously from the smaller-framed Naledi species with longer arms and legs with the wolf line cape. She had dark skin, and she wore her hair in tight kinky dreadlocks; her eyes set her apart from the others. She and her two sisters were the collective recipients of unique genes. Because of their uniqueness, they would become highly desirable women for breeding.

Noolan stood tall, his skin was red with evidence of being well burnt by the sun. Hair covered his body, and he wore an eagle talon tied to a thin leather strap around his neck. His muscles were strong, and he was lean. For a man of seventeen seasons, he had already survived a lot of challenges. He wore his hair in a tangled braid and possessed numerous scars on his body. He was also a desirable mate. They possessed a strong bond of evolving evolutionary traits that would eventually sustain the generational hominoid trajectory for eons to come.

CHAPTER 25

THAT EVENING THERE WAS A LARGE CAMPFIRE. A DRUMMER from a small clan began a rhythmic call that echoed deep into the forest. Noolan and Caek were held in high regard since each was one of triplets. As they sat around the fire, Caek talked about the others they encountered and how she floated down a large river into the ocean. She told them how they were stranded in the pelican cave. She became animated in her movements telling the story, her arms moving in graceful flowing patterns in descriptive gestures. Noolan listened and was drawn to her with an emotion of bonding and thankfulness for her partnership to get to this point. He wanted to be with her. He felt desire. This was an unusual emotion for the developing hominoids. The brain case was not quite as large as the homo sapiens, but it was growing. Neural connections were being made and those connections would become the genetic code for the next generation of people and then the next.

The sensation and recognition of emotions was at its infancy. That is how every organic living cell started. What made the connection between Noolan and Caek unique was the fact that it was the point in time when the hominids became aware. The encounter with the radiation from the fireball changed their minds, bodies, and DNA. The organic conglomeration genetic code was no longer an animal in the purest sense of the word. They started the ability reason with each other and created and shared ideas. Knowledge of plant medicines would be shared and remembered for their respective value. But it would not last. Along with this evolutionary pattern, anger, gluttonous traits, hate, bias, and greed would manifest in their brain and genetic codes would be written for the homo sapiens.

Over the next few days, the couple rested, mended clothing, made arrow shafts, knapped new points, and traded some for a new yew wood bow. They mated numerous times. Noolan found a long thin shaft of black and white seashells in a small cove by the water. He strung several on a string of leather and gave it to Caek. She put it around her neck, immediately smiling. In the evening, they would sit by their campfire as visitors came by. They talked about their past as best they could. Almost on cue, they would stand up at the same time and head to the hot springs. It was a place of healing. There would be silence as the small group soaked for a while, immersing themselves in the evening, and then leaving in silence. Occasionally a small whisper would signal it was time to go. Many of the people understood the body language of others. It was a special event that embedded itself into their collective DNA. After several evenings Noolan told Caek he wanted to find his brothers and she should want to find her sisters. It was the first time they acknowledged the importance of finding their families. They both possessed a feeling that their siblings were still lived. She was excited by the hope of being reunited with her sisters and Drot. It was time to leave and find the rest of their clans.

As they packed their belongings during the next day and told several of the people, they would be leaving. Huki told the couple to go up the coastline for many days. There was a well-worn trail easy to follow. He told them they would likely encounter others coming this way and perhaps overtake larger groups traveling in the same direction they were going, because they were traveling lighter. The larger groups tended to move slower due to older people and small children. Huki also said Kazan had a short leg and slowed the group significantly. Noolan smiled, remembering Kazan's short leg. Huki tried to describe the wheelbarrow invention. Neither Caek nor Noolan clearly understood what he was describing, but they stared with focused curiosity. Huki went on to tell the two they would come to a great river and from there, they would walk towards the rising sun for many days. They would need to look for a safe place to cross. He said Kazan describe his home in valley regions alongside large volcanos. There they would find the shelters of Kazan's clan. The last thing Huki told them was to keep an eye out for the Jakkar. It would be watching them.

Early the next morning Noolan and Caek said goodbye to Huki. Huki told the couple that they would always be part of his Ohana, just as he told Kazan. They turned and started down the trail. The sun was just cresting over the trees and the air was incredibly fresh. A slight breeze blew inland, and a variety of birds darted across the forest canopy, delivering squawks, chirps, or caws that echoed through the valley. Small chipmunks darted across the path, chattering alarms to its own kind. They walked swiftly and quietly noting the vegetation, always keeping focused eyes for unique treats to eat. Their packs were constructed from the rib-bones of an elk with the frame and large skin sections sewn into a single bag. Inside the pack they each carried an assortment of foods and additional arrow tips, extra-long obsidian spear tips, and good amount of braided leather rope. Noolan carried a spear flung over his shoulder. Caek carried the arrow launcher strapped to her pack and a well-made spear, a little longer than she was tall. She used it as a walking stick. Around their waists, tied with a leather strap, they both carried a sheath with a well-knapped knife and a small pouch with fire making materials.

Around noon they came to a small clearing and Noolan noticed a curious track in the soft dirt. It was flat and about the width of his hand. He had never seen a track of this kind and wondered what kind of animal possessed a foot or paw of this nature? He could clearly see other hominoid tracks in front of it and behind it. Noolan could not understand it. Caek looked at it and was puzzled as well but did not take much notice. She was eagerly eating strips of meat they packed and some watercress they came across while walking.

They worked efficiently together. They each found new sensations with each other as their bond continued to grow. Occasionally a feeling of awkwardness emerged, but other times pleasure. They felt good with each other and knew that the only thing that could separate them at this time was death. There was a sense of trust developing. A feeling of safety engulfed them. They began to anticipate the other's thoughts and actions. They began to develop a sense of responsibility for legacy and proliferation. It was with this bold new perspective that they found the courage to walk together and find enjoyment in each other.

This was a time of peaceful co-existence with their environment. Hazards were always present, and death was unpredictable. Noolan and Caek felt committed to take care of each other. A new type of relationship was beginning. One that would be lasting and based on trust and loyalty and truth. New neural connections were being made and would prove to be written into the genetic code of homo sapiens. There were questions of the universe. Sparks of curiosity were emerging in the brain and bringing the hominoids to the recognition of a spiritual world. It was a new pathway to understanding what forces inside their developing brain could master. It was a new way of embracing their world.

Late in the afternoon of the third day the path flattened out and they came to a caramel-colored sandy beach area. The dunes and grasses stretched off on a spit of land and trailed into a frothing ocean. Large coniferous driftwood trees littered the shoreline and great elephant seals basked in the fading sunlight on half submerged branches. Sea otters jumped and swam in the kelp forests, breaching the waves and snapping at the ocean perch, seagulls followed close behind, searching for scraps. Climbing through the dunes, Caek found the small mushrooms growing in the underbrush of the grasses. Noolan helped her picked many of the little brown capped fungi. They wrapped them in a soft tanned rabbit skin and placed the supply in her backpack. She understood how special they were and wanted to share them with her sisters. She knew the mushrooms were powerful and would bring new insights to whomever ingested them.

As the sun began to set, they camped back from the beach near a massive, long cypress tree. It had washed far up on the dunes and grasses grew all around it. They could hear the roar of the waves crashing on the beach as a herd of elk meandered nearby without any sense of fear. A large contingent of seagulls crossed their field of vision, looking for handouts and screaming the familiar squawk of the hunt for scraps of dead crabs and fish remains. The fire Noolan built was larger than usual and its heat felt good. Driftwood was plentiful. For some reason Noolan felt fear. He felt something was watching them. Caek nudged him acknowledging his thoughts. As evening slowly descended, a quiet darkness shrouded the area. There was no moon, and the stars began their brilliant flickering dance. The haunting hoot from a great horned owl echoed in the distance, calling for its lost mate. Noolan did not sleep the entire night.

The path leading up the coastline was well worn. As they kept moving, paralleling the ocean, the area started to look familiar to Caek and then to Noolan. It was near where they would have crossed with Ovla, Hetra, and Vena, had they not been washed out to sea. They kept finding signs of others who had recently passed this way. There were so many footprints in the sand that it was difficult to tell if people were going towards the ocean or leaving. Numerous used campsites started to appear; one they came across had hot coals that still smoldered. The odd flat track crisscrossed the area. Even though Huki describe the wheelbarrow to the couple, they had no idea what they were looking at, though it did spark a profound curiosity with them. At this stop, they also noticed some lines in the soft dirt. They were in uniform patterns and seemed to indicate an artistic rendering of many things. Noolan traced the lines with his finger, contemplating the meaning.

By late afternoon, they came into a clearing and found other travelers camping. With a gesture of friendship, and simple greetings they moved a little further down the trail and setup camped nearby. After Noolan and Caek set up camp, they walked back down the trail and started to communicate with the others. The travelers explained they were going in the opposite direction and told them about a rope bridge used to across the river. It was a short distance upriver. They went on to say their forefathers built it, but it was in a hidden part of the canyon and difficult to find. Noolan asked if they came across others, specifically a shaman with a short leg. The leader of the group said they had not seen anyone else on this side of the river. He went on to say they did meet three others on the opposite side of the river long ago. Two women and one man going north to find their clan. With this news, Noolan and Caek knew their friends Ovla, Hetra, and Vena made it back to land safely, but they were now a long way away.

The next morning the people parted company. Caek and Noolan were hopeful they could catchup with Kazan. Caek did not know it yet, but she was pregnant with triplets. The offspring would have vivid green eyes and the mutation in their genetic code would bring them a consciousness and intellect never seen in the evolution of the human genome.

CHAPTER 26

O N June 6, 2023, Hamster Dunnigan's court case finally concluded he was a free man. He was cleared of multiple charges under the Native American Graves Protection and Repatriation Act (NAGPRA). He argued that the items found were not from a grave, but rather a time capsule. He argued that they belonged to him and his relatives because, as was noted in the record, his small size, vivid green eyes, and his DNA were an obvious link to his Naledi ancestors. He smiled as he walked out into the Seattle sunshine reaching for the small golden disk that he wore around his neck on a leather lace. It was the first wheel in the history of the hominoids, and he had a buyer.

NAGPRA was signed into law in 1990 by President George H.W. Bush. The law describes the rights of Native American lineal descendants, Indian tribes, and Native Hawaiians with respect to the treatment, repatriation, and disposition of Native American human remains, ceremonial objects and cultural patrimony. It is illegal in the United States to disturb, collect, and or sell culturally related objects that show a relationship to a lineal decent or ancient cultural affiliation. A second part of the statue was designed to provide greater protection for Native American burial sites and to provide for strict control over the removal of ancient remains, funerary objects, sacred objects, and items of cultural patrimony.

Title 18 of the United States Code—Crimes and Criminal Procedure

§1170. Illegal trafficking in Native American human remains and cultural items

(a) Whoever knowingly collects, sells, purchases, uses for profit, or transports for sale or profit, the human remains or cultural artifacts of a Native American without the right of possession to those remains as provided in the Native American Graves Protection and Repatriation Act shall be fined in accordance with this title, or imprisoned not more than 12 months, or both, and in the case of a second or subsequent violation, be fined in accordance with this title, or imprisoned not more than 5 years, or both.

ABOUT THE AUTHOR

IN A WORLD WHERE ENVIRONMENTAL WARRIORS OFTEN EMERGE from predictable backgrounds, Hector M. Rodriguez stands as a compelling paradox. His journey began in the strategic corridors of the U.S. Army's III Corps Engineering unit, where he commanded terrain intelligence, before evolving into a pivotal force in environmental protection at both the Hanford Nuclear Reservation and the National Energy Technology Laboratory complex.

The 1980s saw Rodriguez, a geologist by training, spearheading revolutionary projects under the Resource Conservation Reclamation Act. His work on identifying and mitigating the risks of leaking underground storage tanks became instrumental in understanding and safeguarding America's groundwater resources. This expertise catapulted him into a three-decade tenure with the Department of Energy, where he coordinated and managed environmental clean-up projects at some of the nation's most sensitive facilities.

Yet Rodriguez defies simple categorization. Beyond his environmental crusades, he embodies the spirit of a modern Renaissance man. His creative spirit flows through multiple channels: as an award-winning cook whose culinary creations delight palates, a musician who coaxes melodies from both guitar and mandolin, a cycling enthusiast who finds joy in the open road, and a master gardener who understands the subtle language of soil and seasons. His role as a Scout leader and teacher reveals his deep commitment to nurturing young minds, while his decades-long involvement with Kiwanis International has made him a fierce champion of children's literacy.

In what others might call retirement, Rodriguez has embarked on perhaps his most ambitious role yet – that of a visionary writer. His works transcend traditional environmental literature, weaving together threads of ancient wisdom, cutting-edge sustainability practices, and profound insights into the human condition. Drawing from his unique vantage point as both an environmental insider and change agent, his narratives offer readers a rare glimpse into humanity's most pressing challenges.

This self-proclaimed "disruptive boomer" continues to challenge conventional wisdom, crafting stories that bridge the gap between technical expertise and accessible storytelling. Through his written works, Rodriguez advocates for a future where environmental stewardship, educational equity, and human dignity coexist harmoniously. His approach combines deep technical knowledge with an infectious sense of humor and an unwavering commitment to future generations, proving that the most effective advocates are those who can translate complex challenges into compelling narratives for self-realization and positive change.

9 781735 558462